*She breathed gently upon
the woman's sleeping face . . .*

The woman opened her eyes and looked into the
mare's blue gaze. She seemed confused but not
frightened, and after a moment she sat up slowly,
moving cautiously as if for fear of alarming the horse.
The horse was not alarmed. She suffered the woman
to stroke her nose and pat her face before she backed
away. . . . She had timed it perfectly. The woman
came after her as if drawn on a rope, making soft,
affectionate noises. The mare moved as if uneasy, still
backing, and then, abruptly flirtatious, offered her
back, an invitation to the woman to mount. . . .

Feeling her rider in place, legs clasped firmly on
her sides, the mare leaped skyward with more speed
than grace. She felt the woman gasp. . . .

—from "Riding the Nightmare" by Lisa Tuttle

Magic Tales Anthologies
Edited by Jack Dann & Gardner Dozois

UNICORNS!
MAGICATS!
BESTIARY!
MERMAIDS!
SORCERERS!
DEMONS!
DOGTALES!
SEASERPENTS!
DINOSAURS!
LITTLE PEOPLE!
MAGICATS II
UNICORNS II
DRAGONS!
HORSES!

Edited by Terri Windling

FAERY!

HORSES!

EDITED BY
JACK DANN & GARDNER DOZOIS

ACE BOOKS, NEW YORK

This book is an Ace original edition,
and has never been previously published.

HORSES!

An Ace Book/published by arrangement with
the editors

PRINTING HISTORY
Ace edition/May 1994

For
Mike Resnick
and
Maria Vallone
—Two People Who Know Their Horses
and
in memory of
Vivian Smith
—Who Would Have Liked This Book

ACKNOWLEDGMENTS

The editors would like to thank the following people for their help and support:

Susan Casper; Jeanne Van Buren Dann; Janet Kagan; Ricky Kagan; Jim Cappio; Lawrence Person; Ellen Datlow; Ed and Audrey Ferman; Kristine Kathryn Rusch; Jane Yolen; Mike Resnick; Michael Swanwick; Sheila Williams; Ian Randal Strock; Tina Lee; Scott Towner; Judith Tarr; Josepha Sherman; Diana de Avalle-Acre; Barbara Delaplace; Scott Edleman; George Alec Effinger; Nina Kiriki Hoffman; all the folks on the Delphi and GEnie computer networks who offered suggestions; and special thanks to our own editors, Susan Allison and Ginjer Buchanan.

Contents

HORSES!

Classical Horses
by
Judith Tarr

One of the most popular and respected fantasists of the 1980s, Judith Tarr is also a medieval scholar with a Ph.D. in medieval studies from Yale University, which background has served her well in creating the richly detailed milieus of her critically acclaimed novels. Her many books include The Isle of Glass, The Golden Horn, The Hounds of God, The Hall of the Mountain King, The Lady of Han-Gilen, A Fall of Princes, A Wind in Cairo, Ars Magica, Alamut, *and* The Dagger and the Cross: A Novel of the Crusades. *Born in Augusta, Maine, she now lives in Tucson, Arizona.*

In the brilliant story that follows, she offers us a fascinating look at a tranquil country estate where nothing is quite *what it seems to be . . .*

* * *

I

The yard was full of Lipizzans.

I'd been driving by, missing my old mare and thinking maybe it was time to find another horse, and I'd slowed because I always do, going along any row of fence with horses behind it, and there they were. Not the usual bays and chestnuts and occasional gray, but a herd of little thick white horses that weren't—but couldn't be—but were.

They weren't the Vienna School. They came from somewhere in Florida, Janna told me afterward, and they'd been doing something at the armory, and they needed a place to board for the night. I didn't know Janna then. I wouldn't have stopped, either, just gone down to a crawl and stared, except for the two horses in the paddock. It wasn't that they were wild with all the running and clattering. It was that they were quiet. A chestnut and a gray, not big, just about Morgan-sized, and maybe Morgan-built, too, but finer in the leg and shorter in the back than most I'd seen—and of course you don't see a gray

1

Morgan. But as upheaded as any Morgan you'd want to look at, with a good arch to their necks, and ears pricked sharply forward, watching the show.

I pulled over without even thinking about it. I remember wondering that it was odd, me staring at two perfectly nice but perfectly normal horses, with all those white stallions taking turns around the yard and being walked into the barn. The gray would be white when he was older, there was that. He had a bright eye, but calm. When one of the Lipps circled past his fence, his head came up higher and he stamped. Then he lifted himself up, smooth and sweet as you please, and held for a long breathless while. He was, I couldn't help but notice, a stallion.

The chestnut watched him with what I could have sworn was amusement. His ears flicked back and then forward. His muscles bunched. He soared up, even smoother than the gray, and lashed back hard enough to take the head off anyone who might have dared to stand behind him.

Levade, capriole. Then they were quiet again, head to tail, rubbing one another's withers like any old plow horses.

I got out of the car. No one looked at me or even seemed to have noticed the demonstration in the paddock. I wandered toward the fence. The chestnut spared me a glance. The gray was too busy having his neck rubbed. I didn't try to lure them over. I leaned against the post and watched the stallions, but with a corner of an eye for the ones in the paddock.

There was an old surrey on the other side, with a tarp half draped over it, half folded back. Someone sat in the seat. She was old, how old I couldn't tell; just that she was over sixty, and probably over seventy, and maybe eighty, too. It didn't keep her from sitting perfectly straight, or from looking at me with eyes as young as her face was old, large in their big round sockets, and a quite beautiful shade of gray. She didn't smile. If she had, I might have ducked and left.

As it was, I took my time, but after a while I went over. "Hello," I said.

She nodded.

I supposed I knew who she was. I'd heard about a woman who had a farm out this way. She was ninety, people said, if she was a day, and she still drove her own horses. Had even been riding them up till a little while ago, when she broke her hip—not riding, either, but falling down in her house like any other very old lady. She had a cane beside her, with a brass horse's head.

"Nice horses," I said, cocking my head at the two in the paddock.

She nodded again. I wondered if she could talk. She didn't look as if she'd had a stroke, and no one had said anything about her being mute.

"Not often you see two stallions in a paddock together," I went on.

"They've always been together."

Her voice was quiet and a little thin, but it wasn't the old-lady voice I might have expected. She had an interesting accent. European, more or less.

"Brothers?" I asked.

"Twins."

I stared at them. They did look a lot alike, except for the color: bright copper chestnut, almost gold, and dapple gray, with the mane and tail already silver.

"That's rare," I said.

"Very."

I stuck out a hand, a little late, and introduced myself. Her hand was thin and knobby, but she had a respectable grip. "You're Mrs. Tiffney, of course."

She laughed, which was surprising. She sounded impossibly young. "Of course! I'm the only antique human on the farm." She kept on smiling at me. "My yard is full of Lipizzans, and you notice my two ponies?"

"Big ponies," I said. "If they're that. Morgans?"

"No," she said. She didn't tell me what they were. I didn't, at that point, ask. Someone was standing behind me. Janna, I knew later. She wanted to know what to do about someone named Ragweed, who was in heat, and Florence had categorically refused to move her Warmblood for any silly circus horse, and the show manager wanted to know if he could use the shavings in the new barn, but she wasn't sure what to charge him for them, if she let him have them at all, since no one had told her if there was going to be a delivery this week.

It went on like that. I found myself dumping feed in nervous boarders' bins and helping Janna pitch hay to the horses that had been put out to pasture for the night. There were people around—this was a big barn, and the guests had plenty of grooms of their own—but one way and another I seemed to have been adopted. Or to have adopted the place.

"Do you always take in strangers?" I asked Janna. It was late by then. We were up in the office, drinking coffee from the urn and feeling fairly comfortable. Feeding horses together can do that to people. She'd sent the kids home, and the grooms were gone to their hotel or bedded down in the barn. Even Mrs. Tiffney had gone to the house that stood on the hill behind the barns.

Janna yawned till her jaw cracked. She didn't apologize. She was comfortable people, about my age and about my size, with the no-nonsense air that stable managers either learn early or give up and become bitchy instead. "We take in strays," she said. "Plenty of cats. Too damn many dogs. Horses, as often as not. People, not that often. People are a bad lot."

"Maybe I am, too," I said.

"Mrs. Tiffney likes you," said Janna.

"Just like that?"

Janna shrugged. "She's good at judging animals."

"People-type animals, too?"

Janna didn't answer. She poured more coffee instead, first for me, then for herself. "Do you ride?" she asked.

"Not since the winter. I had a mare up at Meadow Farm; Arab. Did dressage with her. She got twisted intestine. Had to put her down." It still hurt to say that.

Janna was horse people. She understood. "Looking for another?"

"Starting to."

"None for sale here right now," she said. "But some of the boarders take leases. There's always someone wanting a horse ridden. If you want to try one of them, take a lesson. . . ."

I tried one, and then another. I took a lesson. I took two. Pretty soon I was a regular, though I didn't settle on any particular horse. The ones that came up weren't quite what I was looking for, and the ones I might have been interested in weren't for sale or lease, but I had plenty of chances to ride them.

What I was mostly interested in was just being there. Someone had put up a sampler in the tackroom: "Peaceable Kingdom." Tacky and sentimental, but it fit. There were always dogs around and cats underfoot. Janna gave most of the lessons, but she had a couple of older kids to help with the beginners. I didn't do any teaching. I did enough of that every day, down in the trenches.

There were thirty horses in the two barns, minus the one-night stand of Lipizzans. The farm owned a few ponies and a couple of school horses, and Mrs. Tiffney's pair of stallions, who had a corner of the old barn to themselves. They weren't kept for stud, weren't anything registered that anyone knew of. They were just Mrs. Tiffney's horses, the red and the gray— Zan and Bali. She drove them as a team, pulling a surrey in the summer and a sleigh in the winter. Janna rode them every day if she could. Bali was a pretty decent jumper. Zan was happier as a dressage horse, though he'd jump if Janna asked; and I'd seen what he could do in the way of caprioles. Bali was the quiet one, though that wasn't saying he was gentle—he had plenty of spirit. Zan was the one you had to watch. He'd snake his head out if you walked by his stall, and get titchy if he thought you owed him a carrot or a bit of apple. Bali was more likely to charm it out of you. Zan expected it, or else.

I got friendly with most of the horses, even Florence's precious Warmblood, but those two had brought me in first, and I always had a soft spot for them. They seemed to know who I was, too, and Bali started to nicker when I came, though I thought that was more for his daily apple than for me. If Mrs. Tiffney was there, I'd help her and Janna harness them up for her to take her drive around the pastures and down the road, or sit with her while she watched Janna ride one or the other of them. The day she asked me if I'd like to ride Bali—Janna was saddling Zan then—I should have been prepared, and in a way I was, but I was surprised. I had my saddle, I was wearing my boots; I'd been riding Sam for his owner, who was jetsetting in Atlantic City. But people didn't just ride Mrs. Tiffney's horses.

I said so. She laughed at me. "No, they don't. Unless I tell

them to. Go and saddle Bali. He'll be much happier to be with
his brother."

He was that. I felt as if I was all over his back—first-ride
nerves, I always get them in front of the owner. But he had
lovely gaits, and he seemed determined to show me all of them.
Fourteen. I'd counted once at Meadow Farm, when I watched
the riding master. Walk: collected, working, medium, extended.
Trot: ditto. Canter: ditto. And then, because Mrs. Tiffney told
me to do it, and because Janna was there to set my legs where
they belonged and to guide my hands, the two gaits almost no
one ever gets to ride: passage, the graceful, elevated, slow-
motion trot; and piaffe, "Spanish trot" that in Vienna they do
between the pillars, not an inch forward, but all that power and
impulsion concentrated in one place, in perfect control, to the
touch of the leg and the support of the hand and the will of the
rider that by then is perfectly melded with that of the horse.

I dropped down and hugged Bali till he snorted. I was
grinning like an idiot. Janna was grinning, too. I could have
sworn even Zan was, flirting his tail at his brother as he went
by.

Mrs. Tiffney smiled. She looked quite as satisfied as Bali did
when I pulled back to look at him, though I thought he might
be laughing, too. And told myself to stop anthropomorphizing,
but how often does anyone get to ride a high-school horse?

II

Not long after that, Mrs. Tiffney taught me to drive. I'd never
learned that, had always been out riding when chances came
up. It was easier than riding in some ways. Harder in others,
with two horses to think of, and turning axes, and all those bits
and pieces of harness.

We didn't talk much through all of this. The horses were
enough. Sometimes I mentioned something that had happened
at school, or said I'd have to leave early to have dinner with a
friend, or mentioned that I was thinking of going back to grad
school.

"In what?" she asked me.

"Classics, probably," I said. "I've got the Masters in it, but all I teach is Latin. I'd like to get my Greek back before I lose it. And teach in college. High school's a war zone, most of the time. You can't really teach. Mostly you just play policeman and hope most of your classes can read."

"Surely," she said, "if they can take Latin, they can read English?"

She sounded properly shocked. I laughed sourly. "You'd think so, wouldn't you? But we're egalitarian at Jonathan Small. Anyone who wants anything can take it. Can't be elitist, now, can we? Though I finally got them to give me a remedial Latin class—remedial reading, for kids who can't read English. It does work. And it keeps them from going nuts in a regular class."

"Democracy," said Mrs. Tiffney, "was never intended for everyone."

I couldn't help it. I laughed. I couldn't stop. When I finally did manage to suck in a breath, she was watching me patiently. She didn't look offended. She didn't say anything further, either, except to ask me to turn around and put the team into a trot.

When we'd cooled the horses and cleaned the harness—she insisted on doing it herself, no matter what anyone said—she invited me to the house. I almost refused. I'm shy about things like that, and I had classes in the morning. But maybe I had amends to make. I shouldn't have laughed at her.

From the outside it was nothing in particular. A big white farm house with pillars in front: New England Neoclassical. Janna had the upstairs rear, which I'd seen already, steep twisty staircases and rooms with interesting ceilings, dipping and swooping at the roof's whim, and a fireplace that worked.

Downstairs was much the same, but the ceilings were halfway to the sky, rimmed with ornate moldings, and there seemed to be a fireplace in every room, even the kitchen. There were books everywhere, on shelves to the ceiling, on revolving shelves beside the big comfortable chairs, between bookends on tables and mantelpieces. And in through the books there were wonderful things: a bust of a Roman senator, a medieval triptych of angels and saints around a Madonna and child, an

African mask, a Greek krater, a bronze horse that must have
been Greek, too, and hanging from the ceiling, so surprising
that I laughed, a papier-maché pterodactyl with carefully
painted-in silvery-gray fur.

Mrs. Tiffney wasn't going to let me help her with the cups
and cookies, but she didn't try too hard to stop me. She did
insist that I get comfortable in the living room while she waited
for the water to boil. I wandered where she pointed, past the
den and the library I'd already seen, to the front room with its
wide windows and its Oriental carpet. It was full of books as all
the other rooms were, and its fireplace was marble, cream-pale
in the light from the tall windows. There was a painting over it,
an odd one, perfectly round, with what must have been
hundreds of figures in concentric circles.

When I came closer I saw that it wasn't a painting, precisely.
More of a bas-relief, with a rim that must have been gold leaf,
and inside it a rim of beautiful blue shading to green and gray
and white, sea-colors, and in the center a field of stars—I
picked out the gold dots of constellations, Orion and the
Dipper, and the moon in silver phases—and between them
more people than I could begin to count, doing more things
than a glance could take in. They had a classical look,
neoclassical more probably, not quite elaborate enough to be
baroque, not quite off-center enough to be medieval.

I found my finger creeping up to touch, to see if it was really
real. I shoved my hand in the pocket of my jacket.

A kettle shrieked in the kitchen. I almost bolted toward it.
Hating to leave that wonderful thing, but glad to escape the
temptation to touch it.

"Did you know," I said to Mrs. Tiffney as she filled the
teapot, "that you have the shield of Achilles in your living
room?"

She didn't look at me oddly. Just smiled. "Yes," she said. "I
thought you'd recognize it."

I picked up the tray before she could do it, and carried it back
through the rooms. The shield—yes, it was a shield, or meant
to be one, clearly and, now that I noticed, rather markedly
convex—glowed at me while Mrs. Tiffney poured tea and I ate
cookies. I don't remember what the cookies tasted like. They

were good, I suppose. I was counting circles. There was the city at peace, yes. And the city at war. The wedding and the battle. The trial, the ambush. The field and the vineyard. The cattle and the lions. The sheep and the shepherds. The dancing floor and the dancers.

"Someone," I said, "made himself a masterpiece."

Mrs. Tiffney nodded. She was still smiling, sipping tea, looking sometimes at me and sometimes at the marvel over her mantel.

"People argue," I said. "Over how it really was supposed to be. Your artist went for the simplest way out—the circles."

"Sometimes simplest is best," Mrs. Tiffney said.

I nodded. The cattle were gold, I noticed, with a patina that made them look like real animals, and their horns looked like tin, or something else grayish-silvery. Base metal, probably, gilded or foiled over. Whoever this artist was, whenever he worked—I was almost ready to say seventeenth century, or very good twentieth with a very large budget—he knew his Homer. Loved him, to do every detail, wrinkles of snarls on the lion's muzzles, curls of hair on the bulls' foreheads, bright red flashes of blood where the lions had struck.

"This should be in a museum," I said.

Mrs. Tiffney didn't frown, but her smile was gone. "I suppose it should. But I'm selfish. I think it's happier here, where people live, and can touch it if they want to, and it can know the air and the light."

Pure heresy, of course. A wonder like this should have the best protection money could buy, controlled climate, controlled access, everything and anything to preserve it for the ages.

But it was beautiful up there in this living room, with late daylight on it and a bit of breeze blowing through. I got up without thinking and went over to it, and touched it. The figures were cool, raised so that I could have seen them without eyes, and they wove and flowed around one another, a long undulating line that came back to where it began.

I wasn't breathing. I drew a breath in slowly. "I've never," I said, "seen a thing like this. Or anything that came close to it."

"There's only one like it in the world," Mrs. Tiffney said.

She bent forward to fill my cup again. I sat back down, took another cookie.

"And you say you don't believe in democracy," I said. "If keeping this out of a museum isn't democratic, then what is?"

"This is simple sense, and giving a masterpiece the setting it loves best." She sipped delicately from the little china cup. "It's been in my family for a very long time. When it first came to us, we promised its maker that we would care for it as he asked us to do, never to hide it away and never to sell it, or to give it except as a gift to one who could love it as he loved it. It was the eldest daughter's dowry, when such things were done. Now I'm the last," she said, "and it goes to no daughter after me."

I was still wrapped up in the wonder of the thing, or I would never have said what came into my head. "Janna says you have daughters. Two of them. And granddaughters."

"Stepdaughters," she said. She didn't seem offended. "I was my husband's second wife. We had a son, but he died early, and he had no children. My husband's children were never quite sure what to make of me. Now that I'm old, you see, I'm permitted to be eccentric. But when I was younger, with children who resented their father's marrying again so soon after their mother died, I was simply too odd for words. All my antiquities, and my books, and that dreadful garish thing that I *would* hang in the parlor—"

"It's not garish!"

She laughed. "It's hardly in the most contemporary of taste; especially when contemporary was Art Deco. And pockets full of coins of the Caesars, and gowns out of the *Très Riches Heures*, and once, as a favor to a friend, a mummy in the basement: oh, I was odd. Alarmingly so. The mummy went back home with as many of her treasures as we could find. I, unfortunately, lacked the grace to do the same."

"So you are Greek," I said.

She nodded.

"The artist—he was, too?"

"Yes," she said, "very. He wouldn't sign his work. He said that it would speak for itself."

"It does," I said, looking at it again, as if I could begin to help myself. "Oh, it does."

III

That was in the early spring. In late spring, just after lilac time, I came to ride Bali—those days, I was riding him almost every day, or driving them both with Mrs. Tiffney—and found the place deserted except for one of the stablehands. She was new and a bit shy, just waved and kept on with the stall she was cleaning.

The stallions were both in their stalls. Usually they were out at this time of day. I wondered if they'd come up lame, or got sick. Zan didn't whip his head out the way he usually did and snap his teeth in my face. Bali didn't nicker, though he came to the door when I opened it. His eyes were clear. So was his nose. He didn't limp as I brought him out. But he wasn't himself. He didn't throw his head around on the crossties, he didn't flag his tail, he didn't grab for the back of my shirt the way he'd taken to, to see me jump. He just stood there, letting me groom him.

I looked in Zan's stall. Zan looked back at me. Nothing wrong with him, either, that I could see or feel. Except that the spirit had gone out of him. He actually looked old. So did Bali, who was still young enough to be more a dapple than a gray.

"You look as if you lost a friend," I said.

Zan's ears went flat. Bali grabbed the right crosstie in his teeth and shook it, hard.

I had a little sense left. I remembered to get him back in his stall before I bolted.

Mrs. Tiffney was in the hospital. She'd had another fall, and maybe a heart attack. They weren't sure yet. I wouldn't have got that much out of anybody if Janna hadn't driven in as I came haring out of the barn. She looked as worn as the horses did, as if she hadn't slept in a week.

"Last night," she said when I'd dragged her up to the office and got coffee into her. "I was downstairs borrowing some milk, or she'd have gone on lying there till God knows when. The ambulance took forever to come. Then she wanted the paramedics to carry her up to her own bed. I thought she'd have another heart attack, fighting them when they took her out."

I gulped coffee. It was just barely warm. My throat hurt. "Is she going to be all right?"

Janna shrugged. "They don't know yet. The harpies came in this morning—her daughters, I mean. Aileen isn't so bad, but Celia . . ." She rubbed her eyes. They must have felt as if they were full of sand. "Celia has been trying for years to make her mother live somewhere, as she puts it, 'appropriate.' A nursing home, she means. She's old enough for one herself, if you ask me."

"Maybe she thinks she's doing what's best," I said.

"I'm sure she is," said Janna. "What's best for Celia. She'd love to have this place. She'd sell it for a golf course, probably. Or condos. Horses are a big waste of money, she says. So's that great big house up there on the hill, with just two women living in it."

"And kids," I said, "in the summer, when you have camp."

"Not enough profit in that." Janna put down her half-empty cup. "She married a stockbroker, but Mrs. Tiffney always said Celia did the thinking for the pair of them, in and out of the office. If she'd been born forty years later, *she'd* have been the broker, and she probably wouldn't have married at all."

It still wouldn't have done Mrs. Tiffney any good, I thought, after I'd bullied Janna into bed and done what needed doing in the barn and driven slowly home. Mrs. Tiffney's horses didn't look any brighter when I looked in on them, just before I left, though, Bali let his nose rest in my palm for a minute. Thanking me, I imagined, for understanding. Just being a horse, actually, with a human he'd adopted into his personal herd.

Mrs. Tiffney wasn't allowed visitors, except for immediate family. In Janna's opinion, and I admit in mine, the hospital would have done better to bar the family and let in the friends. Aileen did answer Janna's calls, which was more than Celia would do; so we knew that Mrs. Tiffney hadn't broken her hip again but she had had a heart attack, and she was supposed to stay very, very quiet. She'd been asking after her horses. Janna was able to pass on some of the news, though Aileen wasn't horse people; she didn't understand half of what Janna told her, and she probably mixed up the rest.

I actually saw her with her sister, a few days after Mrs. Tiffney went to the hospital. They'd come to the house, they said, to get a few things their mother needed. I think Celia was checking out the property. They were a bit of a surprise. The slim blade of a woman in the Chanel suit turned out to be Aileen. Celia was the plump matronly lady in sensible brogues. She knew about horses and asked sharp questions about the barn's expenses. Aileen looked a little green at the dirt and the smell. She didn't touch anything, and she walked very carefully, watching where she put her feet.

I was walking Bali down after a ride. He was still a bit off, but he'd been willing enough to work. If he'd been human, I'd have said he was drowning his sorrows. I brought him out of the ring for some of the good grass along the fence, and there was Aileen, stubbing out a cigarette and looking a little alarmed at the huge animal coming toward her. Little Bali, not quite fifteen hands, kept on coming, though I did my best to encourage him with a patch of clover. He had his sights set on another one a precise foot from Aileen's right shoe. She backed away.

"I'm sorry," I said. "He's got a mind of his own."

"He always did," said Aileen. She eyed him. He flopped his ears at a fly and took another mouthful of clover. "You must be Laura—Ms. Michaels, that is. My mother has told me about you."

For some reason I wanted to cry. "Has she? She's talking, then?"

"She's very frail, but she's quite lucid. All she can talk about, most days, is her horses, and that dreadful platter of hers. You've seen it, she says. Isn't it gaudy?"

"I think it's quite beautiful," I said a bit stiffly—jerkily, too. Bali had thrown up his head on the other end of the leadrope, near knocking me off my feet, and attacked a fly on his flank. For an instant I thought he was going after Aileen. So did she: she beat a rapid retreat.

But she didn't run away completely. She seemed to come to a decision. "Mother has asked to see you. Celia said no, but I think you should go."

I stood flatfooted. Bali was cropping grass again, not a care
in the world. "Why?" was all I could think to ask.

"You ride her horses," said Aileen.

IV

Mrs. Tiffney looked even frailer than Aileen had warned me
she would, white face and white hair against the white sheet,
and tubes and wires and machines all doing their inscrutable
business while she simply tried to stay alive. I'd been not-
thinking, up till then. I'd been expecting that this would go
away, she'd come back, everything would be the way it was
before.

Looking at her, I knew she wasn't coming back. She might
go to a nursing home first, for a little while, but not for long.
The life was ebbing out of her even while I stood there.

She'd been asleep, I thought, till her eyes opened. They were
still the same, bigger than ever in her shrunken face. Her smile
made me almost forget all the rest of it. She reached out her
arms to me. I hugged her, being very careful with her tubes and
wires, and her brittle bones in the midst of them.

Aileen had come in with me. When I glanced back to where
she'd been, she was gone.

"Aileen was always tactful," Mrs. Tiffney said. "Brave,
even, if she saw a way to get by Celia."

Her voice was an old-lady voice as it never had been before,
thin and reedy. But no quaver in it.

"And how are my horses?" she asked me.

I had fifteen minutes, the nurse at the desk had told me. I
spent them telling her what she most wanted to know. I
babbled, maybe, to get it all in. She didn't seem to mind.

"And my ponies?" she asked. "My Xanthos and Balios?"

I'd been saving them for last. I started a little at their names.
No one had told me that was what they were. Then I smiled. Of
course the woman who had Achilles' shield—as genius had
imagined it, long after Achilles was dead—would name her
horses after Achilles' horses. She'd had a pair like them, Janna
had told me, for as long as anyone had known her. Maybe it
was part of the family tradition, like the shield on the wall.

"They're well," I answered her, once I remembered to stop maundering and talk. "They miss you. I had Bali out this morning; Janna and I did a pas-de-deux. We walked them past the surrey after, and they both stopped. I swear, they were asking where you were."

"You haven't told them?"

She sounded so severe, and so stern, that I stared at her.

She closed her eyes. The lids looked as thin as parchment. "No. Of course you wouldn't know. And they'd have heard people talking."

"We've been pretty quiet," I said. And when she opened her eyes and fixed them on me: "We did talk about it while we put the horses out. We'll tell them properly if you like."

"It would be a courtesy," she said, still severely. Then, with a glint: "However silly you may feel."

I didn't know about feeling silly. I talked to my cats at home. I talked to the horses when I rode them or brushed them. "I'll tell them," I said.

She shut her eyes again. I stood up. I was past my fifteen minutes. The nurse would be coming in to chase me out, unless I got myself out first. But when I started to draw back, she reached and caught my hand. I hadn't known there was so much strength in her.

"Look after my horses," she said. "Whatever happens, look after them. Promise me."

I'm not proud to admit that the first thing I thought of was how much it would cost to keep two horses. And the second was that Celia might have something to say about that. The third was something like a proper thought. "I'll do my best," I said..

"You'll do it," she said. "Promise!"

Her machines were starting to jerk and flicker. "I promise," I said, to calm her down mostly. But meaning it.

"And the shield," she said. "That, too. They go together, the horses and the shield. When I die—"

"You're not going to die."

She ignored me. "When I die, they choose to whom they go. It will be you, I think. The horses have chosen you already."

"But—"

"Look to Xanthos. Balios is the sweet one, the one who loves more easily, who gives himself first and without reservation. Xanthos is as wise as he is wicked. He was silenced long ago, and never spoke again, but his wits are as sharp as they ever were."

I opened my mouth. Closed it. She'd gone out of her head. She was dreaming old dreams, taking the name for the thing, and making her very real if by no means ordinary horses into horses out of a story. I'd done it myself when I was younger: little rafter-hipped cranky-tempered Katisha was the Prophet's own chosen mare, because she was a bay with one white foot and a star. But that hadn't made her the first of the Khamsa, any more than Mrs. Tiffney's wishing made her horses Achilles' horses. Or her shield—her neoclassical masterpiece— Achilles's shield.

They were treasures enough by themselves. I almost said so. But she was holding so tight, and looking so urgent, that I just nodded.

She nodded back. "The first moonlit night after I die, make sure you're at the barn. Watch the horses. Do whatever they ask you to do."

What could I do, except nod?

She let me go so suddenly that I gasped. But she was still breathing. "Remember," she said, no more than a whisper.

Then the nurse came charging in, took a look at the monitors, and ordered me out. The last I saw of Mrs. Tiffney was the nurse's white back and Mrs. Tiffney's white face, and her eyes on me, willing me to remember.

V

She died two days later, early in the morning of a gray and rainy day. She went in her sleep, Janna told me, and she went without pain. When I saw her laid out in the casket—and how Celia could think the shield was gaudy and reckon peach satin and mahogany with brass fittings tasteful, I would never understand—she was smiling. The funeral parlor was so full of flowers I could barely breathe, and so full of people I couldn't move, though it tended to flow toward the casket and then away into clumps on the edges. I recognized people from the barn, wide-eyed, white-faced kids with their parents, older ones alone or with friends, looking intensely uncomfortable but very determined, and the boarders in a cluster near the door. They all looked odd and half-complete in suits and dresses, without horses beside them or peering over their shoulders.

I said a proper few words to Celia, who didn't seem to recognize me, and to Aileen, who did. Celia didn't look as triumphant as I suspected she felt. He mother had been such a trial to her for so long, and now the trial was over. She'd get the property and the estate—she'd have to share with Aileen, of course, and there'd be bequests, but she'd hardly care for that. She'd administer it all, if she had anything to say about it.

"She lived a full life," a woman said behind me in the syrupy voice some people reserve for funerals. "She died happy. Doesn't she look wonderful, Celia?"

There was a knot in my throat, so thick and so solid that I couldn't swallow. I said something to somebody—it might have been Janna, who didn't look wonderful, either—and got out of there.

The horses were real. They didn't make empty noises, or drown me in flowers. Bali stood still while I cried in his mane, and when I wrapped my arms around his neck, he wrapped his neck around me.

Finally I pulled back. He had an infection, or something in the new hay had got to him: his eyes were streaming. So, when I turned around, were Zan's. I sniffed hard and got a cloth for them and a tissue for me, and wiped us all dry. "All right," I said. "So you're crying, too. Horses don't cry. You've got an allergy. What is it, mold in the hay?"

Bali bit me. Not hard enough to do damage, but hard enough to hurt. I was so shocked that I didn't even whack his nose; just stood there. And he shouldered past me. He didn't have a halter on. I'd come in to the stall to get him, forgotten the halter on its hook, and starting bawling. I grabbed for him. He kept on going.

Zan arched his neck, oh so delicately, and bared his long yellow teeth, and slid the bar on his door. I lunged. He was out, not moving fast at all, just fast enough to stay out of my reach.

I snatched halters on the way by. Zan pirouetted in the aisle and plucked them both out of my hands, and gave me a look that said as clear as if he'd spoken, "Not those, stupid." Then he spun again and waited.

I heard Mrs. Tiffney's voice. I was imagining it, of course. *Watch the horses. Do whatever they ask you to do.*

They certainly weren't acting like normal stallions on the loose. Bali was waiting, up past Zan, with his most melting expression. Zan—there was no other word for it—glared. His opinion of my intelligence, never very high to begin with, was dropping fast.

And it was dark, but there was a moon, a white half-moon in a field of stars like the ones in the center of the shield. Which was resting against the barn wall, just outside the door to the yard. And where the surrey used to stand was something else. I told myself it was the moon that made the old-fashioned black carriage look like something ages older and much smaller, and not black at all. Not in the least. That was gold, glimmering in the light from the aisle. And gold on the harness that lay on the ground beside it.

"But," I said, "I don't know *how* to yoke up a chariot."

Zan snorted at me. Bali was kinder. He went up to the pole that rested on the ground and positioned himself just so, and cocked an ear. After a minute Zan did the same, but his ears were flat in disgust. If he was choosing me, whatever that meant, he wasn't going to make it easy.

The harness wasn't that hard to figure out, once I'd had a good look at it. Or as good as moonlight and aislelight would give me. The yoke, of course, instead of collars. The bridles were familiar enough, and the reins. I ran those the way they seemed to want to run. The horses were patient, even Zan.

When they were harnessed, I stood back. I don't know what I was thinking. Nothing, by then. Except maybe that this wasn't happening. Something in the combination of moonlight and barn light made the horses shine. Bali, of course, with his silver mane and tail and his pewter coat. But Zan, too, a light that seemed to grow the longer I stood there, not silver but gold, lambent in the dark.

"Immortal horses," I said. "Bright gifts the gods gave to Peleus, and he to his son, and his son—" I broke off. "But the gods are dead!"

Zan shook his head in the bridle, baring his teeth at me. Bali watched me quietly. His ear slanted back. *Get in the chariot,* he meant. And how I knew that, I didn't want to know. No more than how I knew to pick up the shield—heavy as all heaven, but lighter than I'd expected, even so—and hang it where it best seemed to fit, by the left side of the chariot. I picked up the reins. They weren't any different from driving the surrey, though I was standing up in a vehicle that seemed no heavier than an eggshell, and no better sprung than one either, for all its pretty gilding. I didn't pretend that I was telling the horses where to go. They started at a walk, maneuvering carefully out of the yard where I'd seen Lipizzans, so long ago it seemed now, though it wasn't even nine months. Hardly long enough to carry a baby to term.

They took the way I'd driven so often, down the road a bit and into the woods. The moon didn't quite reach through the new leaves, but the horses were shining, silver and red-gold, bright enough to light the woods around them. The track was clear and smooth. They stretched into a trot.

The wind was soft in my face. It was a warm night, the first after a week of damp and rain, and everything smelled green, with sweetness that was apple blossoms, growing stronger as we went on. By the time we came out into the orchard, my lungs were full of it.

The trees were all in bloom, and the moon made them shine as bright almost as Bali's coat. He was cantering now, he and his brother, and the chariot rocked and rattled. I wrapped the reins around the post that seemed made for just that, and concentrated on hanging on. If I'd had any sense at all I would have hauled the horses down to a walk, turned them around and made them go back home. But all the strangeness had caught up with me. My head was full of moon and night and apple blossoms, and old, old stories, and the shield-rim under my left hand and the chariot's side under my right, and the horses running ahead of me, the chestnut, the gray, Xanthos, Balios, who couldn't be, who couldn't begin to be, but who surely were.

And I'd inherited them. I'd had the letter this morning, in her firm clear hand, with a date on it that made me start: the day after I'd first seen the shield. The shield was mine, if the horses chose me; and they were mine, too, and the wherewithal to keep and house them. That was how she put it. Tonight, in the way the moon's light fell, I knew that Janna had an inheritance, too; that Celia would be very surprised when the will was read. Oh, she'd have a handsome sum, and she'd grow richer than she'd been to begin with, once she'd invested it. And Aileen had a sum as large, which she wouldn't manage a tenth as well, unless she handed it over to Celia. But the land was Janna's, and the barn, and the horses, and the house, and everything that went with them, except Xanthos and Balios and the shield that a god had made to protect a legend in battle.

The moon had made a seer of me. I'd wake up in the morning with a headache and a sour stomach, and maybe a little regret for the dream I'd lost in waking.

It didn't feel like a dream, for all its strangeness. The night air was real, and the branch that whipped my face as the horses turned, mounting the hill. From the top of it, over the orchard that surrounded it, you could see for miles, down to the river on one side and over the ridges on the other, rolling outward in circles, with towns in the hollows, and fields full of cows, and the Riccis' vineyard with its rows of vines on poles; and maybe, through a gap in the last ridge, a glimmer that was the ocean. Here was higher than the hill Mrs. Tiffney's house stood on: it lay just below, with the barns beyond it. In the daytime you could see the rings and the hunt course, and the riders going through their paces like a dance.

Tonight the orchard was like a field of snow, and the hills were dark with once in a while a glimmer of light, and where Mrs. Tiffney's house stood, a shadow with a light at the top of it. Janna, home where she belonged, alone in the quiet rooms.

I found I couldn't care that she might be checking the barn, and she'd find the lights on and Mrs. Tiffney's horses missing. Or maybe she wouldn't. Maybe it was all dark and quiet, the doors shut, the horses asleep, everything asleep but me, and the horses who had brought me here. I got down from the chariot and went to their heads, smoothing Bali's forelock, venturing—carefully—to stroke Zan's neck. He allowed it. I slid my hand to the poll, round the ear, down past the plate of the cheek. He didn't nip or pull away. I touched the velvet of his nose. He blew into my palm. His eyes were bright. Immortal eyes. "How do you stand it?" I asked him. "Bound to mortal flesh that withers and dies, and you never age a day? How many have you loved, and however long they lived, in the end, all too soon, they died?"

He didn't speak. He'd been able to, once. I saw it in his eyes. Dust and clamor and a terrible roil of war, the charioteer cut down, the loved one—loved more than the master, for the master owned them, but the charioteer belonged to them, Patroklos who was never strong enough to fight his prince's battle—and the bitterness after, the prince taking vengeance, and the stallion speaking, foretelling the master's death. He'd grieved for the prince, too, and the prince's son in his time, and his son's son, and how it had come to daughters instead of sons—that he wasn't telling me. It was enough that it had been.

Bali rested his nose on my shoulder. Zan nipped lightly, very lightly, at my palm. Claiming me. The wind blew over us. West wind.

I laughed, up there on the hilltop, with the wind in my hair. Little no-name no-pedigree horses: by west wind out of storm wind, or maybe she had been a Harpy, like Celia and her sister. I belonged to them now. And a gaudy great platter that owned me as much as they did.

I'd cry again in a little while. I'd lost a friend; I owed her grief. But she'd be glad that I could laugh, who'd known exactly what she was doing when she filled her yard with Lipizzans and lured me in, and snared me for her stallions.

I leaned on Xanthos' shoulder, and Balios leaned lightly on mine. They were shining still, and brighter than the moon, but they were warm to the touch, real and solid horses. We stood there, the three of us, mortal I and immortal they, and watched the moon go down.

The Wonder Horse
by
George Byram

Here's one of the classic SF stories of horses and horse racing—and a quintessential demonstration of that old adage, Blood Will Tell . . .

As far as we can tell, this clever little story, from a 1957 Atlantic Monthly, *is George Byram's only venture into the science fiction field, although he has also sold stories to* Colliers, the Saturday Evening Post, True West, *and* Sports Afield, *among other markets. He has been a television announcer, a horse breeder, and has published two novels,* The Piper's Tune *and* Tomorrow's Hidden Season.

* * *

Webster says a mutation is a sudden variation, the offspring differing from the parents in some well-marked character or characters—and that certainly fits Red Eagle. He was foaled of registered parents, both his sire and dam descending from two of the best bloodlines in the breed. But the only thing normal about this colt was his color, a beautiful chestnut.

I attended Red Eagle's arrival into the world. He was kicking at the sac that enclosed him as I freed his nostrils from the membrane. He was on his feet in one minute. He was straight and steady on his pasterns by the time his dam had him licked dry. He had his first feeding before he was five minutes old, and he was beginning to buck and rear and prance by the time I got my wits about me and called Ben.

Ben came in the other end of the ramshackle barn from the feed lot. He was small as men go, but big for a jockey. Not really old at forty-two, his hair was gray and he was old in experience of horses.

Ben came into the box stall and as he saw the colt he stopped and whistled. He pushed back his hat and studied the red colt for a full five minutes. Even only minutes old a horseman could see he was markedly different. The bones from stifle to hock

22

and elbow to knee were abnormally long. There was unusual
length and slope of shoulder. He stood high in the croup and
looked like he was running downhill. He had a very long
underline and short back. All this spelled uniquely efficient
bone levers, and these levers were connected and powered by
the deepest hard-twisted muscles a colt ever brought into this
world. Unbelievable depth at the girth and immense spring to
the ribs meant an engine of heart and lungs capable of driving
those muscled levers to their maximum. Red Eagle's nostrils
were a third larger than any we had ever seen and he had a
large, loose windpipe between his broad jaws. He would be
able to fuel the engine with all the oxygen it could use. Most
important of all, the clean, sharp modeling of his head and the
bigness and luster of his eyes indicated courage, will to win.
But because of his strange proportions he looked weird.

"Holy Mary," said Ben softly, and I nodded agreement.

Ben and I had followed horses all our lives. I as a veterinarian
and trainer for big breeders, Ben as a jockey. Each of us had
outserved his usefulness. Ben had got too heavy to ride; I had got
too cantankerous for the owners to put up with. I had studied
bloodlines and knew the breeders were no longer improving the
breed, but I could never make anyone believe in my theories. One
owner after another had decided he could do without my services.
Ben and I had pooled our savings and bought a small ranch in
Colorado. We had taken the mare that had just foaled in lieu of
salary from our last employer. Barton Croupwell had laughed
when we had asked for the mare rather than our money.

"Costello," he said to me, "you and Ben have twenty-five
hundred coming. That mare is nineteen years old. She could
drop dead tomorrow."

"She could have one more foal too," I said.

"She could, but it's five to two she won't."

"That's good enough odds for the kind of blood she's
carrying."

Croupwell was a gambler who raised horses for only one
reason: to make money. He shook his head. "I've seen old
codgers set in their thinking, but you're the worst. I suppose
you've got a stallion picked out—in case this mare'll breed."

"He doesn't belong to you," I said.

That needled him. "I've got stallions that bring five thousand for a stud fee. Don't tell me they aren't good enough."

"Their bloodlines are wrong," I answered. "Mr. Carvelliers has a stallion called Wing Away."

"Carvelliers' stallions cost money. Are you and Ben that flush?" He already knew what I had in mind.

"You and Carvelliers trade services," I said. "It wouldn't cost you anything to have the mare bred."

He threw back his head and laughed. He was a tall, thin man, always beautifully tailored, with black hair and a line of mustache. "I'm not a philanthropist," he said. "Do you really want this mare?"

"I said I did."

"You really think she'll get with foal?"

"I'll turn your odds around. I say it's five to two she will."

"I'll gamble with you," he said. "I'll send the mare over to Carvelliers'. If she settles I'll take care of the stud fee. If she doesn't, I keep the mare."

"And my and Ben's twenty-five hundred?"

"Of course."

"You're no gambler," I said, looking him in the eye, "but I'll take the bet."

Now, Ben and I were looking at a running machine that was something new on the face of the earth.

Our ranch was perfect for training the colt. It was out of the way and we took particular care that no one ever saw Red Eagle. By the time he was a yearling, our wildest estimate of what he would be had fallen short. Ben began to ride him when he was a coming two-year-old. By that time he had reached seventeen hands, weighed twelve hundred pounds, and could carry Ben's hundred and twenty-six as if Ben were nothing. Every time Ben stepped off him he was gibbering like an idiot. I was little better. This horse didn't run; he flowed. Morning after morning as Ben began to open him up I would watch him coming down the track we had dozed out of the prairie and he looked like a great wheel with flashing spokes rolling irresistibly forward. Carrying as much weight as mature horses are asked to carry, our stop watch told us Red Eagle had broken every world record for all distances and this on an imperfect track. Ben and I were scared.

One night when the racing season was close upon us, Ben said nervously, "I've made a few calls to some jockeys I know. Croupwell's and Carvelliers' and some others. The best two-year-olds they got are just normal, good colts. Red Eagle will beat them twenty lengths."

"You've got to keep him under restraint, Ben. You can't let anybody know what he can do."

"I can do anything with him out here by himself. But who knows what he'll do with other horses?"

"You've got to hold him."

"Listen, Cos, I've ridden some of the best and some of the toughest. I know what I can hold and what I can't. If Eagle ever takes it in his head to run, there'll not be a hell of a lot I can do about it."

"We've trained him careful."

"Yes, but if I've got him figured, he'll go crazy if a horse starts to crowd him. Another thing, any horseman will see at a glance what we've got. They'll know we're not letting him extend himself."

We were standing out by the pine pole paddock and I turned and looked at Red Eagle. Have you ever seen a cheetah? It's a cat. It runs faster than any other living creature. It's long-legged and long-bodied and it moves soft and graceful until it starts to run; then it becomes a streak with a blur of legs beneath. Red Eagle looked more like a twelve-hundred-pound cheetah than a horse and he ran the same way.

"Well, he's a race horse," I said. "If we don't race him, what'll we do with him?"

"We'll race him," said Ben, "but things ain't ever goin' to be the same again."

That turned out to be pure prophecy.

We decided to start him on a western track. We had to mortgage the ranch to get the money for his entry fee, but we had him entered in plenty of time. Two days before the race we hauled him, blanketed, in a closed trailer and put him into his stall without anyone getting a good look at him. We worked him out at dawn each morning before any other riders were exercising their horses.

This track was one where a lot of breeders tried their two-year-olds. The day of the race the first person I saw was Croupwell. His mild interest told me he already knew we had an entry. He looked at my worn Levis and string-bean frame. "What's happened these three years, Costello? You don't appear to have eaten regular."

"After today it'll be different," I told him.

"That colt you have entered, eh? He's not the bet you won from me, is he?"

"The same."

"I see by the papers Ben's riding. Ben must have lost weight too."

"Not so's you'd notice."

"You're not asking a two-year-old to carry a hundred and twenty-eight pounds on its first start!"

"He's used to Ben," I said casually.

"Costello, I happen to know you mortgaged your place to get the entry fee." He was looking at me speculatively. His gambler's instinct told him something was amiss. "Let's have a look at the colt."

"You'll see him when we bring him out to be saddled," I said and walked away.

You can't lead a horse like that among a group of horsemen without things happening. Men who spend their lives with horses know what gives a horse reach and speed and staying power. It didn't take an expert to see what Red Eagle had. When we took the blanket off him in the saddle paddock every jockey and owner began to move close. In no time there was a milling group of horsemen in front of where Ben and I were saddling Eagle.

Carvelliers, a handsome, white-haired Southern gentleman, called me to him. "Costello, is that Wing Away's colt?"

"Your signature's on his papers," I said.

"I'll give you fifty thousand dollars for his dam."

"She's dead," I said. "She died two weeks after we'd weaned this colt."

"Put a price on the colt," he said without hesitation.

"He's not for sale," I answered.

"We'll talk later," he said and turned and headed for the
betting windows. Every man in the crowd followed him. I saw
several stable hands pleading with acquaintances to borrow
money to bet on Eagle despite the extra weight he would be
spotting the other horses. By the time the parimutuel windows
closed, our horse was the odds-on favorite and nobody had
seen him run.

"I'm glad we didn't have any money to bet," said Ben, as I
legged him up. "A dollar'll only make you a dime after what
they've done to the odds."

The falling odds on Red Eagle had alerted the crowd to
watch for him. As the horses paraded before the stands there
was a rippling murmur of applause. He looked entirely unlike
the other eight horses on the track. He padded along, his head
bobbing easily, his long hind legs making him look like he was
going downhill. He took one step to the other mincing
thoroughbreds' three.

I had gone down to the rail and as Ben brought him by,
heading for the backstretch where the six-furlong race would
start, I could see the Eagle watching the other horses, his ears
flicking curiously. I looked at Ben. He was pale. "How is he?"
I called.

Ben glanced at me out of the corners of his eyes. "He's
different."

"Different!" I called back edgily. "How?"

"Your guess is as good as mine," Ben called over his
shoulder.

Eagle went into the gate at his assigned place on the outside
as docilely as we'd trained him to. But when the gate flew
open, the rush of horses startled him. Breaking on top, he
opened up five lengths on the field in the first sixteenth of a
mile. The crowd went whoosh with a concerted sigh of
amazement.

"Father in heaven, hold him," I heard myself saying.

Through my binoculars, I could see the riders on the other
horses studying the red horse ahead of them. Many two-year-
olds break wild, but no horse opens five lengths in less than
two hundred yards. I saw Ben steadying him gently, and as they

went around the first turn, Ben had slowed him until the pack moved up to within a length.

That was as close as any horse ever got. Around the turn a couple of riders went after Eagle and the pack spread briefly into groups of three and two and two singles. I could see the two horses behind Eagle make their move. Eagle opened another three lengths before they hit the turn into the stretch and I could see Ben fighting him. The two that had tried to take the lead were used up and the pack came by them as all the riders turned their horses on for the stretch drive. Eagle seemed to sense the concerted effort behind him and his rate of flow changed. It was as if a racing car had its accelerator floor-boarded. He came into the stretch gaining a half length every time his feet hit the turf.

When he hit the wire he was a hundred yards ahead of the nearest horse and still going away. Ben had to take him completely around the track before Eagle realized there were no horses behind him. By the time Ben walked him into the winner's circle, Eagle's sides were rising and falling evenly. He was only damp, not having got himself hot enough to sweat.

The first thing I remember seeing was Ben's guilty expression. "I tried to hold him," he said. "When he realized something was trying to outrun him he got so damn mad he didn't even know I was there."

The loudspeaker had gone into a stuttering frenzy. Yes, the world's record for six furlongs had been broken. Not only broken, ladies and gentlemen; five seconds had been cut from it. No, the win was not official. Track veterinarians had to examine the horse. Please keep your seats, ladies and gentlemen.

Keep their seats, hell! Every man, woman, and child was going to see at close range the horse that could run like that. There had been tears in my eyes as Eagle rolled down the stretch. You couldn't stay calm when you saw what these people had seen.

The rest of that day sorts itself into blurred episodes. First, the vets checked Eagle's teeth, his registration papers, his date of foaling, and finally rechecked the number tattooed in his lip to make sure he was a two-year-old. Then they found that he had not been stimulated. They also found measurements so unbelievable they seriously questioned whether this animal was a horse. They went into a huddle with the track officials.

There was loose talk of trying to rule the Eagle off the tracks. Carvelliers pointed out that Eagle's papers were in perfect order, his own stallion had sired him, he was a thoroughbred of accepted bloodlines, and there was no way he could legally be ruled ineligible.

"If that horse is allowed to run," said one track official, "who will race against him?"

Croupwell was seated at the conference table, as were most of the other owners. "Gentlemen," he said suavely, "aren't you forgetting the handicapper?"

The job of a handicapper is to figure how much weight each horse is to carry. It is a known fact that a good handicapper can make any field of horses come in almost nose and nose by imposing greater weights on the faster horses. But Croupwell was forgetting something. Usually, only older horses run in handicaps.

I jumped to my feet. "You know two-year-olds are not generally handicapped," I said. "They race under allowance conditions."

"True," said Croupwell. "Two-year-olds usually do run under arbitrary weights. But it is a flexible rule, devised to fit the existing situation. Now that the situation has changed, arbitrarily the weights must be changed."

Carvelliers frowned angrily. "Red Eagle was carrying a hundred and twenty-eight against a hundred and four for the other colts. You would have to impose such weights to bring him down to an ordinary horse that you'd break him down."

Croupwell shrugged. "If that should be true, it is unfortunate. But we have to think of the good of racing. You know that its lifeblood is betting. There will be no betting against this horse in any race it's entered."

Carvelliers rose. "Gentlemen," and the way he said it was an insult, "I have been breeding and racing horses all my life. It has always been my belief that racing was to improve the breed, not kill the best horses." He turned to Ben and me. "At your convenience I would like to speak with you."

Ben and I paid off the loan we'd used for the entry fee, bought ourselves some presentable clothes, and went up to Carvelliers' hotel.

"Hello, Ben, good to see you," he said. "Costello, I owe you an apology. I've disagreed with you on bloodlines for years. You've proven me wrong."

"You've been wrong," I agreed, "but Red Eagle is not the proof. He would have been a good colt if he was normal— maybe the best, but what he actually is has nothing to do with bloodlines."

"Do you think he's a mutation—something new?"

"Completely."

"How much weight do you think he can carry and still win?"

I turned to Ben and Ben said, "He'll win carrying any weight. He'll kill himself to win."

"It's too bad you couldn't have held him," said Carvelliers. "My God, five seconds cut from the record. Don't fool yourself, they'll weight him until even tendons and joints such as his can't stand it. Will you run him regardless?"

"What else will there be to do?"

"Hmmmm. Yes. Well, maybe you're right. But if they break him down, I have a proposition to make you."

We thanked him and left.

Ben and I planned our campaign carefully. "We've got to train him with other horses," Ben told me. "If I can get him used to letting a horse stay a few lengths behind, I can hold him down."

We bought two fairly good platers with the rest of our first winnings and hired neighboring ranch kids to ride them. We began to see men with binoculars on the hills around our track. We let the Eagle loaf and the boys with the binoculars never saw any great times.

The racing world had gone crazy over what Red Eagle had done to the records. But as time passed and the binocular boys reported he wasn't burning up his home track, the writers began to hint that it had been a freak performance—certainly

remarkable, but could he do it again? This was the attitude we
wanted. Then we put Red Eagle in his second race, this one a
mile and a sixteenth.

It was a big stakes race for two-year-olds. We didn't enter
him until the last minute. Even so, the news got around and the
track had never had such a large attendance and such little
betting. The people didn't dare bet against the Eagle, but he had
only run at six furlongs and they weren't ready to believe in
him and bet on him to run a distance. Because of the low
pari-mutuel take, we were very unpopular with the officials of
that track.

"If there's any way you can do it," I told Ben, "hold him at
the gate."

"I'll hold him if I can."

By this time Red Eagle had become used to other horses and
would come out of the gate running easily. When they sprung
the gate on those crack two-year-olds that day, Ben had a tight
rein and the pack opened a length on the Eagle before he
understood he'd been double-crossed. When he saw horses
ahead of him he went crazy.

He swung far outside and caught the pack before they were
in front of the stands. He'd opened five lengths at the first turn.
He continued to accelerate in the back stretch, and the crowd
had gone crazy too. When he turned into the stretch the nearest
thing to him was the starting gate the attendants hadn't quite
had time to pull out of the way. Eagle swerved wide to miss the
gate and then, as if the gate had made him madder, really turned
it on. When he crossed the finish line the first horse behind him
hadn't entered the stretch. I sat down weakly and cried. He had
cut *ten* seconds off the world's record for a mile and a
sixteenth.

The pandemonium did not subside when the race was over.
Front-page headlines all over the world said, "New Wonder
Horse Turns Racing World Topsy-turvy." That was an under-
statement.

"The next time we run him," I told Ben, "they'll put two
sacks of feed and a bale of hay on him."

Ben was gazing off into the distance. "You can't imagine
what it's like to sit on all that power and watch a field of horses

go by you backward, blip, like that. You know something, Cos? He still wasn't flat out."

"Fine," I said, sarcastically. "We'll run him against Mercedes and Jaguars."

Well, they weighted him. The handicapper called for one hundred thirty-seven pounds. It was an unheard-of weight for a two-year-old to carry, but it wasn't as bad as I had expected.

At home we put the one thirty-seven on him and eased him along for a few weeks. He didn't seem to notice the weight. The first time Ben let him out he broke his own record. I kept tabs on his legs and he never heated in the joints or swelled.

We entered him in the next race to come up. It rained for two days before the race and the track was a sea of mud. Some thought the "flying machine," as Red Eagle was beginning to be called, could not set his blazing pace in mud.

"What do you think?" I asked Ben. "He's never run in mud."

"Hell, Cos, that horse don't notice what he's running on. He just feels the pressure of something behind him trying to outrun him and it pushes him like a jet."

Ben was right. When the pack came out of the gate that day, Red Eagle squirted ahead like a watermelon seed squeezed from between your fingers. He sprayed the pack briefly with mud, then blithely left them, and when he came down the stretch he was completely alone.

During the next several races, three things became apparent. First, the handicapper had no measuring stick to figure what weight Eagle should carry. They called for one hundred forty, forty-two, then forty-five, and Eagle came down the stretch alone. The second thing became apparent after Eagle had won carrying one forty-five. His next race, he started alone. No one would enter against him. Third, Eagle was drawing the greatest crowds in the history of racing.

There were two big races left that season. They were one day and a thousand miles apart. The officials at both tracks were in a dilemma. Whichever race Eagle entered would have a huge crowd, but it would be a walkaway and that crowd would bet its last dollar on Eagle, because the track was required by law to pay ten cents on the dollar. The officials resolved their dilemma by using the old adage: *You can stop a fright train if*

you put enough weight on it. Red Eagle was required to carry
the unheard-of weight of one hundred and seventy pounds.
Thus they hoped to encourage other owners to race against us
and at the same time they'd have Eagle's drawing power.

Ben grew obstinate. "I don't want to hurt him and that
weight'll break him down."

"Great," I replied. "Two worn-out old duffers with the
world's greatest horse end up with two platers, a sand-hills
ranch, and the winnings from a few races."

"I know how you feel," said Ben. "The only thing you could
have got out of this was money, but I get to ride him."

"Well," I said, trying to be philosophical about it, "I get to
watch him and that's almost as good as riding him." I stopped
and grabbed Ben's arm. "What did I say?"

Ben jerked his arm away. "You gone nuts?"

"Get to watch him! Ben, what's happened every time the
Eagle's run?"

"He's broke a record," said Ben matter-of-factly.

"He's sent several thousand people into hysterics," I
amended.

Ben looked at me. "Are you thinking people would pay to
see just one horse run?"

"Has there ever been more than one when the Eagle's run?
Come on. We're going to enter him."

We entered Eagle in the next to the last race of the season.
What I'd expected happened. All the other owners pulled out.
They weren't having any of the Eagle even carrying a hundred
and seventy pounds. They all entered in the last race. No horse,
not even the Eagle—they thought—had the kind of stamina to
make two efforts on successive days with a plane trip sand-
wiched between, so they felt safe.

The officials at the second track were jubilant. They had the
largest field they had ever run. The officials at the first track
had apoplexy. They wanted to talk to us. They offered plane
fare and I flew down.

"Would you consider an agreement," they asked, "whereby
you would withdraw your horse?"

"I would not," I replied.

"The public won't attend a walkaway," they groaned, "even with the drawing power of your horse." What they were thinking of was that ten cents on the dollar.

"That's where you're wrong," I told them. "Advertise that the wonder horse is running unweighted against his own record and you'll have a sellout."

Legally, they could not call off the race, so they had to agree.

On the way home I stopped off at Carvelliers'. We had a long talk and drew up an agreement. "It'll work," I said. "I know it will."

"Yes," agreed Carvelliers, "it will work, but you must persuade Ben to run him just once carrying the hundred and seventy. We've got to scare the whole racing world to death."

"I'll persuade him," I promised.

When I got home I took Ben aside. "Ben," I said, "every cow horse has to carry more than a hundred and seventy pounds."

"Yeah, but a cow horse don't run a mile in just over a minute."

"Nevertheless," I said, "he'll run as fast as he can carrying that weight and it doesn't hurt him."

"But a cow horse has pasterns and joints like a work horse. They just ain't built like a thoroughbred."

"Neither is Red Eagle," I answered.

"What's this all about? You already arranged for him not to carry any weight."

"That's for the first race."

"*First race!* You ain't thinkin' of runnin' in both of them?"

"Yes, and that second one will be his last race. I'll never ask you to ride him carrying that kind of weight again."

"You ought to be ashamed to ask me to ride him carrying it at all." Then what I had said sun in. "*Last* race! How do you know it'll be his last race?"

"I forgot to tell you I had a talk with Carvelliers."

"So you had a talk with Carvelliers. So what?"

"Ben," I pleaded, "trust me. See what the Eagle can do with a hundred and seventy."

"All right," said Ben grudgingly, "but I ain't going to turn him on."

"Turn him on!" I snorted. "You ain't ever been able to turn him off."

Ben was surprised but I wasn't when Red Eagle galloped easily under the weight. Ben rode him for a week before he got up the nerve to let him run. Eagle was still way ahead of every record except his own. He stayed sound.

When we entered him in the second race all but five owners withdrew their horses. These five knew their animals were the best of that season, barring our colt. And they believed that the Eagle after a plane ride, a run the day before, and carrying a hundred and seventy pounds was fair competition.

At the first track Eagle ran unweighted before a packed stand. The people jumped and shouted with excitement as the red streak flowed around the track, racing the second hand of the huge clock that had been erected in front of the odds board. Ben was worried about the coming race and only let him cut a second off his previous record. But that was enough. The crowd went mad. And I had the last ammunition I needed.

The next day dawned clear and sunny. The track was fast. Every seat in the stand was sold and the infield was packed. The press boxes overflowed with writers, anxiously writing to report to the world what the wonder horse would do. The crowd that day didn't have to be told. They bet their last dollar on him to win.

Well, it's all history now. Red Eagle, carrying one hundred and seventy pounds, beat the next fastest horse five lengths. All the fences in front of the stands were torn down by the crowd trying to get a close look at the Eagle. The track lost a fortune and three officials had heart attacks.

A meeting was called and they pleaded with us to remove our horse from competition.

"Gentlemen," I said, "we'll make you a proposition. You noticed yesterday that the gate for Eagle's exhibition was the largest that track ever had. Do you understand? People will pay to watch Eagle run against time. If you'll guarantee us two exhibitions a season at each major track and give us sixty per cent of the gate, we'll agree never to run the Eagle in competition."

It was such a logical move that they wondered they hadn't

thought of it themselves. It worked out beautifully. Owners of ordinary horses could run them with the conviction that they would at least be somewhere in the stretch when the race finished. The officials were happy, because not only was racing secure again, but they made money out of their forty per cent of the gates of Eagle's exhibitions. And we were happy, because we made even more money. Everything has been serene for three seasons. But I'm a little concerned about next year.

I forgot to tell you the arrangement Carvelliers and I had made. First, we had discussed a little-known aspect of mutations: namely, that they pass on to their offspring their new characteristics. Carvelliers has fifty brood mares on his breeding farm, and Red Eagle proved so sure at stud that next season fifty carbon copies of him will be hitting the tracks. You'd never believe it, but they run just like their sire, and Ben and I own fifty per cent of each of them. Ben feels somewhat badly about it, but, as I pointed out, we only promised not to run the Eagle.

On the Gem Planet
by
Cordwainer Smith

The late Cordwainer Smith—in "real" life Dr. Paul M.A. Linebarger, scholar and statesman—created a science fiction cosmology unique in its scope and complexity: a millennia-spanning future history, logically outlandish and elegantly strange, set against a vivid, richly colored, mythically intense universe where animals assume the shape of men, vast plano-form ships whisper through multidimensional space, immortality can be bought, and the mysterious Lords of the Instrumentality rule a haunted Earth too old for history.

"On the Gem Planet" is a slice of that universe, one with an immortal horse at its heart: an adventure on the strange planet Pontoppidan, an airless world made of rubies and emeralds and amethysts, where the really *valuable things are flowers and earthworms (which cost eight carats of diamond per worm), and nothing is more precious than dirt . . . except, perhaps, life itself.*

* * *

I

When Casher O'Neill came to Pontoppidan, he found that the capital city was appropriately called Andersen.

This was the second century of the Rediscovery of Man. People everywhere had taken up old names, old languages, old customs, as fast as the robots and the underpeople could retrieve the data from the rubbish of forgotten starlanes or the subsurface ruins of Manhome itself.

Casher knew this very well, to his bitter cost. Re-acculturation had brought him revolution and exile. He came from the dry, beautiful planet of Mizzer. He was himself the nephew of the ruined ex-ruler, Kuraf, whose collection of objectionable books had at one time been unmatched in the settled galaxy; he had stood aside, half-assenting, when the colonels Gibna and Wedder took over the planet in the name of reform; he had implored the Instrumentality, vainly, for help when Wedder became a tyrant; and now he traveled among the stars, looking for men or weapons who might destroy Wedder and make Kaheer again the luxurious, happy city which it once had been.

He felt that his cause was hopeless when he landed on Pontoppidan. The people were warm-hearted, friendly, intelligent, but they had no motives to fight for, no weapons to fight with, no enemies to fight against. They had little public spirit, such as Casher O'Neill had seen back on his native planet of Mizzer. They were concerned about little things.

Indeed, at the time of his arrival, the Pontoppidans were wildly excited about a horse.

A horse! Who worries about one horse?

Casher O'Neill himself said so. "Why bother about a horse? We have lots of them on Mizzer. They are four-handed beings, eight times the weight of a man, with only one finger on each of the four hands. The fingernail is very heavy and permits them to run fast. That's why our people have them, for running."

"Why run?" said the Hereditary Dictator of Pontoppidan. "Why run, when you can fly? Don't you have ornithopters?"

"We don't run with them," said Casher indignantly. "We make them run against each other and then we pay prizes to the one which runs fastest."

"But then," said Philip Vincent, the Hereditary Dictator, "you get a very illogical situation. When you have tried out these four-fingered beings, you know how fast each one goes. So what? Why bother?"

His niece interrupted. She was a fragile little thing, smaller than Casher O'Neill liked women to be. She had clear gray eyes, well-marked eyebrows, a very artificial coiffure of silver-blonde hair and the most sensitive little mouth he had ever seen. She conformed to the local fashion by wearing some kind of powder or face cream which was flesh-pink in color but which had overtones of lilac. On a woman as old as twenty-two, such a coloration would have made the wearer look like an old hag, but on Genevieve it was pleasant, if rather startling. It gave the effect of a happy child playing grown-up and doing the job joyfully and well. Casher knew that it was hard to tell ages in these off-trail planets. Genevieve might be a grand dame in her third or fourth rejuvenation.

He doubted it, on second glance. What she said was sensible, young, and pert:

"But uncle, they're *animals*!"

"I know that," he rumbled.

"But uncle, don't you see it?"

"Stop saying 'but uncle' and tell me what you mean," growled the Dictator, very fondly.

"Animals are always *uncertain*."

"Of course," said the uncle.

"That makes it a game, uncle," said Genevieve. "They're never sure that any one of them would do the same thing twice. Imagine the excitement—the beautiful big beings from earth running around and around on their four middle fingers, the big fingernails making the gems jump loose from the ground."

"I'm not at all sure it's that way. Besides, Mizzer may be covered with something valuable, such as earth or sand, instead of gemstones like the ones we have here on Pontoppidan. You know your flowerpots with their rich, warm, wet, soft earth?"

"Of course I do, uncle. And I know what you paid for them. You were very generous. And still are," she added diplomatically, glancing quickly at Casher O'Neill to see how the familial piety went across with the visitor.

"We're not that rich on Mizzer. It's mostly sand, with farmland along the Twelve Niles, our big rivers."

"I've seen pictures of rivers," said Genevieve. "Imagine living on a whole world full of flowerpot stuff!"

"You're getting off the subject, darling. We were wondering why anyone would bring one horse, just one horse, to Pontoppidan. I suppose you could race a horse against himself, if you had a stopwatch. But would it be fun? Would you do that, young man?"

Casher O'Neill tried to be respectful. "In my home we used to have a lot of horses. I've seen my uncle time them one by one."

"Your uncle?" said the Dictator interestedly. "Who was your

uncle that he had all these four-fingered 'horses' running around? They're all Earth animals and very expensive."

Casher felt the coming of the low, slow blow he had met so many times before, right from the whole outside world into the pit of his stomach. "My uncle"—he stammered—"my uncle—I thought you knew—was the old Dictator of Mizzer, Kuraf."

Philip Vincent jumped to his feet, very lightly for so well-fleshed a man. The young mistress, Genevieve, clutched at the throat of her dress.

"Kuraf!" cried the old Dictator. "Kuraf! We know about him, even here. But you were supposed to be a Mizzer patriot, not one of Kuraf's people."

"He doesn't have any children—" Casher began to explain.

"I should think not, not with those habits!" snapped the old man.

"—so I'm his nephew and his heir. But I'm not trying to put the Dictatorship back, even though I should be dictator. I just want to get rid of Colonel Wedder. He has ruined my people, and I am looking for money or weapons or help to make my home-world free." This was the point, Casher O'Neill knew, at which people either started believing him or did not. If they did not, there was not much he could do about it. If they did, he was sure to get some sympathy. So far, no help. Just sympathy.

But the Instrumentality, while refusing to take action against Colonel Wedder, had given young Casher O'Neill an all-world travel pass—something which a hundred lifetimes of savings could not have purchased for the ordinary man. (His obscene old uncle had gone off to Sunvale, on Ttiollé, the resort planet, to live out his years between the casino and the beach.) Casher O'Neill held the conscience of Mizzer in his hand. Only he, among the star travelers, cared enough to fight for the freedom of the Twelve Niles. Here, now, in this room, there was a turning point.

"I won't give you anything," said the Hereditary Dictator, but he said it in a friendly voice. His niece started tugging at his sleeve.

The older man went on. "Stop it, girl. I won't give you

anything, not if you're part of that rotten lot of Kuraf's, not unless—"

"Anything, sir, anything, just so that I get help or weapons to go home to the Twelve Niles!"

"All right, then. Unless you open your mind to me. I'm a good telepath myself."

"Open my mind! Whatever for?" The incongruous indecency of it shocked Casher O'Neill. He'd had men and women and governments ask a lot of strange things from him, but no one before had had the cold impudence to ask him to open his mind. "And why you?" he went on. "What would you get out of it? There's nothing much in my mind."

"To make sure," said the Hereditary Dictator, "that you are not too honest and sharp in your beliefs. If you're positive that you know what to do, you might be another Colonel Wedder, putting your people through a dozen torments for a Utopia which never quite comes true. If you don't care at all, you might be like your uncle. He did no real harm. He just stole his planet blind and he had some extraordinary habits which got him talked about between the stars. He never killed a man in his life, did he?"

"No, sir," said Casher O'Neill, "he never did." It relieved him to tell the one little good thing about his uncle; there was so very, very little which could be said in Kuraf's favor.

"I don't like slobbering old libertines like your uncle," said Philip Vincent, "but I don't hate them either. They don't hurt other people much. As a matter of actual fact, they don't hurt anyone but themselves. They waste property, though. Like these horses you have on Mizzer. We'd never bring living beings to this world of Pontoppidan, just to play games with. And you know we're not poor. We're no Old North Australia, but we have a good income here."

That, thought Casher O'Neill, is the understatement of the year, but he was a careful young man with a great deal at stake, so he said nothing.

The Dictator looked at him shrewdly. He appreciated the value of Casher's tactful silence. Genevieve tugged at his sleeve, but he frowned her interruption away.

"If," said the Hereditary Dictator, "*if*," he repeated, "you

pass two tests, I will give you a green ruby as big as my head.
If my Committee will allow me to do so. But I think I can talk
them around. One test is that you let me peep all over your
mind, to make sure that I am not dealing with one more honest
fool. If you're too honest, you're a fool and a danger to
mankind. I'll give you a dinner and ship you off-planet as fast
as I can. And the other test is—solve the puzzle of this horse.
The one horse on Pontoppidan. Why is the animal here? What
should we do with it? If it's good to eat, how should we cook
it? Or can we trade it to some other world, like your planet
Mizzer, which seems to set a value on horses?"

"Thank you, sir—" said Casher O'Neill.

"But, uncle—" said Genevieve.

"Keep quiet, my darling, and let the young man speak," said
the Dictator.

"—all I was going to ask, is," said Casher O'Neill, "what's
a green ruby good for? I didn't even know they came green."

"That, young man, is a Pontoppidan specialty. We have a
geology based on ultra-heavy chemistry. This planet was once
a fragment from a giant planet which imploded. The use is
simple. With a green ruby you can make a laser beam which
will boil away your city of Kaheer in a single sweep. We don't
have weapons here and we don't believe in them, so I won't
give you a weapon. You'll have to travel further to find a ship
and to get the apparatus for mounting your green ruby. *If* I give
it to you. But you will be one more step along in your fight with
Colonel Wedder."

"Thank you, thank you, most honorable sir!" cried Casher
O'Neill.

"But uncle," said Genevieve, "you shouldn't have picked
those two things because I know the answers."

"You know all about *him*," said the Hereditary Dictator, "by
some means of your own?"

Genevieve flushed under her lilac-hued foundation cream. "I
know enough for us to know."

"How do you know it, my darling?"

"I just know," said Genevieve.

Her uncle made no comment, but he smiled widely and
indulgently as if he had heard that particular phrase before.

She stamped her foot. "And I know about the horse, too. *All* about it."

"Have you seen it?"

"No."

"Have you talked to it?"

"Horses don't talk, uncle."

"Most underpeople do," he said.

"This isn't an underperson, uncle. It's a plain unmodified old Earth animal. It never did talk."

"Then what do you know, my honey?" The uncle was affectionate, but there was the crackle of impatience under his voice.

"I taped it. The whole thing. The story of the horse of Pontoppidan. And I've edited it, too. I was going to show it to you this morning, but your staff sent that young man in."

Casher O'Neill looked his apologies at Genevieve.

She did not notice him. Her eyes were on her uncle.

"Since you've done this much, we might as well see it." He turned to the attendants. "Bring chairs. And drinks. You know mine. The young lady will take tea with lemon. Real tea. Will you have coffee, young man?"

"You have coffee!" cried Casher O'Neill. As soon as he said it, he felt like a fool. Pontoppidan was a *rich* planet. On most worlds' exchanges, coffee came out to about two man-years per kilo. Here halftracks crunched their way through gems as they went to load up the frequent trading vessels.

The chairs were put in place. The drinks arrived. The Hereditary Dictator had been momentarily lost in a brown study, as though he were wondering about his promise to Casher O'Neill. He had even murmured to the young man, "Our bargain stands? Never mind what my niece says." Casher had nodded vigorously. The old man had gone back to frowning at the servants and did not relax until a tiger-man bounded into the room, carrying a tray with acrobatic precision. The chairs were already in place.

The uncle held his niece's chair for her as a command that she sit down. He nodded Casher O'Neill into a chair on the other side of himself.

He commanded, "Dim the lights . . ."

The room plunged into semi-darkness.

Without being told, the people took their places immediately behind the three main seats and the underpeople perched or sat on benches and tables behind them. Very little was spoken. Casher O'Neill could sense that Pontoppidan was a well-run place. He began to wonder if the Hereditary Dictator had much real work left to do, if he could fuss that much over a single horse. Perhaps all he did was boss his niece and watch the robots load truckloads of gems into sacks while the underpeople weighed them, listed them and wrote out the bills for the customers.

II

There was no screen; this was a good machine.

The planet Pontoppidan came into view, its airless brightness giving strong hints of the mineral riches which might be found.

Here and there enormous domes, such as the one in which this palace was located, came into view.

Genevieve's own voice, girlish, impulsive and yet didactic, rang out with the story of her planet. It was as though she had prepared the picture not only for her own uncle but for off-world visitors as well. *By Joan, that's it!* thought Casher O'Neill. *If they don't raise much food here, outside of the hydroponics, and don't have any real People Places, they have to trade: that does mean visitors and many, many of them.*

The story was interesting, but the girl herself was more interesting. Her face shone in the shifting light which the images—a meter, perhaps a little more, from the floor—reflected across the room. Casher O'Neill thought that he had never before seen a woman who so peculiarly combined intelligence and charm. She was girl, girl, girl, all the way through; but she was also very smart and pleased with being smart. It betokened a happy life. He found himself glancing covertly at her. Once he caught her glancing, equally covertly, at him. The darkness of the scene enabled them both to pass it off as an accident without embarrassment.

Her viewtape had come to the story of the *dipsies,* enormous canyons which lay like deep gashes on the surface of the planet. Some of the color views were spectacular beyond belief. Casher O'Neill, as the "appointed one" of Mizzer, had had plenty of time to wander through the nonsalacious parts of his uncle's collections, and he had seen pictures of the most notable worlds.

Never had he seen anything like this. One view showed a sunset against a six-kilometer cliff of a material which looked like a solid emerald. The peculiar bright sunshine of Pontoppidan's small, penetrating, lilac-hued sun ran like living water over the precipice of gems. Even the reduced image, one meter by one meter, was enough to make him catch his breath.

The bottom of the dipsy had vapor emerging in curious cylindrical columns which seemed to erode as they reached two or three times the height of a man. The recorded voice of Genevieve was explaining that the very thin atmosphere of Pontoppidan would not be breathable for another 2,520 years, since the settlers did not wish to squander their resources on a luxury like breathing when the whole planet only had 60,000 inhabitants; they would rather go on with masks and use their wealth in other ways. After all, it was not as though they did not have their domed cities, some of them many kilometers in radius. Besides the usual hydroponics, they had even imported 7.2 hectares of garden soil, 5.5 centimeters deep, together with enough water to make the gardens rich and fruitful. They had brought worms, too, at the price of eight carats of diamond per living worm, in order to keep the soil of the gardens loose and living.

Genevieve's transcribed voice rang out with pride as she listed these accomplishments of her people, but a note of sadness came in when she returned to the subject of the dipsies. ". . . and though we would like to live in them and develop their atmosphere, we dare not. There is too much escape of radioactivity. The geysers themselves may or may not be contaminated from one hour to the next. So we just look at them. Not one of them has ever been settled, except for the Hippy Dipsy, where the horse came from. Watch this next picture."

The camera sheered up, up, up from the surface of the planet. Where it had wandered among mountains of diamonds and valleys of tourmalines, it now took to the blue-black of near, inner space. One of the canyons showed (from high altitude) the grotesque pattern of a human woman's hips and legs, though what might have been the upper body was lost in a confusion of broken hills which ended in a bright almost-iridescent plain to the North.

"That," said the real Genevieve, overriding her own voice on the screen, "is the Hippy Dipsy. There, see the blue? That's the only lake on all of Pontoppidan. And here we drop to the hermit's house."

Casher O'Neill almost felt vertigo as the camera plummeted from off-planet into the depths of that immense canyon. The edges of the canyon almost seemed to move like lips with the plunge, opening and folding inward to swallow him up.

Suddenly they were beside a beautiful little lake.

A small hut stood beside the shore.

In the doorway there sat a man, dead.

His body had been there a long time; it was already mummified.

Genevieve's recorded voice explained the matter: ". . . in Norstrilian law and custom, they told him that his time had come. They told him to go to the Dying House, since he was no longer fit to live. In Old North Australia, they are so rich that they let everyone live as long as he wants, unless the old person can't take rejuvenation any more, even with stroon, and unless he or she gets to be a real pest to the living. If that happens, they are invited to go to the Dying House, where they shriek and pant with delirious joy for weeks or days until they finally die of an overload of sheer happiness and excitement. . . ." There was a hesitation, even in the recording. "We never knew why this man refused. He stood off-planet and said that he had seen views of the Hippy Dispy. He said it was the most beautiful on all the worlds, and that he wanted to build a cabin there, to live alone, except for his non-human friend. We thought it was some small pet. When we told him that the Hippy Dipsy was very dangerous, he said that this did not matter in the least to him, since he was old and dying anyhow. Then he offered to pay us twelve times our planetary income if we would lease him twelve hectares on the condition of absolute privacy. No pictures, no scanners, no help, no visitors. Just solitude and scenery. His name was Perinö. My great-grandfather asked for nothing more, except the written transfer of credit. When he paid it, Perinö even asked that he be left alone after he was dead. Not even a vault rocket so that he could either orbit Pontoppidan forever or start a very slow journey to nowhere, the way so many people like it. So this is our first picture of him. We took it when the light went off in the People Room and one of the tiger-men told us that he was sure a human consciousness had come to an end in the Hippy Dipsy.

"And we never even thought of the pet. After all, we had never made a picture of him. This is the way he arrived from Perinö's shack."

A robot was shown in a control room, calling excitedly in the old Common Tongue.

"People, people! Judgment needed! Moving object coming out of the Hippy Dipsy. Object has improper shape. Not a correct object. Should not rise. Does so anyhow. People, tell me, people, tell me! Destroy or not destroy? This is an improper subject. It should fall, not rise. Coming out of the Hippy Dipsy."

A firm click shut off the robot's chatter. A well-shaped woman took over. From the nature of her work and the lithe, smooth tread with which she walked, Casher O'Neill suspected that she was of cat origin, but there was nothing in her dress or in her manner to show that she was underpeople.

The woman in the picture lighted a screen.

She moved her hands in the air in front of her, like a blind person feeling his way through open day.

The picture on the inner screen came to resolution.

A face showed in it.

What a face! thought Casher O'Neill, and he heard the other people around him in the viewing room.

The horse!

Imagine a face like that of a newborn cat, thought Casher. Mizzer is full of cats. But imagine the face with a huge mouth, with big yellow teeth—a nose long beyond imagination. Imagine eyes which look friendly. In the picture they were rolling back and forth with exertion, but even there—when they did not feel observed—there was nothing hostile about

the set of the eyes. They were tame, companionable eyes. Two
ridiculous ears stood high, and a little tuft of golden hair
showed on the crest of the head between the ears.

The viewed scene was comical, too. The cat-woman was as
astonished as the viewers. It was lucky that she had touched the
emergency switch, so that she not only saw the horse, but had
recorded herself and her own actions while bringing him into
view.

Genevieve whispered across the chest of the Hereditary
Dictator: "Later we found he was a palomino pony. That's a
very special kind of horse. And Perinö had made him immortal,
or almost immortal."

"Sh-h!" said her uncle.

The screen-within-the-screen showed the cat-woman waving
her hands in the air some more. The view broadened.

The horse had four hands and no legs, or four legs and no
hands, whichever way you want to count them.

The horse was fighting his way up a narrow cleft of rubies
which led out of the Hippy Dipsy. He panted heavily. The
oxygen bottles on his sides swung wildly as he clambered. He
must have seen something, perhaps the image of the cat-
woman, because he said a word:

Whay-yay-yay-yay-whay-yay!

The cat-woman in the nearer picture spoke very distinctly:

"Give your name, age, species and authority for being on the
planet." She spoke clearly and with the utmost possible
authority.

The horse obviously heard her. His ears tipped forward. But
his reply was the same as before:

Whay-yay-yay!

Casher O'Neill realized that he had followed the mood of the
picture and had seen the horse the way that the people on
Pontoppidan would have seen him. On second thought, the
horse was nothing special, by the standards of the Twelve Niles
or the Little Horse Market in the city of Kaheer. It was an old
pony stallion, no longer fit for breeding and probably not for
riding either. The hair had whitened among the gold; the teeth
were worn. The animal showed many injuries and burns. Its
only use was to be killed, cut up and fed to the racing dogs. But

he said nothing to the people around him. They were still spell-bound by the picture.

The cat-woman repeated:

"Your name isn't Whayayay. Identify yourself properly; name first."

The horse answered her with the same word in a higher key.

Apparently forgetting that she had recorded herself as well as the emergency screen, the cat-woman said, "I'll call real people if you don't answer! They'll be annoyed at being bothered."

The horse rolled his eyes at her and said nothing.

The cat-woman pressed an emergency button on the side of the room. One could not see the other communication screen which lighted up, but her end of the conversation was plain.

"I want an ornithopter. Big one. Emergency."

A mumble from the side screen.

"To go to the Hippy Dipsy. There's an underperson there, and he's in so much trouble that he won't talk." From the screen beside her, the horse seemed to have understood the sense of the message, if not the words, because he repeated:

Whay-yay-whay-yay-yay!

"See," said the cat-woman to the person in the other screen, "that's what he's doing. It's obviously an emergency."

The voice from the other screen came through, tinny and remote by double recording:

"Fool, yourself, cat-woman! Nobody can fly an ornithopter into a dipsy. Tell your silly friend to go back to the floor of the dipsy and we'll pick him up by space rocket."

Whay-yay-yay! said the horse impatiently.

"He's not my *friend*," said the cat-woman with brisk annoyance. "I just discovered him a couple of minutes ago. He's asking for help. Any idiot can see that, even if we don't know his language."

The picture snapped off.

The next scene showed tiny human figures working with searchlights at the top of an immeasurably high cliff. Here and there, the beam of the searchlight caught the cliff face; the translucent faceted material of the cliff looked almost like rows of eerie windows, their lights snapping on and off, as the searchlight moved.

Far down there was a red glow. Fire came from inside the mountain.

Even with telescopic lenses the cameraman could not get the close-up of the glow. On one side there was the figure of the horse, his four arms stretched at impossible angles as he held himself firm in the crevasse; on the other side of the fire there were the even tinier figures of men, laboring to fit some sort of sling to reach the horse.

For some odd reason having to do with the techniques of recording, the voices came through very plainly, even the heavy, tired breathing of the old horse. Now and then he uttered one of the special horse-words which seemed to be the limit of his vocabulary. He was obviously watching the men, and was firmly persuaded of their friendliness to him. His large, tame, yellow eyes rolled wildly in the light of the searchlight and every time the horse looked down, he seemed to shudder.

Casher O'Neill found this entirely understandable. The bottom of the Hippy Dipsy was nowhere in sight; the horse, even with nothing more than the enlarged fingernails of his middle fingers to help him climb, had managed to get about four of the six kilometers' height off the cliff face behind him.

The voice of a tiger-man sounded clearly from among the shift of men, underpeople and robots who were struggling on the face of the cliff.

"It's a gamble, but not much of a gamble. I weigh six hundred kilos myself, and, do you know, I don't think I've ever had to use my full strength since I was a kitten. I *know* that I can jump across the fire and help that thing be more comfortable. I can even tie a rope around him so that he won't slip and fall after all the work we've done. And the work he's done, too," added the tiger-man grimly. "*Perhaps* I can just take him in my arms and jump back with him. It will be perfectly safe if you have a safety rope around each of us. After all, I never saw a less prehensile creature in my life. You can't call those fingers of his 'fingers.' They look like little boxes of bone, designed for running around and not much good for anything else."

There was a murmur of other voices and then the command of the supervisor. "Go ahead."

No one was prepared for what happened next.

The cameraman got the tiger-man right in the middle of his frame, showing the attachment of one rope around the tiger-man's broad waist. The tiger-man was a modified type whom the authorities had not bothered to put into human cosmetic form. He still had his ears on top of his head, yellow and black fur over his face, huge incisors overlapping his lower jaw and enormous antenna-like whiskers sticking out from his moustache. He must have been thoroughly modified inside, however, because his temperament was calm, friendly and even a little humorous; he must have had a carefully re-done mouth, because the utterance of human speech came to him clearly and without distortion.

He jumped—a mighty jump, right through the top edges of the flame.

The horse saw him.

The horse jumped too, almost in the same moment, also through the top of the flame, going the other way.

The horse had feared the tiger-man more than he did the cliff.

The horse landed right in the group of workers. He tried not to hurt them with his flailing limbs, but he did knock one man—a true man, at that—off the cliff. The man's scream faded as he crashed into the impenetrable darkness below.

The robots were quick. Having no emotions except *on, off,* and *high,* they did not get excited. They had the horse trussed and, before the true man and underpeople had ensured their footing, they had signaled the crane operator at the top of the cliff. The horse, his four arms swinging limply, disappeared upward.

The tiger-man jumped back through the flames to the nearer ledge. The picture went off.

In the viewing room, the Hereditary Dictator Philip Vincent stood up. He stretched, looking around.

Genevieve looked at Casher O'Neill expectantly.

"That's the story," said the Dictator mildly. "Now you solve it."

"Where is the horse now?" said Casher O'Neill.

"In the hospital, of course. My niece can take you to see him."

III

After a short, painful and very thorough peeping of his own mind by the Hereditary Dictator, Casher O'Neill and Genevieve set off for the hospital in which the horse was being kept in bed. The people of Pontoppidan had not known what else to do with him, so they had placed him under strong sedation and were trying to feed him with sugar-water compounds going directly into his veins. Genevieve told Casher that the horse was wasting away.

They walked to the hospital over amethyst pebbles.

Instead of wearing his space suit, Casher wore a surface helmet which enriched his oxygen. His hosts had not counted on his getting spells of uncontrollable itching from the sharply reduced atmospheric pressure. He did not dare mention the matter, because he was still hoping to get the green ruby as a weapon in his private war for the liberation of the Twelve Niles from the rule of Colonel Wedder. Whenever the itching became less than excruciating, he enjoyed the walk and the company of the slight, beautiful girl who accompanied him across the field of jewels to the hospital. (In later years, he sometimes wondered what might have happened. Was the itching a part of his destiny, which saved him for the freedom of the city of Kaheer and the planet Mizzer? Might not the innocent brilliant loveliness of the girl have otherwise tempted him to forswear his duty and stay forever on Pontoppidan?)

The girl wore a new kind of cosmetic for outdoor walking—a warm peach-hued powder which let the natural pink of her cheeks show through. Her eyes, he saw, were a living, deep gray; her eyelashes, long; her smile, innocently provocative beyond all ordinary belief. It was a wonder that the Hereditary Dictator had not had to stop duels and murders between young men vying for her favor.

They finally reached the hospital, just as Casher O'Neill thought he could stand it no longer and would have to ask

Genevieve for some kind of help or carriage to get indoors and away from the frightful itching.

The building was underground.

The entrance was sumptuous. Diamonds and rubies, the size of building-bricks on Mizzer, had been set to frame the doorway, which was apparently enameled steel. Kuraf at his most lavish had never wasted money on anything like this door-frame. Genevieve saw his glance.

"It did cost a lot of credits. We had to bring a blind artist all the way from Olympia to paint that enamel-work. The poor man. He spent most of his time trying to steal extra gemstones when he should have known that we pay justly and never allowed anyone to get away with stealing."

"What do you do?" asked Casher O'Neill.

"We cut thieves up in space, just at the edge of the atmosphere. We have more manned boats in orbit than any other planet I know of. Maybe Old North Australia has more, but, then, nobody ever gets close enough to Old North Australia to come back alive and tell."

They went on into the hospital.

A respectful chief surgeon insisted on keeping them in the office and entertaining them with tea and confectionery, when they both wanted to go see the horse; common politeness prohibited their pushing through. Finally they got past the ceremony and into the room in which the horse was kept.

Close up, they could see how much he had suffered. There were cuts and abrasions over almost all of his body. One of his *hooves*—the doctor told them that was the correct name, *hoof*, for the big middle fingernail on which he walked—was split; the doctor had put a cadmium-silver bar through it. The horse lifted his head when they entered, but he saw that they were just more people, not horsey people, so he put his head down, very patiently.

"What's the prospect, doctor?" asked Casher O'Neill, turning away from the animal.

"Could I ask you, sir, a foolish question first?"

Surprised, Casher could only say yes.

"You're an O'Neill. Your uncle is Kuraf. How do you happen to be called 'Casher'?"

"That's simple," laughed Casher. "This is my young-man-name. On Mizzer, everybody gets a baby name, which nobody uses. Then he gets a nickname. Then he gets a young-man-name, based on some characteristic or some friendly joke, until he picks out his career. When he enters his profession, he picks out his own career name. If I liberate Mizzer and overthrow Colonel Wedder, I'll have to think up a suitable career name for myself."

"But why 'Casher,' sir?" persisted the doctor.

"When I was a little boy and people asked me what I wanted, I always asked for cash. I guess that contrasted with my uncle's wastefulness, so they called me Casher."

"But what is cash? One of your crops?"

It was Casher's time to look amazed. "Cash is money. Paper credits. People pass them back and forth when they buy things."

"Here on Pontoppidan, all the money belongs to me. All of it," said Genevieve. "My uncle is trustee for me. But I have never been allowed to touch it or to spend it. It's all just planet business."

The doctor blinked respectfully. "Now this horse, sir, if you will pardon my asking about your name, is a very strange case. Physiologically he is a pure earth type. He is suited only for a vegetable diet, but otherwise he is a very close relative of man. He has a single stomach and a very large cone-shaped heart. That's where the trouble is. The heart is in bad condition. He is dying."

"Dying?" cried Genevieve.

"That's the sad, horrible part," said the doctor. "He is dying but he cannot die. He could go on like this for many years. Perinö wasted enough stroon on this animal to make a planet immortal. Now the animal is worn out but cannot die."

Casher O'Neill let out a long, low, ululating whistle. Everybody in the room jumped. He disregarded them. It was the whistle he had used near the stables, back among the Twelve Niles, when he wanted to call a horse.

The horse knew it. The large head lifted. The eyes rolled at him so imploringly that he expected tears to fall from them, even though he was pretty sure that horses could not lachrymate.

He squatted on the floor, close to the horse's head, with a hand on its mane.

"Quick," he murmured to the surgeon. "Get me a piece of sugar and an underperson-telepath. The underperson-telepath must not be of carnivorous origin."

The doctor looked stupid. He snapped "Sugar" at an assistant, but he squatted down next to Casher O'Neill and said, "You will have to repeat that about an underperson. This is not an underperson hospital at all. We have very few of them here. The horse is here only by command of His Excellency Philip Vincent, who said that the horse of Perinö should be given the best of all possible care. He even told me," said the doctor, "that if anything wrong happened to this horse, I would ride patrol for it for the next eighty years. So I'll do what I can. Do you find me too talkative? Some people do. What kind of an underperson do you want?"

"I need," said Casher, very calmly, "a telepathic underperson, both to find out what this horse wants and to tell the horse that I am here to help him. Horses are vegetarians and they do not like meat-eaters. Do you have a vegetarian underperson around the hospital?"

"We used to have some squirrel-men," said the chief surgeon, "but when we changed the air circulating system the squirrel-men went away with the old equipment. I think they went to a mine. We have tiger-men, cat-men, and my secretary is a wolf."

"Oh, no!" said Casher O'Neill. "Can you imagine a sick horse confiding in a wolf?"

"It's no more than you are doing," said the surgeon, very softly, glancing up to see if Genevieve were in hearing range, and apparently judging that she was not. "The Hereditary Dictators here sometimes cut suspicious guests to pieces on their way off the planet. That is, unless the guests are licensed, regular traders. You are not. You might be a spy, planning to rob us. How do I know? I wouldn't give a diamond chip for your chances of being alive next week. What do you want to do about the horse? That might please the Dictator. And *you* might live."

Casher O'Neill was so staggered by the confidence of the surgeon that he squatted there thinking about himself, not about the patient. The horse licked him, seemingly sensing that he needed solace.

The surgeon had an idea. "Horses and dogs used to go together, didn't they, back in the old days of Manhome, when all the people lived on Planet Earth?"

"Of course," said Casher. "We still run them together in hunts on Mizzer, but under these new laws of the Instrumentality we've run out of underpeople-criminals to hunt."

"I have a good dog," said the chief surgeon. "She talks pretty well, but she is so sympathetic that she upsets the patients by loving them too much. I have her down in the second underbasement tending the dish-sterilizing machinery."

"Bring her up," said Casher in a whisper.

He remembered that he did not need to whisper about this, so he stood up and spoke to Genevieve:

"They have found a good dog-telepath who may reach through to the mind of the horse. It may give us the answer."

She put her hand on his forearm gently, with the approbatory gesture of a princess. Her fingers dug into his flesh. Was she wishing him well against her uncle's habitual treachery, or was this merely the impulse of a kind young girl who knew nothing of the way the world was run?

IV

The interview went extremely well.

The dog-woman was almost perfectly humaniform. She looked like a tired, cheerful, worn-out old woman, not valuable enough to be given the life-prolonging santaclara drug called *stroon*. Work had been her life and she had had plenty of it. Casher O'Neill felt a twinge of envy when he realized that happiness goes by the petty chances of life and not by the large destiny. This dog-woman, with her haggard face and her stringy gray hair, had more love, happiness and sympathy than Kuraf had found with his pleasures, Colonel Wedder with his powers, or himself with his crusade. Why did life do that? Was there no justice, ever? Why should a worn-out worthless old underwoman be happy when he was not?

"Never mind," she said, "you'll get over it and then you will be happy."

"Over what?" he said. "I didn't say anything."

"I'm not going to say it," she retorted, meaning that she was telepathic. "You're a prisoner of yourself. Some day you will escape to unimportance and happiness. You're a good man. You're trying to save yourself, but you really *like* this horse."

"Of course I do," said Casher O'Neill. "He's a brave old horse, climbing out of that hell to get back to people."

When he said the word *hell* her eyes widened, but she said nothing. In his mind, he saw the sign of a fish scrawled on a dark wall and he felt her think at him, *So you too know something of the "dark wonderful knowledge" which is not yet to be revealed to all mankind?*

He thought a *cross* back at her and then turned his thinking to the horse, lest their telepathy be monitored and strange punishments await them both.

She spoke in words, "Shall we link?"

"Link," he said.

Genevieve stepped up. Her clear-cut, pretty, sensitive face was alight with excitement. "Could I—could I be cut in?"

"Why not?" said the dog-woman, glancing at him. He nodded. The three of them linked hands and then the dog-woman put her left hand on the forehead of the old horse.

The sand splashed beneath their feet as they ran toward Kaheer. The delicious pressure of a man's body was on their backs. The red sky of Mizzer gleamed over them. There came the shout:

"I'm a horse, I'm a horse, I'm a horse!"

"You're from Mizzer," thought Casher O'Neill, "from Kaheer itself!"

"I don't know names," thought the horse, "but you're from my land. The land, the good land."

"What are you doing here?"

"Dying," thought the horse. "Dying for hundreds and thousands of sundowns. The old one brought me. No riding, no running, no people. Just the old one and the small ground. I have been dying since I came here."

Casher O'Neill got a glimpse of Perinö sitting and watching the horse, unconscious of the cruelty and loneliness which he had inflicted on his large pet by making it immortal and then giving it no work to do.

"Do you know what dying is?"

Though the horse promptly: "Certainly. No-horse."

"Do you know what life is?"

"Yes. Being a horse."

"I'm not a horse," thought Casher O'Neill, "but I am alive."

"Don't complicate things," thought the horse at him, though Casher realized it was his own mind and not the horse's which supplied the words.

"Do you want to die?"

"To no-horse? Yes, if this room, forever, is the end of things."

"What would you like better?" thought Genevieve, and her thoughts were like a cascade of newly-minted silver coins falling into all their minds: brilliant, clean, bright, innocent.

The answer was quick: "Dirt beneath my hooves, and wet air again, and a man on my back."

The dog-woman interrupted: "Dear horse, you know me?"

"You're a dog," thought the horse. "Goo-oo-oo-ood dog!"

"Right," thought the happy old slattern, "and I can tell these people how to take care of you. Sleep now, and when you waken you will be on the way to happiness."

She thought the command *sleep* so powerfully at the old horse that Casher O'Neill and Genevieve both started to fall unconscious and had to be caught by the hospital attendants.

As they re-gathered their wits, she was finishing her commands to the surgeon. "—put about 40% supplementary oxygen into the air. He'll have to have a real person to ride him, but some of your orbiting sentries would rather ride a horse up there than do nothing. You can't repair the heart. Don't try it. Hypnosis will take care of the sand in Mizzer. Just load his mind with one or two of the drama-cubes packed full of desert adventure. Now, don't you worry about me. I'm not going to give you any more suggestions. People-man, you!" She laughed. "You can forgive us dogs anything, except for being right. It makes you feel inferior for a few minutes. Never mind. I'm going back downstairs to my dishes. I love them, I really do. Good-bye, you pretty thing," she said to Genevieve. "And good-bye, wanderer! Good luck to you," she said to Casher O'Neill. "You will remain miserable as long as you seek justice, but when you give up, righteousness will come to you and you will be happy. Don't worry. You're young and it won't hurt you to suffer a few more years. Youth is an extremely curable disease, isn't it?"

She gave them a full curtsy, like one Lady of the Instrumentality saying good-bye to another. Her wrinkled old face was lit up with smiles, in which happiness was mixed with a tiniest bit of playful mockery.

"Don't mind me, boss," she said to the surgeon. "Dishes, here I come." She swept out of the room.

"See what I mean?" said the surgeon. "She's so horribly *happy!* How can anyone run a hospital if a dishwasher gets all over the place, making people happy? We'd be out of jobs. Her ideas were good, though."

They were. They worked. Down to the last letter of the dog-woman's instructions.

There was argument from the council. Casher O'Neill went along to see them in session.

One councillor, Bashnack, was particularly vociferous in objecting to any action concerning the horse. "Sire," he cried, "sire! We don't even know the name of the animal! I must protest this action, when we don't know—"

"That we don't," assented Philip Vincent. "But what does a name have to do with it?"

"The horse has no identity, not even the identity of an animal. It is just a pile of meat left over from the estate of Perinö. We should kill the horse and eat the meat ourselves. Or, if we do not want to eat the meat, then we should sell it off-planet. There are plenty of peoples around here who would pay a pretty price for genuine earth meat. Pay no attention to me, sire! You are the Hereditary Dictator and I am nothing. I have no power, no property, nothing. I am at your mercy. All I can tell you is to follow your own best interests. I have only a voice. You cannot reproach me for using my voice when I am trying to help you, sire, can you? That's all I am doing, helping you. If you spend any credits at all on this animal you will be doing wrong, wrong, wrong. We are not a rich planet. We have to pay for expensive defenses just in order to stay alive. We cannot even afford to pay for air that our children can go out and play. And you want to spend money on a horse which cannot even talk! I tell you, sire, this council is going to vote against you, just to protect your own interests and the interests of the Honorable Genevieve as Eventual Title-holder of all Pontoppidan. You are not going to get away with this, sire! We are helpless before your power, but we will insist on advising you—"

"Hear! Hear!" cried several of the councillors, not the least dismayed by the slight frown of the Hereditary Dictator.

"I would take the word," said Philip Vincent himself.

Several had had their hands raised, asking for the floor. One obstinate man kept his hand up even when the Dictator announced his intention to speak. Philip Vincent took note of him, too:

"You can talk when I am through, if you want to."

He looked calmly around the room, smiled imperceptibly at his niece, gave Casher O'Neill the briefest of nods, and then announced:

"Gentlemen, it's not the horse which is on trial. It's Pontoppidan. It's we who are trying ourselves. And before whom are we trying ourselves, gentlemen? Each of us is before that most awful of courts, his own conscience.

"If we kill that horse, gentlemen, we will not be doing the horse a great wrong. He is an old animal, and I do not think that he will mind dying very much, now that he is away from the ordeal of loneliness which he feared more than death. After all, he had already had his great triumph—the climb up the cliff of gems, the jump across the volcanic vent, the rescue by people whom he wanted to find. The horse has done so well that he is really beyond us. We can help him, a little, or we can hurt him, a little; beside the immensity of his accomplishment, we cannot really do very much either way.

"No, gentlemen, we are not judging the case of the horse. We are judging space. What happens to a man when he moves out into the Big Nothing? Do we leave Old Earth behind? Why did civilization fall? Will it fall again? Is civilization a gun or a blaster or a laser or a rocket? Is it even a planoforming ship or a pinlighter at his work? You know as well as I do, gentlemen, that civilization is not what we can do. If it had been, there would have been no fall of Ancient Man. Even in the Dark Ages they had a few fusion bombs, they could make some small guided missiles and they even had weapons like the Kaskaskis Effect, which we have never been able to rediscover. The Dark Ages weren't dark because people lost techniques or science. They were dark *because people lost people*. It's a lot of work to be human and it's work which must be kept up, or it begins to fade. Gentlemen, the horse judges us.

"Take the word, gentlemen. 'Civilization' is itself a lady's word. There were female writers in a country called France who made that word popular in the third century before space travel. To be 'civilized' meant for people to be tame, to be kind, to be polished. If we kill this horse, we are wild. If we treat the horse gently, we are tame. Gentlemen, I have only one witness and that witness will utter only one word. Then you shall vote and vote freely."

There was a murmur around the table at this announcement. Philip Vincent obviously enjoyed the excitement he had created. He let them murmur on for a full minute or two before he slapped the table gently and said, "Gentlemen, the witness. Are you ready?"

There was a murmur of assent. Bashnack tried to say, "It's still a question of public funds!" but his neighbors shushed him. The table became quiet. All faces turned toward the Hereditary Dictator.

"Gentlemen, the testimony. Genevieve, is that what you yourself told me to say? Is civilization always a woman's choice first, and only later a man?"

"Yes," said Genevieve, with a happy, open smile.

The meeting broke up amid laughter and applause.

V

A month later Casher O'Neill sat in a room in a medium-size planoforming liner. They were out of reach of Pontoppidan. The Hereditary Dictator had not changed his mind and cut him down with green beams. Casher had strange memories, not bad ones for a young man.

He remembered Genevieve weeping in the garden.

"I'm romantic," she cried, and wiped her eyes on the sleeve of his cape. "Legally I'm the owner of this planet, rich, powerful, free. But I can't leave here. I'm too important. I can't marry whom I want to marry. I'm too important. My uncle can't do what *he* wants to do—he's Hereditary Dictator and he always must do what the Council decides after weeks of chatter. I can't love you. You're a prince and a wanderer, with travels and battles and justice and strange things ahead of you. I can't go. I'm too important. I'm too sweet! I'm too nice; I hate, hate, hate myself sometimes. Please, Casher, could you take a flier and run away with me into space?"

"Your uncle's lasers could cut us to pieces before we got out."

He held her hands and looked gently down into her face. At this moment he did not feel the fierce, aggressive, happy glow which an able young man feels in the presence of a beautiful and tender young woman. He felt something much stranger, softer, quieter—an emotion very sweet to the mind and restful to the nerves. It was the simple, clear compassion of one person for another. He took a chance for her sake, because the "dark knowledge" was wonderful but very dangerous in the wrong hands.

He took both her beautiful little hands in his, so that she looked up at him and realized that he was not going to kiss her. Something about his stance made her realize that she was being offered a more precious gift than a sky-lit romantic kiss in a garden. Besides, it was just touching helmets.

He said to her, with passion and kindness in his voice:

"You remember that dog-woman, the one who works with the dishes in the hospital?"

"Of course. She was good and bright and happy, and helped us all."

"Go work with her, now and then. Ask her nothing. Tell her nothing. Just work with her at her machines. Tell her I said so. Happiness is catching. You might catch it. I think I did myself, a little."

"I think I understand you," said Genevieve softly. "Casher, good-bye and good, good luck to you. My uncle expects us."

Together they went back into the palace.

Another memory was the farewell to Philip Vincent, the Hereditary Dictator of Pontoppidan. The calm, clean-shaven, ruddy, well-fleshed face looked at him with benign regard. Casher O'Neill felt more respect for this man when he realized that ruthlessness is often the price of peace, and vigilance the price of wealth.

"You're a clever young man. A very clever young man. You may win back the power of your Uncle Kuraf."

"I don't want *that* power!" cried Casher O'Neill.

"I have advice for you," said the Hereditary Dictator, "and it is good advice or I would not be here to give it. I have learned the political arts well: otherwise I would not be alive. Do not refuse power. Just take it and use it wisely. Do not hide from your wicked uncle's name. Obliterate it. Take the name yourself and rule so well that, in a few decades, no one will remember your uncle. Just you. You are young. You can't win now. But it is in your fate to grow and to triumph. I know it. I am good at these things. I have given you your weapon. I am not tricking you. It is packed safely and you may leave with it."

Casher O'Neill was breathing softly, believing it all, and trying to think of words to thank the stout, powerful older man when the dictator added, with a little laugh in his voice:

"Thank you, too, for saving me money. You've lived up to your name, Casher."

"Saved you money?"

"The alfalfa. The horse wanted alfalfa."

"Oh, that idea!" said Casher O'Neill. "It was obvious. I don't deserve much credit for that."

"*I* didn't think of it," said the Hereditary Dictator, "and my

staff didn't either. We're not stupid. That shows you are bright.
You realized that Perinö must have had a food converter to
keep the horse alive in the Hippy Dipsy. All we did was set it
to alfalfa and we saved ourselves the cost of a shipload of horse
food twice a year. We're glad to save that credit. We're well off
here, but we don't like to waste things. You may bow to me
now, and leave."

Casher O'Neill had done so, with one last glance at the
lovely Genevieve, standing fragile and beautiful beside her
uncle's chair.

His last memory was very recent.

He had paid two hundred thousand credits for it, right on this
liner. He had found the Stop-Captain, bored now that the ship
was in flight and the Go-Captain had taken over.

"Can you get me a telepathic fix on a horse?"

"What's a horse?" said the Go-Captian. "Where is it? Do you
want to pay for it?"

"A horse," said Casher O'Neill patiently, "is an unmodified
earth animal. Not underpeople. A big one, but quite intelligent.
This one is in orbit right around Pontoppidan. And I will pay
the usual price."

"A million Earth credits," said the Stop-Captain.

"Ridiculous!" cried Casher O'Neill.

They settled on two hundred thousand credits for a good fix
and ten thousand for the use of the ship's equipment even if
there were failure. It was not a failure. The technician was a
snake-man: he was deft, cool, and superb at his job. In only a
few minutes he passed the headset to Casher O'Neill, saying
politely, "This is it, I think."

It was. He had reached right into the horse's mind.

The endless sands of Mizzer swam before Casher O'Neill.
The long lines of the Twelve Niles converged in the distance.
He galloped steadily and powerfully. There were other horses
nearby, other riders, other things, but he himself was conscious
only of the beat of the hooves against the strong moist sand, the
firmness of the appreciative rider upon his back. Dimly, as in
a hallucination, Casher O'Neill could also see the little orbital
ship in which the old horse cantered in mid-air, with an amused

cadet sitting on his back. Up there, with no weight, the old worn-out heart would be good for many, many years. Then he saw the horse's paradise again. The flash of hooves threatened to overtake him, but he outran them all. There was the expectation of a stable at the end, a rubdown, good succulent green food, and the glimpse of a filly in the morning.

The horse of Pontoppidan felt extremely wise. He had trusted *people*—people, the source of all kindness, all cruelty, all power among the stars. And the people had been good. The horse felt very much horse again. Casher felt the old body course along the river's edge like a dream of power, like a completion of service, like an ultimate fulfillment of companionship.

The Thunder of
the Captains
by
Garry Kilworth

Garry Kilworth is a British writer who began to publish in the mid-1970s upon retiring after eighteen years of service as a cryptographer in the Royal Air Force. Raised partly in Aden, he has traveled and worked in the Far East, and after living for a number of years in Hong Kong, is now residing in England again. He sold his first SF story in 1975, and has subsequently become a frequent contributor to Omni, Interzone, Asimov's Science Fiction, *and many other magazines and anthologies; his short fiction has been assembled in* The Songbirds of Pain, *and in the upcoming collection* In the Country of Tattooed Men. *His many novels include* Witchwater Country, *a mainstream novel, and, among many others, the science fiction novels* In Solitary, The Night of Kadar, Split Second, Gemini God, A Theatre of Timesmiths, Cloudrock, *and* Abandonati. *His most recent work is a trilogy of popular fantasy novels,* The Foxes of First Dark, Midnight's Sun: A Story of Wolves, *and* Frost Dancers: A Story of Hares.*

Here he gives us a harrowing look at the seduction and corruption of the innocent, at the misuses of power, and at the dread consequences that inexorably follow that misuse . . .

*　　*　　*

Those who have never experienced the rigid discipline of a military school cannot imagine how assiduously such establishments work to destroy one's identity. There is not a single minute of the seventeen-hour day that is not filled with gruelling physical training, base manual labor or academic study. One might work through the remaining hours of the night in order to be immaculate for a morning parade and an inspection, then, desperate for sleep, stand by with a tense frame while someone in authority destroys the kit layout because a toothbrush is still damp, or is facing the wrong way, and orders a re-inspection within the hour. Even during sleep one's head still rings with the bawling voices and bugle calls that pass for communication. There are nightmares that are formed from a state of extreme order as well as chaos.

There are more terrors than are found in the established hierarchy. Just as terrible as the hostile oppressions of the authorities are the attentions of the senior boys whose brutality belongs to street gangs. They choose a victim with care and, physically and mentally, annihilate their character with a systematic cruelty found only in a mind disciplined beyond thinking or feeling. I have seen boys beaten, then hung by their legs from third story windows by drum cords. I have seen boys stripped and rubbed raw with wet wire pads. When the lights go out in the dormitories, the manufactured adolescent—a creature possessed and fashioned by inflexible ritual, by set rules and regulations—exercises an ungovernable free will and prowls through sleeping forms, looking for the youth who is solitary, friendless and weak. It is a calculated destruction that has all the hallmarks of insanity. There are those who try to fight both formal and informal authority openly, and are broken, at the age of fifteen or sixteen, into items useless to any society except that of a service life. There are those who bend with the system, like malleable strips of copper, hoping that though they allow themselves to be distorted during their years at the school, they can reshape, reform themselves later. There are those who feign mental illness or deliberately cause themselves to be physically disabled, in order to escape. There are those whom the life suits and who have no desire to retain any individuality. Then there are those like Jake and I, who fight in secret, fight insidiously in the dark, with mysticism, black magic, and souls the color of pitchblende.

There were two activities which kept us sane, Jake and I, during those hellish years at the school: horses and witchcraft. Possibly a strange combination, but while we were out horse-riding we had the freedom of the open air, the exhilaration of animal-powered speed and a proximity with the natural, chaotic elements of weather and nature to contrast to the order and discipline. At night, behind the closed doors of the drying-room, we lit tinlids of rags soaked in brass cleaner and chanted incantations to unhallowed gods: to Satan, to Nahemah the princess of succubi, to Seddim, to Astaroth, to Bael, to Praslus, to Furfur the demon winged stag, to Glasyalobalus, to Kobal, to Ukoback the stoker of Hell's fires—but most of all, to Cimeries, the demon who rides a black horse. We studied the works of Alister Crowley, Mathers, W. B. Yeats and others of the Order of Golden Dawn.

After our initial explorations into the art of the occult, Jake and I finally formed our own bastard religion, linking our two favorite activities. We began to pray to the spirits of dead horses. Bucephalus, Alexander's charger, and King Richard's mount, Barbary. Other famous steeds. Almost from the dawn of its creation, the destiny of humanity has been closely interwoven with the horse. Together we have forged civilizations out of wildernesses, have pushed back frontiers, have ploughed the land and made it fertile, have conquered wastelands and formed unions stronger than marriages.

In the dim light and foul gases of our homemade brands, we would try to conjure up visions of these beasts in the unsanctified air of the drying-room, murmuring invented chants into its dark corners. Perhaps it was a trick of the mind, brought about by the atmosphere we created, but on certain occasions my heartbeat quickened to see horse-like shapes in the wispy fumes of burning rags. We found the passage in Job, Chapter 39, which says, "Hast thou given the horse strength? Hast though clothed his neck with thunder? He mocketh at fear. He swalloweth the ground with fierceness and rage. He saith among the trumpets, Ha, ha; and he smelleth the battle afar off, the thunder of the Captains, and the shouting."

How we loved those words, would recite them backwards in an attempt to produce this wonderful creature, Jake more enthusiastically than I, for he was the leader and I his lieutenant. No one could touch our souls, we were sure of that, for we had blackened them beyond any stains the school could overprint. We heard the thunder of the Captains, but not from afar. We heard them as their vicious faces pressed to ours. We smelt their breath as their mouths contorted with threats and obscenities. We, with stiff bodies, wooden expressions, heard their booming break close to our ears and had held down our heartbeats for fear of betraying fear. We were afraid of being afraid. We ran ten miles in mud and rain; scrubbed toilet pans with nail brushes; scraped, cleaned, polished, washed, ironed, oiled; we slaughtered cardboard enemies; we marched and drilled to distorted commands; we prayed in rigid rows, the words mechanical; we sat with poker spines in disinfected classrooms; we ate our meals in unison; we knew sudden light or instant darkness to the minute—all to the thunder of the Captains.

Of course, we did as we were told, avoided the bullies as best we could and outwardly appeared pliable to the system's manipulations. But beneath our disciplined shells, deep beneath the fear, were dark smiles that mocked the authorities as surely as Job's horse mocked at fear. We said our "Yes, sirs" and "No, sirs" with the correctness of groomed students, and once on our own prayed to Pegasus, the flying horse that rose from the drops of blood of the decapitated Gorgon. We prayed for deliverance from those who would destroy we. We prayed for the destruction of our enemies. We prayed for power over the lives of the oppressors, the persecutors, the hated authorities.

Somehow I made it through two years at military school and then escaped on the death of my father. My mother required my support at home and money was short. I had to go to work to help with the household expenses. Father had left many debts, God bless him. Jake stayed on, of course, and the last I saw of him at the school was his wan face beneath the cropped tar-black hair, watching me through the barred gates as I walked away. He looked thin and wasted, his prominent front teeth giving him the curious paradoxical appearance of combined predacity and piteousness. For Jake, there was no escape. His father was wealthy and determined to have a soldier for a son. I was sorry for him but that sorrow extended only as far as common human kindness. We had never been friends in the true sense of the word. We had combined our forces to fight a common enemy: had shared experiences as soldiers do in the trenches, only seeing a single facet of a many faceted character. I did not *know* Jake, the way one knows a friend, because life at the school produced narrow viewpoints on personalities. It is like looking at a folded map. One sees small sections of rivers and roads, but their sources and destinations are hidden somewhere behind the sharp creases and edges of the folds. Jake, the whole Jake, was a folded chart and it was only years later that I was to be allowed another study of the regions and contours of the man.

Over the subsequent years my memories of school and its horrors were obliterated from my mind piece by piece. People speak of memories as fading, like sepia photographs under a desert sun, but memories do not fade—they are either there, or they are not. In order to retain memories one has to recharge them from time to time by re-running them through conscious thought. In this way we remember the good old days and not the bad ones, because we muse on pleasant hours and reject uncomfortable ones. Of course, had I wanted to, I could have recalled them—but the desire was not there. Even Jake, with his pinched, eager expression and quick gestures was sliced from my mind, like celluloid film in a cutting room. So too were my tentative ventures into the world of the occult. Consequently, when he came back into my life again, it was a while before I recognized him.

By the time I was thirty I had worked at a number of jobs and finally settled into a niche that I hoped would remain available to me for the rest of my life. I became a gamekeeper to John Sutton, a gentleman farmer in the district of Rochford in Essex. The date I took up employment with him was August the 17th, 1952, five months before the great flood, when high winds and a spring tide encouraged the sea to new, temporary conquests of the east coast of Britain. My period of military school had revealed an aptitude for marksmanship—not something I was especially proud of because of its limited worth in civilian life; but it seemed to impress my employer. The morals of breeding birds to shoot them did not impinge upon my principles either. Most people ate meat and it seemed to me that the only difference between putting a bolt into the brain of a calf, or shot into a bird, was that the latter had some chance of escape, especially from the myopic, cack-handed gentry that sported shotguns on John Sutton's estate every year. In the main they were flaccid, gin-soaked bankers and politicians who had never grown out of playing with guns.

I was needed, among other things, to keep out poachers. East Essex is a settling place for gypsies and John Sutton was convinced that the bulk of local gypsy mealtables was gathered from his land. It was not true, of course. Gypsies are shrewd business people, and if you are looking for a bargain, you stay clear of them, but they have no more thieves amongst them than house dwellers. A pheasant in the bush by the road is considered wild fruit to gypsies and country folk alike, but concentrated poaching is usually carried out by organized gangs from the towns. It was the gypsies that drew Jake back into my life again. They are, traditionally, horse traders and it was on a Thursday in October, market day in Rochford Square, that I felt a lean hand on my shoulder.

"It *is* you!"

I had turned to face a gaunt man of my own age and attempted to place him in front of one of the bars of the Plough and Sail, my local pub.

"Jake! Jake Dorstern," he cried.

Still nothing registered and I felt a little stupid.

"Are you sure . . ." I began, but he interrupted me, saying, "God, fancy seeing you after all these years. How many? Fifteen . . . it must be fifteen. You lucky bastard—you escaped early, didn't you? I had two more years of that . . . well, no sense in raking the ashes, now they're thankfully dead. How are you anyway?"

Then I had him of course. *Jake*. I shook his hand and asked the inevitable question.

"I'm buying a horse for my girlfriend. We're in London now that the old man's gone. Yes, died a year ago. Left me quite a bit, which is lucky. I'm not good for much. Went into the army, of course. Had to. Wouldn't have inherited otherwise and it's the only thing I've ever been any good at, inheriting money. Not easy, you know. You have to graft like hell at it. People seem to think an inheritance drops in one's lap. Instead one has to slog one's guts out doing all sorts of unpleasant things, like soldiering, in order to keep the source sweet. Captain Dorstern." He smiled grimly. "I nearly became one of them—one of those who tormented us at school . . . and beyond."

"With us . . . well, it was just a general title, for all superior ranks," I said.

"Yes, but they almost got me then, with those three pips. I nearly became one of them—it seemed easier to bend than buck . . ."

"It was always *easier* to bend," I interrupted. "We had to fight to keep our souls—I remember that."

His eyes brightened. "And we did, didn't we? We never—I never let them get *my* soul. You didn't have to contend with their bribes. When the thunder has run its course, the persuasion starts, and it's harder to resist, believe me. Their *acceptance* of you—their admittance to their damned—I kept on fighting though, as I always had—as we did." He paused.

"Still, got it now." He patted a pocket which no doubt contained the check book. All the while he spoke to me his eyes were roaming over faces in the bustling crowd of farmers, horse dealers, and market types. I wondered then how I could have failed to recognize him. That ambivalent look of the snake in a suspended moment—the second in which it is between the decision to strike or slither away out of danger—was in Jake's expression. That same mixture I had witnessed before, only this time it was fear and excitement, one pressing him forward, the other urging him away. And so he was captured in a perfect balance between the two, seeming to be caught, not in physical motion, but in spiritual argument, between two strong desires.

"Can you help me?" he said. "Which of those people are Romanies?"

"True Romanies? Or just gypsies?" I asked, surprised.

"Either. Which are the horse dealers?"

I nodded towards a short, swarthy man close by. "Him. He's one. His name's Henry Troupe."

"How do you know? Is he known to you?"

"I see him around and he's carrying his stick. If a gypsy's ready to trade, he carries a stick to indicate it. Do you want to speak to him?"

"In a moment." He paused, then said, "Where do they get their horses? They breed them, I suppose?"

"Yes. Much of the stock comes from Spain, Andalucía. There's a horse fair there once a year. Most of the gypsies go."

"And what do you do?" he asked, suddenly confronting me with a question more direct than polite, and I was taken aback a little.

"Gamekeeping. I'm a gamekeeper."

"Ah. Yes. You always did like the outdoor life. Bit of a nature freak, yes?"

I felt affronted. "I don't see . . . what's freakish about it. I like to be in the woods and fields . . . it's a living."

"But you have an affinity with nature, don't you? Bit like a church to you, isn't it? Sanctified woods, sacred fields, the sepulchral mound of the mole?" The tone was mocking.

"Rubbish, man." I was beginning to get annoyed with him. He turned his attention back to the gypsy.

"Well, never mind, anyway. Those fellows—they have an affinity with horses. Superstitious as well—to the back teeth. Power over horses, and under the power of superstition. Remind you of anything?"

I started. "Good God, you're not *still* . . . you can't be. You *are*. You're serious."

He turned to face me again.

"I couldn't give it up like you, you see. Oh, you can sneer, but you escaped, damn you. I still had it all . . . the bloody kit to polish, the inane drills, the fucking lot . . . I still had it, up to here." His eyes burned with a feverish anger and in spite of myself, my own irritation, I winced inwardly. Suddenly, he smiled, but somehow the smile seemed more threatening than the fury it had replaced. He said in a pleasant tone, "So, I continued our experiments, alone. Look, I'm going to have a word with that chap. You wait here. Afterwards I'll buy you a pint—for old times' sake. We'll celebrate my final escape. Don't go away . . ."

He left me and walked across the cobbled, strawstrewn square to speak to the gypsy. I watched as the big-boned, stocky man brought his face up to answer Jake, while Jake himself seemed to curve over, as if he were about to swallow the fellow. I wondered whether it would be prudent to just walk away, thinking that the bargaining would take some time—

gypsies will haggle over a penny in a hundred pounds—but Jake was soon back.

"Made an appointment for later," he said. "Come on. Where's the nearest alehouse? What about over there?" He pointed to The King's Head.

"Not my local," I said, "but it sells beer."

"Good. Let's to it, man." He slapped my back and led the way.

We drank steadily, until evening came upon us, sifting through scattered incidents that were best left lying where they had fallen in earlier years. Finally I asked the question that I knew he had been waiting for.

"The gypsy. What do you really want with him?"

Jake's eyes glittered, partly with excitement and partly through having drunk more than his share.

"They know something I need to know. Our old religion, man . . . it still runs thick in my veins. Can't get it out now. Runs too deep. Mingled with my blood. Have you ever heard of the Gytrash?"

"The Gytrash?"

"That's it. No, you haven't, have you? Well, it's . . . it's a horse. A phantom horse. The gypsies believe in it—so do I. Surprises you, eh? The old hocus-pocus rubbish, yes? Well, I do believe it. The Gytrash. It appears . . . look, when you see it, it's a warning that a loved one, your nearest and dearest, is going to die. The Gytrash appears, black-coated and white-eyed and you know that death is at hand, ready to swat." He swallowed more of his beer at a rapid pace, his Adam's apple bobbing away in front of me.

I said, "Did you come here to buy a horse?"

His eyes met mine. They were the eyes I remembered, from the old Jake. Eyes do not change—they are the exception in the aging process of the human body. Old people can have clear blue eyes that look as though they belong to a baby.

"After you left I took the whole thing a little more seriously—began to explore libraries for the right kind of books. I learned a great deal. I thought we . . . well, the horse is a magnificent animal. It has grace in speed. It's powerful—

muscularly powerful. Its lines are aesthetic. It has no-
bility . . ."

"Are you here to buy a horse?" I persisted.

"No. I'm here to talk—to the gypsies. I need to know certain
things. Then I'll be ready."

I studied his face in the dim light. The dusk filled the
hollows of his cheeks with dark shadows and I felt disturbed,
uneasy in his presence. Here was a man with an obsession. The
kind of obsession that permits no barriers, no morals, no
principles to stand in its way. He had narrowed his perspective
on the future to a bayonet point, and at that point stood the
Gytrash.

I said, "If the . . . Gytrash appears only to those about to
lose a loved one . . ."

"*The* loved one."

"All right. But what happens when you conjure its presence
then? I mean, if it's supposed to be some kind of
premonition—a warning—surely, calling it up might
precipitate . . ."

"Someone has to die. Yes."

The tone was that of a man explaining a logical fact and a
torpor took control of me, long enough to prevent me betraying
my revulsion.

"Who?" I uttered, after a long while.

"In my case, a woman called Catherine." He said it so
casually I almost struck him. Not in anger or disgust, but in
spiritual anguish. His disregard for human feeling was unpal-
atable and I wanted desperately to be out of his influence. I was
afraid that the corruption of his soul might be contagious and
would permeate my own with its close proximity.

Distance. I wanted spiritual distance between us, before the
decay became a shared experience and I was drawn too deeply
into something that was fascinatingly repulsive to me. The
problem was within myself. Since leaving military school I had
lived in a placid pool of unchanging events, but somewhere in
my nature revolution was waiting to erupt. I craved a momen-
tous change, which I had always hoped would come from
meeting someone with whom I would fall in love. Now I was
afraid that something else might draw me out of that pool,

something that was exciting through its sheer repulsiveness. Whether I believed in the Gytrash or not was immaterial. The fact was, Jake did, and he was prepared to sacrifice this Catherine to an indulgence in the black arts. He was offering someone he loved, the woman who presumably loved him, in exchange for a mystical experience. I, who had no one, who had not found such a woman, who would have fought with devils and demons to protect such a precious, rare quality as mutual love, was both appalled and intrigued by Jake's decision.

"Don't you think that this is a little bit insane?" I said.

He smiled. "Don't *you* think that's a rather trite remark? I expected better of you. Catherine is aware of what I'm doing—she's not only agreed to it, she's been a source of encouragement."

"Then you're both mad."

"Perhaps. It doesn't matter, does it? If we are, then nothing will happen. If not . . . well, you may not understand this, but some people are prepared to sacrifice everything they have— even love and life—for the ultimate experience. I know what you're thinking. What does *she* get out of it? What she gets is a special death. For some people, life is not the most precious gift. It's a burden . . ."

My blood felt as sluggish as mercury in my veins and I was finding it difficult to remain upright in my chair. I wanted to rest my head on a soft cushion, go to sleep, try to forget that people like Jake and Catherine existed. A wild thought came to me and I clutched at it.

"Is she a cripple?" I asked. "Or ill? In terrible pain?"

"Not physically. She's . . . spiritually oppressed. As I am. We need more than reality and death is a fantasy . . ."

"My God, I pity you. Both." I could have included myself but my ego would not allow it.

"That's rather arrogant. We don't need it." He glanced at his watch.

"Now I must go. My appointment." He reached across with his hand and when I failed to take it, rested it on my shoulder for a moment.

"Perhaps we'll see each other again," he said. "I hope so."

His face set into a hard mask. "I have to do this thing. You'll probably never understand—but I *have* to." Then he stood up and strode out of the pub, his tall, lean body stooping at the door before disappearing into the gloom beyond. I sat there for a long time, wondering how such a man had survived until now. Yet, as I reasoned, I knew how. He was a product of extremes—a combination of inflexible discipline and complete self-indulgence of spirit—which had resulted in a paradox: the rational lunatic. I did pity him, but I also envied him. He had an inner strength, a confidence that left me in awe of him. Had I that kind of strength, I could have . . . what? Gone on a quest for someone to share my life with me? You don't find that sort of person by searching for them. They happen in your way. The strange thing was, until Jake had mentioned those words— *the* loved one—I had not realized just how lonely I was. Now I felt destitute of emotion—hollow—not a real man at all. I was a walking effigy of men. A scarecrow. A straw man. Jake had revealed to me just how empty, how useless my life was, and had been since I had left the school. Yet, here was someone with the one thing I needed to make me whole, and he was prepared to throw it away for something—something transient, an evanescence, an experience as fleeting as a puff of smoke from a burning log. Somehow I stumbled from my chair and out into the blackness. There was a sharp wind blowing from the east which buffeted the pines that lined the road to Sutton Hall. Not looking up, I could hear them, tossing their dark manes above me, swishing their many tails beneath the lining of the sky.

Three nights later there was an urgent knocking on my cottage door. I put down the book I was reading and rose, reluctantly, to open it. To say I sensed it was Jake would be wrong. I *knew* it was him. I was familiar with the sound of John Sutton's knock and he was the only person who ever came to the cottage.

Jake stood before me, swaying slightly and exhaling plumes of cold air.

"Did you see it?" I cried, unable to prevent myself asking the question that had haunted me since our parting. Again, I knew before he had time to answer. It was evident in his whole demeanor. The suppressed excitement suffused his features until it seemed to me that his face had reverted to its childhood complexion: smooth and glowing like an infant freshly awakened from sleep.

"I saw it. . . ." He stepped inside and pulled at his gloves, feverishly. "I saw it. Let me tell you. I spent two days with the gypsies . . . then last night they took me out to the marshes. Left me there. I was terrified. . . ." He shook his head and laughed, finally managing to pull one of his gloves off. "*Terrified.* It's one thing talking about it, but out there—it's so bleak. Just miles of dark reeds moving to the varying pressures of the wind, unseen hands pressing down the grasses. And desolate creeks of slick mud, shining under the starlight. There are birds out there, you know—of course, you do—but hundreds of them, crouched in banks of saltwort and bladderwrack. They fly out when you disturb them. Startles you. God, this is a lonely place you've chosen . . . the Essex marshes. I never felt so lonely in my life."

"The Gytrash . . ."

"Yes, yes. I know. Let me tell you. I did it all—the incantations, the symbols, the magic rites. Once I had begun I was okay—I felt only excitement. I knew it would come . . . and it did. That place has atmosphere—the perfect atmosphere. It reeks of old religions, pagan worship. I felt the presence of those pre-Christian gods. I smelled their breath on the wind. It stank of their foul odors—rank, yet charged with power. I felt puny and vulnerable under their observations. They cluster in those salt marshes, you know. The primal mud is their last refuge. . . ."

"But . . ."

"I know. Finally, at the termination of the mystical orisons, I called its name—and the sound formed a spiral in the night airs above the marshes, turning faster and faster, increasing its circle, until the sound became a whirlpool of vapor that formed a tunnel back through space and time, to antiquity, to the origin of folklore—and through this celestial tunnel he came, beautiful and black, the height of three houses and eyes white with the fires of death.

"It seemed to me that flying hooves struck the moon, as the

beast descended to earth, set it spinning in a wheel of light—I
was momentarily blinded by a magnificent refulgence which
traveled along the back of the Gytrash—my hands, my face,
my skin were alive with static—every hair on my body was
drawn toward the beast, as if it were charged with a million
volts of electricity. I remember screaming one word, half in
fear, half in exaltation—'Catherine!' ''

"Oh, my God," I cried. This madman was exuding evil,
filling my house with its noxious fumes.

"Yes. It came." He spread his arms and seemed to fill the
room, his dark overcoat still glistening with drops of moisture
from the night mists. "Not just a horse—the Gytrash—I mean,
it was *huge*. There was no mistaking it. I had been prepared for
a trick—those gypsies are wily people, but not this. This
creature—this supernatural beast. *Then* I was afraid. I turned to
run. Like a coward, I turned to run. But it was there before me
again, enormous, its black, muscled flanks shedding flakes of
light, its mane and tail like textured darkness. . . . Each time
I turned, it was there. I couldn't run. There was nowhere to run
to.

"It reared up, over me, filling the sky with its giant form, and
I thought I was going to die. I could see its great hooves,
gleaming dully in the darkness above me, and I was going to be
crushed like a beetle. It made no sound, you know—
completely silent—yet I could see steam rushing from those
cavernous nostrils, like volcanic dust-clouds. I felt the white-
heat of its eyes. This was a god-horse—it was Aeton, Nonios,
Abastor, Malech, Abraxas, all rolled into one. It was the four
horses of the Apocalypse, it was Skinfaxi, it was Balios, it was
Borak. I can't describe my feelings beyond that point—they
were all bound up in that steed. I was part of it. . . .''

"Stop it!" I shouted. There was a ferment inside me. A
terrible sense of doom permeated my spirit. I had a premonition
of some ghastly, evil event that lay in the future, which had no
shape or form, but which gripped my heart like a hand and
threatened to squeeze it dry of blood. I could hardly breathe.
The atmosphere in the room was stifling and I pushed past him
to lean on the doorpost, gulping down draughts of cold air as if

they had miraculous medicinal powers that would remove the stains with which he had darkened my soul. "Stop it, for God's sake."

"There's not much more to tell," he said in a quiet voice. "It came down astride me, and then galloped away, into the night. I'm going back to London now. . . . Perhaps we'll see each other again soon?"

"No," I said flatly. "I don't want to hear from you." I turned to face him and he shrugged.

"Well . . . good luck." He went out into the night, leaving me wretched and miserable in the open doorway. It was difficult to know which of my feelings was most dominant. Horror was there, and anger, and fear—but if there was a ruling passion, it was *envy.* I am ashamed to say I felt an overwhelming envy at having been so close to such an experience, yet not part of it. Damn him, I could have killed him then. He had disturbed my spirit, stirred it into a maelstrom of conflicting emotions, and now that it was active I could not see how I was going to find peace again.

By the next morning I had convinced myself that Jake had taken some drug—something that had produced a hallucination of the image he craved so much. I did not want to believe in the Gytrash because if I did I would never rest easy again. I left the cottage and made my way to Hadleigh Downs, where Henry, the gypsy Jake had spoken to, kept his herd of horses. They were there, grazing on the meadow grass, and as I approached them they began cantering away, some thirty of them—grays, roans, piebalds, and one beautiful palomino with its honey-colored mane and tail floating like satin as it wheeled with the others, away from a corner.

Henry was by the trough with his black and white mongrel, and he looked up as I approached, his swarthy face closing down its natural geniality as he recognized me. My office of gamekeeper had done nothing for my popularity amongst the gypsies, since the time I had to prosecute them for poaching.

"'Morning," I said.

He replied in kind, but guardedly.

I nodded toward his herd. "Nice horses."

He sniffed. "You know about horses, then?"

"Used to do a lot of riding . . . not so now."

"They don't make you some'un who knows about horses. Lots o' people ride 'em, but don't know forelocks from withers."

"I know one man who does—the man that spoke to you about the Gytrash."

Henry nodded. "Him?" The little man squared his chest, stretching the string that served as buttons on his brown waistcoat. "Yep, he knew all right. Knew about horses."

"What did you tell him about the Gytrash, Henry?" I said, coming to the point of my visit.

His eyes crinkled at the corners. He may have been smiling but it was difficult to tell. Thickset and hard, he stood like a proud rock beside the water trough, solid, immovable. In him were all the secrets of the stones. Though a "settled" gypsy he was still closer to the natural, the dark elements of nature, than most men alive.

"Are you going to tell me?" I said.

"You want to know if he saw it?"

My silence conveyed my answer.

"You *have* to know, don't 'un? Desperate passions, those o' yours. Dangerous ones, I think. Well, I'll say this—his soul's damned. I warned 'im. I warned 'im hard, but he took not a bit o' notice. That fellow's a goner. Ain't no saving the lost. Stay away from things like that, gamekeeper. There's more bad in them than a sane man can tell."

"You think he's insane?" I said, hopefully, grasping at the single word I had wanted to hear.

"He will be. Don't you think he won't. You can't pluck things out o' the darkness and then go home an' forget 'em. Once they get a hold of your mind, they don't let go—like my old dog over there," he pointed. "Once he's got 'is teeth into a rag, you won't get 'un back except it's in tatters. A soul in tatters is a mind that's mad, gamekeeper. Stay away from 'un."

He walked off then, without a backward glance. The confirmation I had required had been shredded for me by Henry. And I? I was nothing. A mere bystander content to wear

a blindfold. Then there was Catherine. She was to die, if she
was not already dead. The sacrifice. The willing sacrifice.

For the next two months I spent restless days at my work,
fixing fences, ripping out poachers' snares and generally
carrying on with my duties with half a mind. At night I would
sit up, staring out of the window into the darkness, wondering
about the things that lay in wait out there. I would sit until I was
too tired to keep my eyes open and either fall asleep in the chair
or crawl away to my bed. I saw Henry several times, but we
merely acknowledged each other with a nod or wave of the
finger. Then, one afternoon, I returned to the cottage for a bite
of food, and found Jake sitting outside on my window bench.

His appearance penetrated any security I had salvaged since
our last meeting. He had always been a thin man, but now he
was emaciated, haggard and brittle-looking. He raised two
red-rimmed eyes at my approach and the sorrow I saw in their
depths, the anguish and grief, was frightening.

"You'd better come in," I said, unlocking the door with a
trembling hand.

He entered, a wraith-like figure whose clothes hung from
him. It seemed that if I were to touch him, he would crumble
into nothing but dust and sighs. He sat in the chair; hung from
it rather.

"She died then?" I said, softly.

"Yes." The sound was a mere breath of wind from between
his lips.

"Poor Catherine," I murmured. "I didn't know her, but . . ."

His head jerked up. "Not Catherine." His voice was as dry as
old paper, rustling. "Not her. She's still . . . alive."

"Who then? Somebody died. You just said so." I could feel
something stirring in my blood—that ominous presence that
had been with me on the night he had told me about the
Gytrash.

"I don't know."

"You don't know? I . . . where's the understanding in
this?"

His hands came together like two bundles of sticks. With a
dry, rasping sound he rubbed them together.

"This. Catherine didn't die, therefore someone did. I came to tell you this before . . . There's nothing left for me. Nothing. She's gone, you see. The one person that could have changed my life. I killed her . . . murdered her with my selfish obsession."

"This is ludicrous . . ."

"No. No, it's not." His eyes were a sulphurous yellow, and hot upon my own.

"Meaning what, for God's sake?"

"I called the Gytrash prematurely—that meant someone would have to die . . ."

"Yes, yes. You told me that. A loved one . . . the closest to you."

There were bitter tears now, and I turned away, embarrassed for him.

"Don't you see," he said. "Not someone I *know*—someone I hadn't met. I called it up prematurely. Someone—a woman who would have loved me—whom I would have loved more deeply than I have ever loved anyone—that someone died. I don't even know her name. She died before we met and I destroyed myself with her—any purpose I had in this world— Catherine is still alive. It wasn't her. I spoke to the gypsies thinking that it was just a matter of time, but they said no, the night after. The night after I called the Gytrash, my love . . ." His voice cracked. "She would have died. I killed a woman that could have saved me. The one person on this earth with whom I could have shared this *life*—do you understand now?"

My cheeks were tight against the bone.

"Yes. I think so. Out there, amongst the unknown masses, was . . ."

"Her. I can't even put flowers on her grave. I can't even wet the earth with these useless tears. *I never even knew her! Everywhere I go, each place, I think, did she live here? Was that her house? Perhaps she visited this pub or dined at this restaurant?* I look for signs of her—signs I would not even recognize. I see women in the street and wonder, *was she like that? Did she have blonde hair, or brown? What color were her eyes? Did her laughter sound like that woman's laughter? Was she wise, tender, understanding, serious, humorous, intelli-*

gent? I have nothing but questions, and no answers. How can *you* know . . . ?"

"I don't know. I can't know. Neither can you. Perhaps you're tormenting yourself for nothing, Jake. Maybe . . . maybe what you saw was contained in your own mind? A hallucination. Maybe no one has died."

His sallow cheeks tightened. Bitterness replaced the sorrow in his eyes.

"Yes. I know that much. I saw the Gytrash. A woman died, somewhere, out there in the world. I killed her, whoever she was. You only get one opportunity and I've obliterated mine. I destroyed it before it had a chance to happen. Ugly, isn't it? Terribly, terribly ugly. Well, that's that. I've left Catherine. Not her fault. She's got her chance to come. So have you. Give Catherine a call—you never know—some good might come out of this."

He stood up and walked towards the door. I stretched out a hand to stop him. "Stay here the night, Jake, we'll talk about it in the morning."

He hesitated, then said, "I am so tired. Maybe you're right." He ran a hand through his matted, disheveled hair. There was a bleakness in his expression that worried me. I did not want him doing anything stupid. He was so obviously distraught and under tremendous internal pressure.

He said, "I'm sorry—to drag you into all this."

"It's all right," I lied. "This whole thing could be wrong, you know—you're working on assumptions. Let's get some sleep, then try to rationalize it all."

He smiled grimly. "You can't rationalize emotions, not with talk, not with argument. You—I know what you think—that the human mind is—strange—powerful. You're hoping that what I saw out on the marshes was the product of a distorted reality—perceptions warped by an intense, overactive imagination; by heightened senses in a fever-ridden atmosphere. It's not so. I wish it were. That black beast appeared to me—and I have to take the consequences of promoting that appearance. I feel it here. . . ." He tapped his chest, over his heart. "I *know* she's gone. I know the world is lighter of one human being— the one that could have made me whole, with a relationship that

I can never now experience. You were right—I exchanged a lightning thrill for a complete life. I destroyed two people that night—and I was one of them. The other, I'll never know."

"Sleep," I insisted. "You're worn down to nothing. Let's talk tomorrow."

He nodded and I showed him to my bedroom. I left him there and went down to the sofa, where I spent an uncomfortable and restless night. When the morning came the sparrows woke me, clustering in a tree outside my window. I lay there for a few minutes observing the changing fragments of gray caught between the stark, crazed network of branches and recalled the events of the previous evening. I felt numb inside. What was I going to say to him that would help him in any way? You cannot convince a man whose whole mind has reshaped itself around a negative idea, that he is wrong. I could produce nothing in the way of evidence to substantiate an argument that ran counter to his belief. He believed he had precipitated the death of his one chance of happiness. *You only get one chance.* And what did I believe?—that he had created a state of mind which had enabled him to externalize his subconscious desires: that the scenes on the marshes were fantasies projected through his eyes, onto the screen of an empty landscape: that what he had witnessed was the showing of a celluloid dream filmed by his receptive mind? Yet, his conviction that his future love had perished had formed dark lanes in my rationalization. My mind rejected his beliefs, but my soul absorbed them eagerly, as confirmation of its earlier acceptance of a superphysical world beyond blood, flesh, and bone, where one was safe from the thunder of the Captains; safe from the horrors of ritual and order; safe from a life in which actions were repetitive and timed to precision, and impulsiveness, initiative, spontaneity and eccentricity were taboo. If he could have found love, real love, with its wild, energetic gestures and chaotic motion, he would have been safe. Love plays havoc with order. Love is delightful in its irrationality and its scorn of discipline. Love fashions its clocks from ill-fitting cogs of emotion and wheels of impulse. I rose and made two coffees, taking one upstairs to give to Jake.

He was gone.

I stood there, stupidly holding the hot coffee, and stared at the state of the room. Bewilderment gradually dawned into a kind of comprehension. He had left the room in complete order. The blankets had been folded into an immaculate bedpack, squared and sharply creased, at the top of the bed. He had taken all my toilet articles and laid them out neatly, conforming to the diagrams we had followed for military inspections. My shoes were in a row at the end of the bed, lace-ends tucked tightly into the top two eyeholes. Shirts, suits, underwear, socks, ties—all were folded in the correct military manner and displayed according to regulations. Even my writing materials, pad, envelopes and pens, had been placed precisely in their correct mandatory positions on the bedside cabinet. The whole room had been dusted and straightened to a stark, clean, dull uniformity.

It was a chilling sight.

I knew then that nothing could save him. His determination was evident in that display of regimentation and order. Whether he had done it consciously, as some kind of sign to me, or because of some inner compulsion over which he had no control, I never discovered. The Captains had won after all. They had broken him.

A week later, I went to the funeral. It was a small, dismal affair attended by one or two military types, and Catherine. She and I exchanged only a few words; the guilt, whether justified or not, forced us apart quickly, like two magnets of the same polarities. Neither of us, I am sure, felt we had anything in common that was not linked by Jake—sad to say—for it might have indicated something.

Brothers of the Wind
by
Jane Yolen

*One of the most distinguished of modern fantasists, Jane Yolen
has been compared to writers such as Oscar Wilde and Charles
Perrault, and has been called "the Hans Christian Andersen of
the twentieth century." Primarily known for her work for
children and young adults, Yolen has produced more than sixty
books, including novels, collections of short stories, poetry
collections, picture books, biographies, and a book of essays
on folklore and fairy tales. She has received the Golden Kite
Award and the World Fantasy Award, and has been a finalist
for the National Book Award. In recent years, she has also been
writing more adult-oriented fantasy, work which has appeared
in collections such as* Tales of Wonder, Neptune Rising: Songs
and Tales of the Undersea Folk, Dragonfield and Other Stories,
and Merlin's Booke, *and in novels such as* Cards of Grief,
Sister Light, Sister Dark, *and* White Jenna. *She lives with her
family in Massachusetts.*

*Here she spins a touching tale of how sometimes, against all
odds, loyalty is rewarded with wonder—and with love.*

* * *

The Foal

In the Far Reaches of the Desert, where men and horses are said
to dwell as brothers, a foal was born with wings. The foal was
unremarkable in color, a muted brown with no markings.
However, the wings—small and crumpled, with fragile ribs
and a membrane of gray skin—made it the center of all eyes.

But the sheik who owned the foal was not pleased. He stood
over the newborn, pulling on his graying beard. He shook his head
and furrowed his brow. Then he turned quickly, his white robes
spinning about him, casting dervish shadows on the ground.

"This must be Allah's jest," he said contemptuously to the
slave who tended his horses. "But I do not find it amusing. If
horses were meant to be birds, they would be born with beaks
and an appetite for flies."

"It is so," said the slave.

"Take the foal out into the desert," said the sheik. "Perhaps
the sands will welcome this jest with better humor than I."

"At once, master," said the slave. He spoke to the sheik's
back, for his master had already left the tent.

The slave clapped his hands twice. At the sound, so sharp in
the desert's silence, a boy appeared. His name was Lateef, the
tender one, the one full of pity and tears. He was an orphan's
orphan and small for his age, with dark hair and skin the color
of an old coin. His eyes burned fiercely, black suns in a bronze
sky, but they were always quick to cloud over. And though
Lateef was handsome and hardworking, the sheik's chief slave
knew that the boy's tenderness was a great fault and that he was
often the butt of jokes. Indeed, without a living mother or father
to teach him other ways or to protect him from his tormentors,
he was at the mercy of all. Lateef was always given the hardest
and most unpleasant chores to do. He was the lowest slave in
the sheik's household.

"I am here," Lateef said in his gentle voice.

"Ah, the tender one," said the keeper of horses. "Do you see
this foal? This new one? It is not pleasing to our master. It is
Allah's jest. For if a horse were meant to be a bird, it would
make a nest of sticks and straw."

Lateef looked down at the foal as it sucked contentedly at its
mother's teat. He loved being with the horses, for only with
them did Lateef feel brave and strong. The little foal's sides
moved in and out, and at each movement the fragile, membranous wings seemed to flutter. Lateef's hand moved to touch one
wing, and his heart filled with wonder.

But the keeper of horses spoke cruelly, cutting across
Lateef's thoughts. "You are to take this jest far out beyond the
sight of the oasis and leave it in the sand." He turned in
imitation of the sheik, his robes spinning around him.

Lateef spoke as the turn began. "Perhaps . . ." he said
daringly. "Perhaps it is not Allah's jest at all. Perhaps . . .
perhaps . . ." and he spoke so softly, he almost did not say it
aloud. "Perhaps it is Allah's *test*."

The keeper of horses stopped in midturn, his exit ruined, his
robes collapsing in confused folds and entangling his ankles.

"You piece of carrion," he said in a loud, tight voice. "Do you dare to question the sheik?"

"Yes. No. But I thought . . ." Lateef began.

"You have no thoughts," said the keeper of horses. "You are a slave. A slave of slaves. You will do only as you are ordered."

"So let it be," murmured Lateef, his eyes filling. He looked meekly at the ground until the keeper of horses had left the tent. But though his eyes were on the ground, his mind was not. Questions spun inside his head. This wonder, this foal with wings—might it not truly be Allah's test? And what if he failed this test as he seemed to fail everything else? He *had* to think about it. And, even though a slave must *not* think, he could not stop himself.

"And do it at once!" came the command through the tent flap as the keeper of horses poked his head in for one last word. "You are not only too tender but also too slow."

Lateef took a wineskin that hung from a leather thong on the side of the tent to fill it with milk from the foal's mother. He shouldered the foal aside and softly squeezed the milk in steady streams into an earthen bowl, then carefully poured it from the bowl into the skin flask. While Lateef worked, the foal nuzzled his ear and even tried to suck on it.

When the skin flask was full, Lateef knelt and put his head under the foal's belly, settling the small creature around his shoulders. Then he stood slowly, holding on to the foal's thin legs. The foal made only one tiny sound, between a sigh and a whicker, and then lay still. Lateef kept up a continual flow of words, almost a song.

"Little brother, new and weak," he crooned, "we must go out into the sun. Do not fear the eye of God, for all that has happened, all that will happen, is already written. And if it is written that we brothers will survive, it will surely be so."

Then Lateef walked out of the tent.

The Desert

Lateef and the foal both blinked as the bright sun fell upon them. From the inside of the tent, the mare cried out, an anguished farewell. The foal gave a little shudder and was still.

But Lateef was not still. He looked around once at the village of tents that rimmed the oasis. He watched as some slave girls, younger even than he, bent over the well and drew up water. He had known them all his life, but they were still strangers to him. His mother had died at his birth; her mother had died the same way. He was indeed an orphan's orphan, a no-man's child, a slave of slaves. He would leave this home of familiar strangers with no regrets and take his burden—jest or test—out into the burning sands. He had thought about it, though thinking was not for slaves. He had thought about it and decided that he would stay with the foal. His orders were to take it out into the sands. And perhaps the keeper of horses expected them both to die there. But what if their deaths were not written? Could that be part of Allah's test? He would go out into the sands as ordered, and then turn north to Akbir. Akbir, the city of dreams. If it were written anywhere that the foal was to live, in Akbir that writing could be understood.

It was noon when Lateef set out, and the fierce eye of the sun was at its hottest. It was a time when no son of the desert would ordinarily dare the sands. But Lateef had no choice. If he did not leave at once, he would be beaten for disobedience. If he did not leave at once, his courage—what little there was—would fail him. And if he did not leave at once, some other slave would take the foal and leave it out on the desert, and then the foal with wings would surely die.

North to Akbir. Lateef felt the sand give way beneath his feet. It poured away from his sandals like water. Walking in the desert was hard, and made harder still by the heavy burden he was carrying on his back.

He turned once to look at the oasis. It was now only a shimmering line on the horizon. He could see no movement there. He continued until even that line disappeared, until his legs were weak and his head burned beneath his *dulband*. Only then did he stop, kneel down, and place the foal gently onto the sand. He shaded it with his own shadow.

The foal looked up at the boy, its eyes brown and pleading.

"Only one small drink now," cautioned Lateef. He held the wineskin out and pressed its side. Milk streamed into the foal's mouth and down the sides of its cheeks.

"*Aiee,*" Lateef said to himself, "too quickly!" He gave one more small squeeze on the wineskin, then capped it. All the while he watched the foal. It licked feebly at the remaining milk on its muzzle. Its brown flanks heaved in and out. At each outward breath, the membranous wings were pushed up, but they seemed to have no life of their own.

Lateef sat back on his heels and matched his breathing to the foal's. Then, tentatively, he reached over and touched one wing. It looked like a crumpled veil, silken soft and slightly slippery to the touch. Yet it was tougher than it looked. Lateef was reminded suddenly of the dancing women he had glimpsed going in and out of the sheik's tent. They had that same soft toughness about them.

He touched the wing again. Then, holding it by the thin rib with one hand, he stretched it out as far as it would go. The wing unfolded like a leaf, and Lateef could see the dark brown veins running through it and feel the tiny knobs of bone. The foal gave a sudden soft grunt and, at the same moment, Lateef felt the wing contract. He let it go, and it snapped shut with a soft swishing sound.

"So," he said to the foal, "you *can* move the wing. You can shut it even if you cannot open it. That is good. But now I wonder: will you ever fly? Perhaps *that* is Allah's real test."

He stood up and looked around. All was sand. There was no difference between what was behind him and what was before. Yet he was a boy of the desert. He knew how to find directions from the traveling sun. Akbir lay to the north.

"Come, winged one," he said, bending down to lift the foal to his shoulders again. "Come, little brother. There is no way for us but north."

The foal made no noise as Lateef set out again. And except for Lateef's own breathing, the desert was silent. It drank up all sound. So, with the sand below, the sky above, and only the wind-sculpted dunes to break the unending horizon, Lateef walked on. He felt that he labored across a painted picture, so still was the land.

Then suddenly, rising up from the place where sand and sky meet, Lateef saw a great watery shape. First it was a beast, then a towered city, then an oasis surrounded by trees. The changes were slow, one image running into the next as a river is absorbed into the sea. Something in Lateef leaped with the sight, and for a moment he let himself cry out in hope. But as the tears filled his eyes, Lateef reminded himself: "It is not a beast, not an oasis, not Akbir. It is only a mirage. Sun on the brain and sand in the eye." He spoke over his shoulder to the foal. "And I wonder what it is *you* see there, little brother." Then, closing his eyes and heart to the mocking vision, he trudged on, over the wind-scoured ripples, the changing, changeless designs on the desert floor.

When night came, he walked many miles farther under the light of the indifferent stars. Finally exhausted, he set his burden and slept. But his sleep was fitful and full of dreams. He dreamed of sand, of sun, of stars. But he never once dreamed of the little horse that had curled against his chest, confident of the coming day.

The City

Before dawn, before the sun could once more coax the shadow beasts and cloud cities to rise, Lateef set out again. He let the foal suck on the bottle and allowed himself a few sips as well. He dared not think about the coming heat or that his left foot had a cramp in it, or that his shoulders ached from the burdensome foal, or that his heart could not stop trembling with fear. He refused to let himself think about those things. Instead he thought about Akbir.

Akbir. His great-grandmother had been from Akbir. The daughter of a kitchenmaid, without a father to claim her, she had been sold into slavery. To the father of the father of Lateef's master, the sheik. Lateef understood well that being the son of so many generations of slaves made him a person worth nothing. Less than nothing. Yet he dared to hope that, in Akbir, the home of his ancestors, he might change his position. With the foal as his touchstone, might he not even become a free man? A trainer of horses? An owner of stables?

He closed his eyes against the rising fantasy. Best, he cautioned himself, to think of only one thing at a time. Allah's jest or Allah's test. After all, he had no real idea what he would be able to do when he reached the pebbled streets, the mosaic mosques, the towered palaces of Akbir.

Walking forward quickly, his mind on the desert and not on his dreams, Lateef continued on. Even when he passed some horsemen at last and a caravan that jangled across his path for hours, he did not permit himself to dream. And in all that time, he spoke to no one other than the foal with whom he shared the wineskin.

But Lateef was not fooled into thinking that they had managed to come so far without the help of some unacknowledged miracle. After all, though he was an orphan, the great-grandson of a city dweller, he had been reared in the desert. His people had seventeen different words for sand, and not one of them was a compliment. He well knew that a solitary traveler could not hope to walk across the desert under the sun's unrelenting eye without more to stave off thirst than a single flask of mare's milk. And yet they had done so, the boy and the foal, and were alive as they finally stumbled onto one of the dirt-packed back streets of Akbir. Still, as if afraid of giving tongue to the word "miracle"—as if speech might unmake it—Lateef remained silent. He set the foal down and then, as it stood testing its wobbly legs against the ground, Lateef bowed down and kissed the road at the foal's feet.

The foal took a few steps down a road that led off to one side. Then it turned its head toward Lateef and whickered.

"*Aiee,* brother. That road it shall be," Lateef said. He caught up with the foal easily and gave it the last of the milk. Then he stroked its velvety nose and lifted it for one last ride upon his back.

Surprisingly there was no one in the street, nor in the roadways they crossed, nor in the souk, the marketplace, where stalls and stands carried handwork, and foodstuffs enough to feed a multitude. Puzzling at this, Lateef explored further, passing from dirt roads to pebbled streets, from pebbled streets to roadways studded with colorful patterned stones.

The foal nuzzled his ear, and at that moment Lateef heard a strange moaning. He turned and followed the sound until he came to a line of high walls. Standing in front of the walls were hundreds of people.

Women, dressed in black mourning robes, cried out and
poured sand upon their heads. Men in black pants and ragged
shirts wailed and tore at their own beards. Even the children, in
their best clothes, rolled over and over in the roadway, sobbing.
And the name that he heard on every lip was "Al-Mansur.
Al-Mansur."

Lateef was amazed. He had never seen such extravagant
grief. The dwellers of the desert, with whom he had lived all his
life, were proud of their ability to endure tragedy and pain.
Water, they said, was too precious to be wasted in tears. Their
faces never showed hurt. That was why Lateef, who cried at
another's pain and could not disguise his griefs, had been called
"tender one" and despised by all.

As Lateef watched the wailing men and women and children, he felt tears start down his own cheeks. Embarrassed, he
went over to one young mourner who was rolling in the street
and stopped him gently with his foot.

"Tell me, city brother," said Lateef, "for whom do we
weep?"

The boy looked up. "Oh, boy with horse shawl," he began,
"we cry because our great king of kings, the caliph Al-Mansur,
is dying for want of a strange horse, a horse that he has seen in
his dreams. And though the caliph is a man of mighty dreams,
he has always before been able to have whatever he dreamed.
Only this time he cannot. And none of our doctors—the
greatest physicians in the world—can cure him. They cannot
cure him, for now he dreams of his death and, as it is written,
there is no remedy for death." Then the boy fell back and
pulled up some of the pebbles in the street, digging in the dirt
beneath them. He covered his head with this dirt and began
wailing again, this time louder than before.

"These are strange people," thought Lateef, "the people who
dwell in cities. Yet I am of their blood. My great-grandmother
was a sister to theirs. Surely that is why I am such a tender one.
Still," he mused, "it is true that there is no remedy for death. I
have heard that said many times in the desert. I have looked on
many dead people, even in my short life, and have never known
any of them to be cured."

And thinking about the caliph's approaching death led him to think about the caliph's dream. What could a man as rich and powerful as Al-Mansur desire so much that he might die of wanting? A horse, the boy said. But surely Al-Mansur could have any horse he wanted, any horse he dreamed of, any horse in his land.

"Perhaps the horse I carry is the very horse of the caliph's dream," Lateef said to the weeping boy.

At his words, the boy stopped his noise and looked up. "That is no horse, but a rag around your shoulders. A rag on a rag. The caliph is a great man, a giant. His dreams are big, too. He would laugh at such a jest should he see it." The boy began to laugh, but quickly the laugh turned back into a wail and he lay down again in the dust.

Lateef stroked the nose of the foal with one hand. "You are no jest to me, little brother," he said. Then he stepped over the wailing boy, pushed through the line of weeping people, and entered a gate in the wall.

Inside he saw the palace guards. They had taken off their great scimitars and, after laying the swords carefully on the ground, were rolling in the dirt and crying out their grief in tones even louder than the rest.

Lateef walked past them all and mounted the steps, marveling at the patterns on the stairs and walls. Behind them were the hundreds of grieving people. He wondered what lay ahead.

The Dream

Room upon room seemed to open before Lateef, and he walked through each one as if in a dream. He—who had known only the tents of his sheik, thinking them rich beyond his greatest imaginings—could not even begin to comprehend the wonders that belonged to the caliph. The sheik's desert tents now seemed but tattered remnants of an old beggar's cloak.

He followed a thread of sound, a wailing as thin and pure as a piece of spun gold. And when he found its beginning, he entered a room more splendid than any he had wandered in before.

Pearl-encrusted oil lamps sat on ebony tables. Draperies of wine-and-gold-colored silks hung on the walls. The wind of fifty fans held by fifty slaves made the shadows from the lamplight dance about the floor and over the carved faces of the wooden window screens.

In the center of the room was a mountain of pillows where a man lay, his head back and his bearded face bleached nearly as white as his robes and *dulband*. Only the red jewel of his turban had color. The ghost of his flesh hovered around his bones, for he had once been a large man, but was now shrunken with illness and age. His eyes were closed, but his lips moved in and out as he breathed. Around him were seven weeping women dressed in veils, their noses and mouths covered but their eyes eloquent with tears. Four old men, wringing their hands and making sour mouths, listened by the bed.

As Lateef came closer, he could hear the man on the pillows speaking faintly.

"In my dream," the bearded man said, "I stood upon the brink of a river. I knew that I had to cross to the other side. But there was no boat to take me there, and the waters were too wild and cold to swim. As I stood on the bank, longing for the other side, a wind began to dance around me. It blew sand in my face. I brushed my hand across my eyes to clear them and, when I could see once more, there was a great horse standing before me. The wind came from its huge, shining wings, fanning the air. I leaped onto its back. It pumped those mighty wings once, twice. Then, with a leap, it rose into the air. I looked below, and the river was but a thin ribbon lying across a sandy vastness. I gave a great laugh, threw my hands above my head, and—laughing—fell from the horse and awoke again in my bed."

"It is the same dream, my caliph," said the oldest man there, a man with a long white beard as fine as several silken threads.

"Of course it is," said the caliph. "But if I do not find that horse, I will die." He sighed deeply, and his stomach moved up and down.

The women began to wail again, but the old men shook their heads. The oldest spoke again.

"Be reasonable, my caliph. To die for a dream?" he said.

"Is it better to die of old age? To die of a disease? I think," said the caliph, "that to die for a dream is the noblest course of all."

"Be reasonable, my caliph," the old man tried again. "There is no such horse."

"Then how did I dream it?" asked Al-Mansur. "Can a man dream what is not? What can never be? If there is no such horse, then tell me, you who are the wisest of my people, what is the meaning of my dream?" He looked up at the men.

"The river is the river of death," said one adviser.

"Or the river of life," said the second.

"Or the river of sleep, which runs between," said the third. The women cried out again.

"And the horse is your life," said the one.

"Or your death," said the second.

"Or it is the dream beyond, the great dream that all men and all women dream," said the third.

The caliph sat up straight and smiled at them. "But is it not possible that the dream might come true, that such things could exist? That someday a man will ride in the sky and look down on a river and see it as thin as a ribbon?" The caliph looked pityingly at his advisers. "Can we not dream what *will* be?"

"If men were meant to fly," said the oldest adviser, stroking his thin beard, "they would be born with feathers instead of hair. So it is written. And it is so."

The caliph puffed out his cheeks thoughtfully. "But in the days of my father's fathers," he said, "there were those who dared to dream of great wonders. And in time such wonders came into being in the land: the building of this palace, and of the road that now runs across the sand—these were but dreams once, and now they are real. Why do you tell me I should dream no more?"

"Wonders in one year are commonplaces in another," replied the old man. "And memory has a faulty tongue."

"But do not say this dream is impossible," said the caliph. "I will not have it." Yet even as he spoke the words, he sank back onto the pillows.

Before the men could tell the caliph no once more, Lateef spoke. The horse on his shoulders lent him courage. "In the desert we say nothing is impossible, my caliph. What one man cannot do, another may." He sank to his knees, ducked his head, and set the foal onto the floor. The little horse wobbled, and his tiny hooves clattered against the colorful tiles. "Perhaps, great Al-Mansur, this is the wonder of which you dreamed."

The caliph sat up again and laughed, his eyes nearly hidden in the flaps of his shriveled cheeks. The laugh put false color in his face. "I dreamed of a mighty horse, and you bring me a starveling foal. I dreamed of a flying white-winged wonder, and you bring me a brown mite almost too weak to walk."

But the oldest adviser looked more closely at the foal. He saw its tiny gray wings, frail as those of a dragonfly. And he saw a way to keep his caliph alive for a while longer. He spoke with great care. "Even a wonder may be weak in its youth," he whispered to the caliph. "Look again, Al-Mansur."

The caliph looked again, saw the wings, and clapped his hands. "Perhaps," he said, "I shall put off dying until this foal has grown. You, boy, shall live with it in its stall. You shall eat with it and exercise it. And when the wonder is big enough, you shall bring it to me once again, and I shall have my ride." He sat up and put his feet over the side of the pillows. "And now, bring me some food and tell my people to stop their grieving. Their caliph shall not die for this dream—but live."

The Year

And so it came to pass that Lateef, the slave of slaves, became Lateef the keeper of the winged foal. Yet his life was not so different as one might suppose. He slept in the straw by the side of the horse, warming its body with his own. He was up before dawn drawing water from the well, filling a sack with grain, always feeding the horse before he dared to feed himself. And each day, besides, he brushed the horse's long black mane and tail, grooming its sleek, dark sides.

But he paid the most attention of all to the wondrous wings. He would take the fragile ribs in his hands and gently flex them, stretching the membranes until they were taut. In the cook, dark stable the membranes were a milky white, the color of old pearl. But outside, with the sun shining through, they were as iridescent as insect wings. So the caliph called the horse "Dragonfly." But Lateef did not.

"Brother," he named the foal. "Wind Brother." And he sang the name into the horse's ears and blew a breath gently into the foal's nostrils as was the custom among the desert dwellers. And he made the horse a song:

> Wind rider,
> Sun strider,
> The dreamer's dream,
> Moon leaper,
> Star keeper,
> Are you what you seem?

It was not a great song, but Lateef whispered it over and over in an affectionate tone as he touched the horse, until it twitched its ears in reply. And the horse grew to love Lateef and would respond to his every command.

Often the caliph would stand by the stall, holding on to the door for support while Lateef cleaned the horse. Or he would sit in a chair nearby while the horse's wings were stretched and rubbed with oil. But whenever the caliph tried to come too close, both Lateef and the horse would tremble. Then the caliph would sigh, and a faint blush of color would stain his pale cheeks. "Ah, Dragonfly," Al-Mansur would say, "do not forget that you are my dream. And I must ride my dream or die."

One day, when Lateef and the horse had both trembled at the caliph's approach, and Al-Mansur had sighed and spoken, Lateef could control his tongue no longer. Bowing low, afraid to raise his head, he spoke. "O Caliph, if what you say is so, then you are no more free than I."

The caliph was silent for a moment, and when he spoke his voice was very soft. "No one is entirely free, child. Even I, Caliph Al-Mansur, have never been free to indulge my own dreams. To be good and wise, a ruler must make real the dreams of his people. But now, for once, I would have this dream, this wonder, for myself alone. For in some small way, the dreaming makes me feel I am free, though I know I am not."

Lateef shook his head, for he did not understand the caliph. How could a man who had everything no farther away than a handclap not be free? He raised his head to ask the caliph, but the man was gone. He did not come again to the stable, and his absence troubled Lateef.

When a year had passed and Wind Brother's sides had filled out, his mane and tail grown long and silky, the caliph sent word around to the stables that he would come the very next day to ride the winged horse. Now in all this time Wind Brother had never been mounted, nor had a saddle ever been placed upon his back. And never had he opened and shut his wings on his own. Lateef had been content to walk around the ring with the horse, his hand on Wind Brother's neck. He had feared that if he were to sit on the horse's back, his heels might accidentally do injury to the iridescent wings or that a saddle might crush a fragile rib.

Lateef bowed low to the messenger. "Tell my caliph," he said fearfully, "and with many respects, that the horse is not yet strong enough for a rider."

The messenger looked even more afraid than Lateef. "I dare not deliver such a message myself. You must go."

So Lateef entered the caliph's room for the second time. Al-Mansur lay on the silken pillows as if he were only dreaming of life.

"The horse, your . . . your Dragonfly," stuttered Lateef, "he is not yet ready to be ridden."

"Then make him so," said the caliph, barely raising himself up to speak. He sank back quickly, exhausted from the effort.

Lateef started to protest, but the guards hurried him out of the room. As he walked down the long hall, the caliph's oldest adviser followed him.

"He *must* ride tomorrow," said the old man, his thin beard weaving fantastic patterns in the air as he spoke. "It is his only wish. He is growing weak. Perhaps it will keep him alive. A man is alive as long as he can dream."

"But *his* dream is of *my* horse."

"The horse is not yours, but the caliph's. His grain has kept the horse alive. You are but a slave," said the old man, shaking his finger at Lateef. "A slave cannot own a horse."

"A slave can still be brother to the wind," Lateef whispered, aghast at his tongue's boldness, "as long as the wind wills it so." But even as he spoke, he feared he had failed—failed the horse and failed the caliph—and in failing them both, failed himself.

Allah's Test

In the morning Lateef was up early. He rubbed the horse's sides with scented oils. He wove ribbons into its black mane. And all the while he crooned to the horse, "Oh, my brother, do not fail me as I fear I have failed you. Be humble. Take the caliph onto your back. For you are young and healthy, and he is old and sick. He is the dreamer and you are the dream."

The horse whickered softly and blew its warm breath on Lateef's neck.

Then Lateef took the horse out into the ring.

Soon the caliph came, borne in a chair that was carried by four strong men. Behind them came the caliph's advisers. Then, in order of their importance, came the caliph's wives. Finally, led in by the armed guards, came the men and women and children of Akbir, for the word had gone out to the souks and mosques: "Come see Caliph Al-Mansur ride his dream."

Only then, when Lateef saw how many people waited and watched, did he truly become afraid. What would happen if the caliph failed in front of all these people? Would they blame the horse for not bearing the caliph's weight? Would they blame Lateef for not training the horse well? Or would they blame the caliph? Failure, after all, was for slaves, not for rulers.

The caliph was helped from his chair, but then he signaled his people away. Slowly he approached the horse. Putting his hand to the horse's nose, he let Wind Brother smell him. He moved his hand carefully along the horse's flanks, touching the wings in a curious, tentative gesture, as if he had never really seen them clearly before. He spoke softly, so that only the horse and Lateef could hear: "I am the dreamer, you are the dream. I think I am ready to ride."

Lateef waited.

The horse waited.

All the men and women and children of Akbir waited.

Suddenly, so swiftly it surprised them all, the caliph took a deep breath and leaped onto the horse's back. He sat very tall on Wind Brother, his hands twisted in the horse's mane, his legs carefully in front of the wings. Eyes closed, the caliph smiled. And his smile was a child's, sweetly content.

For a long, breath-held moment, nothing happened. Then the horse gave a mighty shudder and reared back on his hind legs. He spun around and dropped onto all fours, arching his back. The caliph, still smiling, flew into the air and landed heavily on the ground. He did not get up again.

The horse did not move, even when Lateef ran over to him and touched his nose, his neck, his side. But as Lateef swung himself astride, he felt the horse's flanks trembling.

"Be not afraid," Lateef whispered to the horse. "I am here. What they try to do to you, they must do to me first. In this I will not fail you."

The chief of the caliph's guards ran toward the boy and the horse, his great silver scimitar raised above his head. As the scimitar began to sing its death song on the trip down through the air, Lateef leaned forward, guarding the horse's neck with his own. But he did not feel any blow. All he felt was a rush of wind as the horse began to pump its mighty wings for the first time.

Lateef turned his head. Above them he could still see the image of the silver sword. Then at his knee he felt a hand. He looked down. A boy about his own age stood there, in white robes, with a white *dulband* on his head. In the turban's center was the caliph's red jewel.

"I am free and ready to ride," the boy said, a shadowy smile playing at the corners of his mouth.

"Then mount, my brother," whispered Lateef, putting his hand down and pulling the boy up behind him. "Ride your dream."

With a mighty motion, the horse's wings pumped once again, filling with air and sky. He lifted them beyond the sword, beyond the walls of the palace. They circled the minarets once, and Lateef looked down. He could see a crowd gathering around the fallen figures of a caliph, a horse, a ragged boy. Only here and there was a man or a woman or a child who dared to look up, who saw the dream-riders in the sky.

And then they were gone, the three: over a river that was a thin ribbon in the sand, over the changing patterns of the desert, to the place where there are neither slaves nor rulers and where all living beings truly dwell as brothers—the palace of the winds.

Aunt Millicent at the Races
by
Len Guttridge

Here's a gentle, warm-hearted, and very funny look at a family problem—and the ingenious, if not exactly ethical, solution the family finds for that problem . . .

Len Guttridge has published several lyrical and amusing stories about strange doings and supernatural occurrences in the Welsh countryside, most of them in The Magazine of Fantasy and Science Fiction *in the mid-1960s. He lives in Alexandria, Virginia.*

*   *   *

You've heard what they say about the Rhondda Valley. How the spread of industry cast a blight upon the verdant land and just as ineradicably scarred with fear and suspicion the souls of its people, etc. That more or less is the popular romantic notion. But it wasn't the coal mines and smelting furnaces which stamped the faces of Pontypandy at least, my birthplace, with permanent expressions of gall. Instead, I blame the economic crisis which struck following my father's exploitation of Aunt Millicent's overnight transformation into a horse.

Interior alterations may already have begun, so to speak, but the first surface indications that Aunt Milly was not her usual self appeared halfway through my tenth birthday party, forever wrecking my father's long reign as life and soul of such occasions. He had just supervised the usual gamut of infant-games and our carpet was littered with small panting bodies, mine included. His sergeant-major bellow jerked us then into giggling attention and he began his standard trio of funny stories.

We had heard them before, without comprehension. As usual, we sat through the first in grave and baffled silence. As usual, Father convulsed with mirth before he could complete the punch line of the second. The third, not as usual, was rewarded by a spirited neigh from the prim pink lips of my mother's cousin Millicent.

She neighed for several seconds and ended with a triumphant *arpeggio* squeak. It was the squeak, I recall, which flipped us. We spun like cartwheels all over the room, we clawed each other's clothes, we turned crimson and we choked. Had Father told fifty stories, all new and uproarious, he could never have achieved such spectacular effects and by the hand of the Lord, he knew it.

His brow grew blacker than summer thunder clouds over Gerrig Llan and his words spat down like hail. "I'll trouble you, Millicent, to keep your blasted animal impersonations to yourself."

Aunt Milly gulped. Her hands fluttered like blind birds. She hated to be the center of attention. But she could no more retreat from the spotlight now than explain why she occupied it.

From certain of his sulphuric soliloquies, I knew that Father had long felt the time overdue when his wife's cousin should have found herself a husband, preferably one of means. I don't think Millicent was unattractive. But since she swathed herself from chin to ankles in the tweedy puritan garb considered proper uniform for a twenty-five-year-old Welsh assistant librarian, it was hard to tell whether she was emphatically curved or indeed if she had any curves at all.

Anyway, the morning after Father's deposition as life and soul of family parties, Aunt Milly at breakfast was seen to be desperately grappling for her fork with a hoof protruding from one thick sleeve. Mother blinked and prepared to swoon. Father glared. My aunt gave a helpless shrug. "I'm terribly sorry." Her apology tiptoed into the sudden tension. "This . . . this came on in the night." A penitent neigh escaped her. "I rather hoped you wouldn't notice."

She neighed again, abandoned her labors with the cutlery, and fled to her room.

Father adjusted his features into a familiar cast. Upstairs over his bed hung a large Victorian print showing the last stand of the South Wales Borders against the Zulus at Rorke's Drift, its dominant figure the beleaguered lieutenant atop the redoubt, a dashing ideal of pluck and fortitude. Precisely this bearing my father always strove for when confronted by domestic emergency.

"Son." He addressed me with the gruffness of a commander dispatching a scout to bring up the cavalry. "Go and fetch Doctor O'Toole. *On the double!*"

The doctor was for Mother. When I returned with him, Father was buckling his old Sam Browne army belt, another symbolic gesture, and gazing resolutely upstairs where from Aunt Milly's room echoed a rhythmic sound. An anxious drumming. As of hoofbeats.

Doctor O'Toole sighed and turned to Mother but she threw one swoon after another, which quickly infuriated O'Toole and drew forth in a loud Belfast accents his oft-proclaimed intention of quitting this lunatic land for a sane and profitable practice in Harley Street.

Then Milly's room door banged wide and downstairs galloped a great bay mare. With a shriek Mother fainted again and Dr. O'Toole, about to apply brandy, quickly diverted it to his own gaping mouth.

The mare staggered nervously. Her flanks barged into our century-old grandfather clock and she butted an equally antique Welsh oak dresser. Chinaware flew. A silver cup Father had won in a regimental prize fight tournament toppled to the carpet. His ornate pipe-rack (hand-carved in Italy) followed, scattering English briars, Dutch porcelains and rich brown meerschaums. Uncertain hoofs kicked them right and left.

Throughout, Father stood unbowed in the center of the room, Gibraltar against a storm, although the military wingtips of his delta mustache quivered. Twice he muttered, "*Steady, lads, steady,*" and I could almost hear bugles. Behind him the bruised grandfather clock burst into a frantic chiming though it was nowhere near the hour, and then it slid to silence like a half-wound gramophone. And Aunt Milly came to rest and braced on trembling legs, and peered self-consciously over Father's squared shoulder.

Thus Millicent's equine debut. Naturally, it summoned Father's strongest qualities, particularly his instinct for exploiting the unexpected, the at first glance *perplexing*, to his own greedy ends. That afternoon his mind was already exploring ways and means as, watched peaceably by Aunt Milly grazing in our cabbage patch, he made over the toolshed out back into a cozy stable.

After we had pushed and prodded her into it, she turned to survey us with modest complacency, as when she used to relate some minor personal triumph attained at the Pontypandy Reading Circle. Father grinned. "Milly, my gal," he said. "You was never in better shape."

Father of course *accepted* what had happened. Despite his brief career in the army (exaggerated by him in retrospect), he believed whole-heartedly in magic. Name me the Welshman who doesn't. But instead of showing the proper awe for it, he took it like everything else in his military stride. And I'm sure he had felt that sooner or later, something strange was bound to happen to Milly . . .

Shy and demure though she was, Milly had positively wallowed in wizardry. Night upon night she would read to me from books old and full of wonder whose words bewitched the very pages so, I swear, they turned untouched. And I would shiver with dread, that was no west wind keening across the valley but spirit hounds baying at the moon, and once pajamaed for sleep I would keep my eyes from the bedroom window to avoid a fatal glimpse of death candles flickering in procession around the foot of Cerrig Llan or the Little People up to no good among the ash groves. . . .

Well, Pontypandy soon hummed with gossip. Inevitably it reached the vigilant ears of Pastor Goronwy Jones, familiar to his flock as Goronwy the Sin-killer. That Sunday, with hotter than usual eloquence, he kindled a special hellfire for those who would dabble in dark powers, and although he did not mention us by name, all knew that the target for his fiery shafts was the Pritchard brood, of which I was the only one in chapel. Obedient to the hint of its spellbinder, the congregation turned its multiple gaze on me, and as if pinned by a circle of flamethrowers I squirmed, sizzled, and finally melted in shame.

Rumors spread beyond the Welsh border and attracted a sniffing pack of newspapermen. A disarmament conference in Paris, an earthquake in Peru, and the defrocking of a Sussex bishop for scandalous conduct were elbowed off the front pages by speculation upon Aunty Milly, the Pontypandy Wonder. Pontypandy, we would say today, hogged the headlines. But not for long. Alien students of psychic phenomena who camped on the slopes of Cerrig Llan caught pneumonia and went home. A professional ghost-hunter materialized at our front door but was himself so rudely interrogated by Father that he vanished more quickly than any apparition. An attractive lady evangelist from California delivered a sermon on Signs and Portents to Goronwy the Sin-killer's fold, then sailed off to America, her choral retinue augmented by some dozen endlessly singing young miners whose conversion had been instantaneous the moment they emerged from the bituminous depths to behold her.

All the visitors in fact departed before Father had a fair chance to profit from the publicity, for nobody really believed the whirl of stories about Milly. Nobody, I mean, who wasn't Welsh.

But Father was far from dashed. One morning after the fuss had died down, he marched off to the library in his best no-surrender manner while I trotted alongside him. The library staff numbered three, not counting Milly, whose absence they sorely lamented. "How is she?" they asked Father.

"Off her oats this morning," he replied curtly and demanded to see their stock of horse books. It was slim. We left with "Turf and Paddock," "Illustrated Horsebreaking" and "The Complete Horsewoman," all more than thirty years out-of-print. The last title didn't seem wholly appropriate but for some reason Father savored it with great glee.

He also wrote to London and bought a subscription to *Horse and Track*. And that is how we met Arlington Mellish, wealthy horse breeder, patron of the races, frequent contributor to *Horse and Track*. It was something in a Mellish article, we learned later, that led Father to ponder seriously Aunt Milly's track potential.

"I've written to Mr. Mellish," Father announced one evening, "with a view to introducing our Milly to the Sport of Kings."

Important decisions, Father believed, deserved the grandiose phrase.

Mother was horrified. *"Mogwen Sion Pritchard!"* Going the full distance with Father's name shows how shocked she was. "You can't . . . Why, it isn't decent. My own cousin a . . . *racehorse?* Indeed no, not while I still breathe."

Mother's lungs were functioning at their usual robust rate two weeks later as she pored with growing enthusiasm over *Horse and Track* while Father conferred with Arlington Mellish himself, a plump check-suited Englishman addicted to long cigars which he snatched from his mouth at intervals to talk out of partly closed lips as if his every word were guarded. Since security was impossible to maintain in the Red Lion public house, Mellish and my father ascended Cerrig Llan every morning for a week to conduct literally what a later generation would call summit talks. Each afternoon we all gathered to watch Aunt Milly canter in Madoc Meadow, Mellish emitting rapid grunts of approval from the edge of his mouth, Father pleasurably caressing his mustache. And Mother's eyes gleaming. You couldn't, after all, live sixteen years with my father and remain altogether immune to his genial avarice.

Mellish inspected Milly from forelock to fetlocks. He removed his cigar with lightning speed and snapped, "Good lean head. Muscular loins, nice level croup."

"Croup?" Father frowned.

"Rump," explained Mellish. He snapped Milly by way of further amplification then sprang back as she bared her teeth and lunged for his cigar.

"That's good, too," panted Mellish. "High-spirited. Mark of a thoroughbred." He replaced his cigar.

"Naturally Milly's a thoroughbred," Mother murmured a trifle stiffly.

Mellish continued his appraisal. He wrenched the cigar from his teeth. "Sixteen hands at the withers, I'd say. Hindquarters firmly developed." He bent. "Pasterns smooth and true."

"Pasterns?" Father was stroking his mustache almost ferociously.

Mellish straightened. "Ankles, if you like."

And that night, before driving off from Pontypandy, he offered Father the use of his training stables in Somerset.

"Expect you as soon as you can come," he puffed twice then whipped the cigar aside. "And Milly, of course."

A bubbling cold kept me from school. Mother and Father were in the village shopping for suitable stable wear. Aunt Milly grazed placidly in the garden. I had the house to myself. I don't know what impulse moved me, I had not entered Millicent's old room since her transfer to more fitting quarters. But now, in the quiet of a fading day, I pushed open the door and crept in.

It was a pretty room and neat, with a large window overlooking the valley. On a chair beside the bed rested a tattered book, from its decrepit condition obviously one of the collection bequeathed the previous winter to Pontypandy Library by a Welsh bard turned hermit who had dabbled heavily in Druidic mysticism and at the age of 104 was found dead on Cerrig Llan by a posse of town tipplers chasing a mountain goat for fun.

I opened the book where a pink feather marked the pages. They splintered like rust-flakes between my fingers; the print was tiny and half-obscured by footnotes, marginal notes, and notes between the lines, the scribbled interjections of the late bard. But I learned a few things, nevertheless. Aunt Millicent hadn't been the first around these parts to lose human form. Twm Shon Catti, a mountain scamp, had beaten her by a century, though what he had turned *into* wasn't clear. There was also a luscious witch named Blodwenwedd who changed rather pointlessly into an owl. Gilvaethwy hadn't known when to stop: he became a deer, then a hog, then a wolf, then a snake, and finally forgot what he had started out as.

Dusk crept down from Cerrig Llan. I found a match, touched flame to an oil lamp's wick and read on. My tongue fought aloud with the difficult words and the house crouched listening, now and then clearing its throat with wind gusts down the chimney.

What I was reading was nothing less than a text-book on sorcery, a handy "how-to" tome on transmogrification, a step-by-step guide in the art of switching shapes. To that of a lion for strength, a bird for its flight. To a horse for fleetness. A rabbit for . . . for . . . *fecundity*. I didn't know the word but I must have partly divined its meaning for I felt a spasm of regret that Aunt Milly had not become a rabbit.

Transformation was big league magic, attainable only by eating the fruit which grew from the sacred grave of Wyn Ab Nudd, the King of the Little People. While you ate, you wished like blazes. That old bard had eaten and wished, then, but as a mountain goat he'd had the singular bad luck to run into a covey of drunks. And Millicent, she too must have found Wyn Ab Nudd's grave, and . . .

At the approaching footsteps of my parents, I snuffed out the lamp, closed the book and ran downstairs, my mind a riot.

"Why," asked Mr. Conway next morning, "are you so interested in Wyn Ab Nudd's grave?"

Bald and beaked, Mr. Conway was our history teacher. If anybody could tell me where Ab Nudd was buried, it had to be old Beaky Conway. And once I knew, then I would go there, snatch some fruit, smuggle it after bedtime into Milly's stable.

I felt sure she must be wishing herself back in her old shape, she had only transmogrified for a bit of daring, she never got much fun out of life really, but a joke was a joke and time now to end it. Moreover, Milly had been with us since before I was born and she was, in some ways, closer to me than either parent. So I was all for restoring her, library tweeds and all.

"I was reading about him," I answered Beaky Conway thoughtfully.

"Well, child." Conway's nose hooked down at me as if to pierce my heart. I wondered suddenly if Beaky—of course *Beaky*—knew about the grave, had guzzled fruit from it and almost but not quite changed into an eagle. "Nobody knows for sure where King Ab Nudd is buried. Some say beneath Bala Lake. Others, the crown of Cerrig Llan. Personally," he chuckled sepulchrally and I tensed for feathered wings to spread from his underarms and claws to burst through his polished boots. "Personally, I suspect he is buried nearby. Perhaps the mound on Farmer Pugh's land."

The mound. Of course. I had read how in olden times they burned the bodies of the Celtic kings and put the ashes in pots and raised huge heaps of earth and stones over them, and many such mounds we took today to be natural hillocks. "There is such a mound, child," Mr. Conway loomed over me, his eyes flashing down the bony comma between them, "in Farmer Pugh's apple orchard."

The sun was a molten penny dipping beyond distant Bala Lake, the sky overhead a purple silence. The road home to Pontypandy curved out of sight behind the bare slope of Cerrig Llan. I was nearly halfway up the mountain overlooking Farmer Pugh's orchard, and there it was in the middle, the *mound*, crested with apple trees and encircled by ash like petrified high priests. A wind stirred and the trees whispered and scraped their branches on the wall as if they knew someone was watching. It was a lonely spot all right, but I had to go through with it, had to climb that wall . . .

When I shinned back out again, my pockets were stuffed. Dusk had fallen. Rooks cawed above my head and the nearest tiny lamplight in the Pugh farmhouse glimmered a thousand miles far off. Choir practice echoed remotely from Goronwy the Sin-killer's chapel, but holy music was no match for the unnameable force I suddenly felt tug-o'-warring me back to an age of dark ritual among cromlechs, crags and Druids' circles. The apples I'd poached now tingled through good Welsh cloth to my goose-pimpling skin, and with a yell I ran headlong down the mountain and covered the last mile from Cerrig Llan to our safe house faster than any future Bannister.

And I was too late. Father and Aunt Milly had just departed for Somerset.

Just how Arlington Mellish, who had bought part ownership in Millicent, satisfied the Jockey Club, those traditional arbiters of the British turf, concerning her pedigree when none of her ancestors could be found in the General Stud Book, is and will forever remain a tightly guarded Mellish secret. Anyway, Millicent proceeded to win several county events with ease and it was only a matter of time before Father talked of entering her for the Glamorgan Plate. Father was just home from Somerset on what he called a brief furlough from the field.

"The Glamorgan Plate?" Mother glanced up from the *Racing*

Calendar she was studying. "Do you think Milly's ready for the big time yet?"

"Mellish does," replied Father at once, and rewarded Mother with a smacking kiss for her display of professional caution. I could see he was proud of her.

The main event of the South Wales racing season, the Glamorgan Plate was run at Ely, a mile-long oval course not, in those days anyhow, exactly Ascot. Much of it in fact curved out of general view behind huge commercial hoardings.

But my chief worry of course was to get the apples into Aunt Milly. The original looted fruit had gone moldy by now (magic or not), requiring a second poaching foray into Farmer Pugh's orchard.

I took the apples down to Ely with us, but when I thrust one at Milly during the short period Mother and I were permitted to the paddock, Father swept my hand away and Mellish confirmed sagely from the corner of his mouth that whole apples might well give Millicent stomach cramps.

We were briefly introduced to the jockey, Cobey Sharpe, a ginger-headed man no larger than myself whose vocabulary was as stunted as his stature, resulting in a frequent reliance upon the word "strike" and its derivatives. When paddock colleagues warned Sharpe of the odd rumors surrounding Millicent's origin (she went to the post as "Millicent"), he had replied that he had struck a lot of queer things in his lifetime, he didn't care a strike whether she had been a woman, a witch, or even a striking walrus, she was a bay horse now, wasn't she, and strike him happy he would ride her. All the way to victory. This was especially sanguine of Sharpe because he had ridden in the annual Plate for twelve years and never won once.

The crowd roared *they're off*, the sun hurried behind a slab of cloud, and the horses leaped forward.

They thundered past us, streaming down the track, and Millicent shot into the lead at once. Father tossed his hat in the air as if she had already won. Arlington Mellish kept nudging him and firing from the side of his mouth, "Didn't I tell you, Mog?" They were on a first-name basis. "Didn't I ruddy well tell you?"

The horses vanished behind the hoardings. HANCOCK'S—

WALES' BEST BEER blotted Millicent from view briefly but she reappeared still leading by a length and evidently with strength in reserve. They vanished again, behind PLAYERS NAVY CUT TOBACCO. Father rocked gently on his heels. "Got the race in her pocket, Milly has," he murmured happily. "Knew a drop of cider would do the trick."

Under the mottled green canopy of a hat she had bought for Ely, Mother's ears quivered. "Cider, Mog?" She turned to him. "Drinking, were you?"

"Not me, woman." He grinned and pointed. "Milly out there." He winked strenuously at me and his mustache ends oscillated. "Brought a pot of Farmer Pugh's cider down with me. Thought Milly might like some too. Dropped a spit or two in her pail. Give her more spirit, like."

At first, his words didn't register with me. Mother though was pained. "Mogwen Pritchard," she scolded, "you know our Milly never touched—"

"Dash it all, woman, it isn't slowing her, is it?" He lowered his field-glasses and gestured at the distant hoardings. "Besides, Arly said a little spit wouldn't do any harm. Right, Arly?"

"Not to worry," Mellish told Mother. "Apple cider never slowed a thoroughbred in my experience."

Apple cider. *Farmer Pugh's apple cider.*

Grabbing the field-glasses which swung from Father's shoulder I readjusted them and scanned the track. One by one the horses emerged from the shadow of the hoardings. I didn't see Millicent.

"Father." The climax of the race was approaching, and my small voice foundered in the roaring tide of excitement. *"Father,"* I bawled. "Where's Aunt Milly?"

He glared at me, then turned to address nearby spectators. "Is my only son daft?" He retrieved his glasses and squinted. "Where's Aunt Milly indeed." He fingered the focussing screw with mounting panic. "Out in front, she's got to be." His voice trailed off. He rallied gallantly. "Blasted cheap glasses," he snorted. "Blurred or something."

But again he was silent. I looked up. "Not there, is she?" I said briskly.

The race was over. The crowds had gone, except for the Rhondda Valley contingent which had bet heavily on Millicent and were now contemplating Father ominously. Then everyone's gaze turned to the track. A small figure had popped from behind PROTHEROE'S ATHLETIC WEAR and sprinting towards us assumed clarity as Cobey Sharpe. His face was the color of chalk. So now was his hair. He didn't throttle down as he drew near, and every few paces he gasped, *"O strike . . . strike me 'appy."*

Angrily Father stepped forward. "Sharpe," he roared, "pull yourself together. Where's your mount, sir?"

"Struck if I know," panted Sharpe. Dodging Father, he accelerated and vanished over the fields into the sunset.

Father's jaw suddenly sagged. We all stared in silence at Aunt Millicent advancing timorously and unclothed across the turf. She clutched a saddle modestly before her and she trailed reins. She must have been wishing awfully fierce to be herself again, in proper shape. So all it had needed was Farmer Pugh's fruit or the juice thereof. And Father had provided it. Just a little spit, he had said. Trust Father.

He wheeled and stalked from the track. Mother flung herself at Millicent in welcoming embrace. Men nearby gulped, clenched their fists and averted their eyes. Only Arlington Mellish seemed unshaken. That veteran horse fancier continued to measure Milly with a connoisseur's eye but, I know now, there was a somewhat different glow in it.

The lawsuits with which indignant Welsh gamblers threatened Father were dropped when a Jockey Club inquiry into the affair at Ely ended in frustration. Cobey Sharpe, discovered after a nationwide manhunt, proved wholly incapable of coherent testimony. Moreover, it was as well known to the Jockey Club as to everybody else that in Wales odd things are always happening, so due allowances have to be made.

And Father? He was silent for weeks while Mother berated him: Millicent's racing form had been impeccable, what right had he to tamper with it? But then, he had never fully trusted his own wife's relatives. And he was greedy into the bargain. Well, Mother said, that's what you got for overreaching. Teach him a lesson, it would.

Maybe. Then again, maybe not. Affluent Arly Mellish married Millicent following the Ely fiasco and carried her off to his Somerset retreat. And after a decent pause, we Pritchards descended upon the lovebirds for an indefinite stay during which Father freeloaded like wildfire.

They were happy days. Nostalgic perusal of Arlington's bound *Horse and Track* volumes would alternate with merry banter over whether he had lost his heart to a bay mare in Madoc Meadow or a shapely assistant librarian *sans* uniform on the Ely Racetrack. And Father, reaching for the fruit dish to sample one of Arly's unenchanted Somerset apples, would remark with consummate authority that it had, in any case, been love at first sight.

The Circus Horse

by
Amy Bechtel

A relatively new writer, Amy Bechtel attended the Clarion Writers' Workshop in 1984, and in 1988 made her first sale, to Analog. She has since become a frequent contributor to Analog, and has twice won that magazine's AnLab readers' poll for Best Short Story of the Year, once with the thoughtful and incisive story that follows . . . which demonstrates that once a choice is made, all the wishing in the world will not unmake it.

A practicing veterinarian with a doctorate in veterinary medicine from Texas A&M, Bechtel's Hollywood patients have included such movie stars as Mike the Dog and the Persian cat from the Fancy Feast commercials, and she also has performed surgery on a 500-pound tiger. She now lives in Rio Rancho, New Mexico.

* * *

Russell Clark saw a flash of headlights as a pickup and stock trailer pulled into his drive, and he sighed, put down his coffee, and went outside. It was eleven-thirty at night. He'd just crawled into bed and turned out the light when old Fred Brown had called, worried about a cow that wasn't getting on with a calving as she should. Clark supposed he should be glad Fred had brought the cow to the clinic rather than asking for a farm call, but he wasn't; he only wanted to go back to bed.

The truck and trailer maneuvered, backing up to the chute; then the engine ground to a stop and Clark heard a godawful racket of reverberating crashes and bangs coming from the trailer. Fred Brown jumped out of the pickup and peered at his cow as if he'd never seen her before; Clark moved closer and saw the frantic black beast lurching back and forth, slamming her body against the trailer slats as hard as she could. Clark sighed again; he was tired—*so* tired—of unmanageable animals turning up at his clinic in the middle of the night.

"What in the world have you got here, Fred?" he asked.

"I dunno, doc," Fred Brown said. "Can't figure out what's the matter with her. She's my wife's pet, you know? She was calm as could be when I loaded her up."

Clark winced as the cow smashed her head solidly against the trailer door. "You ever trailered her before?" he asked. "Maybe the trip got her all excited."

Fred Brown shook his head, looking puzzled. "I've trailered her plenty of times, and she's never acted like this before."

"Let's wait a couple of minutes, then," Clark said. "See if she'll settle. How long have you seen her straining?"

"All day, doc, and she hasn't got nowhere with it."

The cow suddenly stopped plunging and stood with her face pressed against the trailer slats, sides heaving. She let out a long low bellow, which was answered by a shrill whinny and a crashing noise from within the barn. Fred Brown smiled wanly.

"Guess she's got your patients riled up too, huh, doc?"

"Guess so." Clark frowned and went to the barn to check on the animals within. Fred Brown trotted beside him, talking all the while. "Hope we get a good calf out of her. My wife, she's been looking forward to it. She's been going out to check on this old cow every night, you know?"

Clark nodded absently, listening to the restless shuffle of hooves circling in sandy stalls. He fumbled for the light switch and turned it on. The pony in the nearest stall plunged away from him, eyes rolling, and the goats bleated nervously as they milled about, butting at each other. An old mare pawed the ground, filling the air with dust. A peacock fluttered down from the loft and let loose a bloodcurdling wail.

Clark winced. "Sometimes I hate that damned peacock," he muttered. "I could wring its noisy little neck."

"Know what you mean—my neighbors have one, and my wife keeps thinkin' she hears a baby screaming. Is it little Anny's pet?"

"Yeah. Half the things in here are Anny's pets. They eat me out of house and home, but if I got rid of 'em she'd never understand." Whenever his granddaughter found out that an animal was scheduled to be euthanized, he could rarely bring himself to go through with it; if he did, he had to face Anny's misery for weeks. Anny sometimes understood that animals with incurable illnesses ought to be put to sleep to spare their suffering, but it was useless trying to explain economic situations to her, or worse, owners who simply lost interest in their pets. Clark had gotten stuck with a lot of unwanted animals. The worst one was the big gray hydrocephalic cat which was now Anny's constant companion. Clark had first seen it as a kitten with a bulging head and yellow buglike eyes—severely retarded, dangerously uncoordinated. The owner had wanted to put it to sleep. Clark had actually had a needle in its vein, his thumb pressed against the plunger of a syringe of deathly green T-61, when he had felt Anny's sad, accusing gaze. Anny had not actually been there, but he'd felt her presence—he'd almost seen her: his twelve-year-old granddaughter who acted more like a six year old, her wispy blond hair not quite hiding the soft bulge at the back of her head. Shaken, he had given Anny the kitten, though it still made him ill to see the two of them together.

"How is little Anny?" Fred Brown asked, his tone carefully neutral—the same dutiful question that everyone asked, every time. Clark was sick of people asking how little Anny was. As if she'd ever get any better. She'd had all the surgery and all the medical treatments that were available, but nothing could correct the damage that had already been done.

"She's fine," he said shortly. He put Anny out of his mind and turned his attention to the nervous animals in the stalls. "I wonder what's got them all so jumpy," he muttered.

"Maybe a stray dog roamin' around? They could've picked up a smell they didn't care for."

"Maybe so." Clark looked at his watch. It was going to be a long evening, and with his luck it would be a difficult delivery. "Come on, let's get that cow in the swing-around," he said. As he strode back to the trailer, a cacophony of barks and howls erupted from the kennel in his clinic, and he frowned.

Anny lay underneath the covers of her bed with her cat Ace, holding a dim flashlight on the pages of a picture book about circuses. She smiled at the pictures. She'd never been to a circus but her mother had told her that one had just come to town and that in a couple of days she'd get to see it. It looked like ever such fun. All the pretty animals, glittering with spangles, and the clowns, and the acrobats in their brilliant costumes . . . she couldn't wait! She moved the light to the lines of big print and concentrated hard, but as always the letters meant nothing to her. She banged the flashlight against her head in frustration, and the light dimmed further.

Ace lifted his head suddenly, yellow eyes gleaming, ears pricked forward on his oversized domed head. Anny had rarely seen him look so alert. "Whatsa matter, Ace?" she whispered.

Ace gave her a quick glance when she spoke, then stretched awkwardly and climbed out from under the blanket. He sat on the edge of the bed and stared out the half-open window, where white curtains trimmed with blue fluttered in a soft cool breeze. Anny stroked him, smoothing his thick gray fur over his tensed muscles, scratching his big head.

Ace yowled. It was a low, disturbing sound that she had never heard from him before. His tail twitched.

"Ace?" Anny moved her hand away and stared at him.

The cat sprang from the bed to the windowsill, scrabbling ungracefully for balance, then disappeared out the window.

"Ace!"

Anny threw off the covers, dumping the book on the floor, and ran to the window. In the bright moonlight, she saw her cat trotting across the back pasture in the direction of the woods: he vanished abruptly into the murky blackness among the trees. Tears stung Anny's eyes. She couldn't lose Ace! She had to go after him, but she wasn't allowed to go outside after dark. She whimpered, trying to decide what to do.

From the other side of the house she heard the clattering of gates and the bellowing of a cow: Granpa must have an emergency. Slowly she realized that if he was busy, he'd never know if she slipped outside, and Momma wouldn't be home from work until morning. Anny found her shoes, dumped one of Ace's stuffed mice out of the right one, and put them on, then pulled a coat on over her nightgown. At the last second she remembered the flashlight. She snatched it up and wiggled out the window.

Her breath frosted in front of her as she jogged across the

back pasture. Two cows and a horse saw her coming and bolted, startling her with the loud drum of their hooves. She paused, wondering why they'd run away. The cows were placid beasts, and the horse usually came to be petted. Maybe they didn't realize it was her, since she'd never before been in their pasture at night. She shrugged, crawled through the spiky barbed-wire strands of the far fence, and entered the woods: dark and spooky, filled with rustling twigs and creaking branches. A flurry of leaves brushed against her legs.

"Ace?" Anny stopped and listened. Over the moan of the wind, she heard the soft patter and crunch of small paws running through dead leaves. "Ace!" She ran in the direction of the sound, dodging trees, stumps, and bushes, but she couldn't see the cat. She got out her flashlight and turned it on, but its light was no brighter than that of the full moon. She stopped and listened again. Nothing. She couldn't hear the paw-patter any more. She stuffed the useless flashlight in her pocket and turned slowly around.

The underbrush rustled. Anny turned in the direction of the sound, then froze in place when she realized that the sounds were much too loud to be Ace. Something big was crashing through the trees, coming closer and closer. Frightened, she ran away from the noise, but it followed her, louder every second. She tripped over a dead branch and fell sprawling. A huge dark shape, unrecognizable, flashed past in the nearby trees. Then it was gone, and the noise of its passage slowly receded. Anny gasped for breath. She got up and brushed herself off, trembling all over. What had that thing been? And would it come back?

She started to cry. Now she was too scared to go on looking for Ace, and she'd have to go home, and she might never see Ace again—what if he wandered to the highway and got run over? She covered her face with her hands, shaking and crying, until—suddenly—she realized what the creature had been. She laughed through her tears. Of course. It had been the horse, or one of the cows. Granpa was always complaining about that horse, threatening to sell it, because it was clever enough to open gates with its nose, and was always getting loose along with its pasture-mates. It wasn't anything to be afraid of. She could go on looking for Ace.

But she still felt uneasy. Maybe she'd better make sure. She trotted back through the woods, back in the direction of the house. She crawled through the strands of the fence and peered around the pasture as the wind soughed through the long grass at her feet.

She saw the horse and both cows standing in the middle of the pasture. The horse was nervously pawing the ground.

Anny shivered, the huge black beast running through her mind. A piercing squawk echoed in her ears, and she heard wings flapping vigorously above her. Something dove low over her head, screeching and drumming its wings, then vanished into the blackness of the night.

"Doc, what's wrong with them animals now?" Fred Brown asked.

"Huh?" Clark had the calf-puller fixed on the cow's rear and was hauling out the calf, puffing hard as he cranked the ratchet. He was getting too old for this kind of thing, too old and too tired. He ought to retire properly sometime soon, or at least hire an assistant. He'd tried that once, but the new man's enthusiasm and fresh-learned knowledge had intimidated him. It had jarred him into realizing how out-of-date he was, how out of touch with new methods; made him feel guilty about the stacks of dusty journals that he never quite got around to reading. He hated feeling inadequate, and had solved the problem by getting rid of the assistant. He'd stubbornly kept working on his own. But he couldn't go on like this forever. Aloud, he said, "What'd you say, Fred?"

"All them animals are just settin' there. Staring. Not a one's making a sound."

"Fine by me," Clark muttered, not looking up. "Quieter the better. Grab her tail, willya, Fred? The calf's coming now."

Out in the pasture, the horse stopped its nervous pawing and stood motionless, staring intently in the direction of the woods. One cow stood on either side of it, just as still. Anny slowly walked up to them, touched them and poked them, but they ignored her. All of them were staring in the same direction, and the horse's ears were pricked sharply forward. Anny turned and looked. She saw a soft glow of yellow light coming from deep in the woods. Silhouetted against the light she saw a slow moving line of shadows: animals, walking quietly and sedately toward the source of the light. At the end of the line she saw a shadow that looked like an elephant.

Anny's breath exploded in a huge sigh of relief. They were circus animals! Why hadn't anyone told her that the circus was going to set up so near? Anny scrambled through the fence, ripping the hem of her nightgown on a barb in her hurry. She couldn't wait to see the tent. If she was quick enough maybe she'd get to see the whole line of animals go in, and Ace was bound to be lurking somewhere nearby. She ran through the woods, the light shining brighter and brighter as she neared the clearing where the circus tent had been set up.

She stopped in the bushes at the edge of the clearing, breathless and suddenly shy. She didn't want to meet any of the circus people, didn't want to find out if they would whisper about her behind their backs, or laugh, or call her stupid, or *hey ree-tard!*—the way other people did. She only wanted to watch.

The circus tent was a shiny silver dome, ever so pretty, with gold and blue stripes around its sides, and large black letters which Anny couldn't read. Its flaps were open and inside it Anny could see only darkness. The light was coming from somewhere outside. Two girls, fancily dressed in bright-colored coveralls, were directing the line of animals into the tent. And the animals! Anny had never imagined such a variety; this must surely be the finest circus in all the world, to have such animals.

A long-fanged golden cat marched into the tent and disappeared. It was followed by a big wolf with a pouch like a kangaroo's, then a large pink lizard with maroon wings and a snaky neck. Then two scurrying rodents. A low-flying bird with talons at its wingtips and sharp teeth in its beak. A small antelope with huge mooselike horns that seemed far too heavy for its body. A miniature elephant with an oddly shaped trunk and great yellow tusks . . .

One by one the animals vanished into the tent.

Anny hugged herself in delight, unable to believe that she'd seen such an incredible parade. Would there be any more animals? She didn't see any, but the two girls were still standing by the tent flap as if they expected more creatures to show up. Such pretty girls they were, with their vivid outfits and the sparkly jewels in their hair! But they looked worried. Maybe they'd lost one of their animals.

That thought gave Anny a jolt. She'd almost forgotten Ace! She looked around quickly, but the cat was nowhere to be seen. She'd been so sure she'd find him here. And it was getting awfully late—Granpa would be finished with his emergency any time now, in fact might already *be* finished, looking in Anny's room and finding the bed empty. *Where* could Ace be? Those girls might have seen him, but try as she would, Anny couldn't bring herself to go to them and ask. She was too scared of people, especially of pretty people who emphasized how peculiar she looked. No, she wouldn't ask yet. She'd look for Ace for just a little bit longer first.

She wandered back through the woods, stopping at intervals to listen, but she heard nothing until she neared the pasture fence. Then she heard something rustling in the leaves, thrashing, struggling.

"Ace?"

The sounds stopped for an instant, then began again. Anny pushed her way through the undergrowth. The moon passed behind a cloud, then emerged, shining bright in the sky, reflecting off frightened rolling eyes. At first Anny thought it was Ace, but when she crept closer she saw that it was a tiny dark horse, scarcely any bigger than Ace, with its front leg caught in the bottom strand of the fence. "It's okay," Anny whispered. "Don't be scared, okay?" She reached out to touch the frightened little horse, feeling a plastic collar fastened around the taut muscles of its neck. It belonged to someone, then. Of course! The circus. It was a little circus horse.

Anny tried to pull its leg free from the fence, but was hindered by the little horse's fruitless struggling. "Stop kicking!" she gasped. "I wanta help you out." Tears smarted in her eyes as a barb scraped against her arm. The horse ought to know she was trying to help; it ought to hold still. But it kept on pawing and fighting her. "Stop it!" Anny said. She put her knee against the horse's neck to hold it down, then grasped its trapped foreleg with both hands and finally managed to work it free. It wasn't bleeding very much, but the leg was dangling at a peculiar angle. The horse struggled to push itself to its feet but fell, thrashing and snorting. Anny picked it up, stroked it, tried to soothe it. She felt it trembling in her arms.

"It's okay," she said softly. "I'll take you to my Granpa. He'll fix you. It'll be okay."

Clark watched Fred Brown's truck and trailer rattle off down the road, hauling a cow and a brand-new calf. He dumped the calving chains in the rinse bucket and took a last look around the barn; he was a bit puzzled by the quietness of the animals in the stalls, but was too tired to worry about it. He switched out the light, patted his pockets and found the bottle of tetracycline; he'd better put it back in the clinic cabinet before he forgot about it.

He went in and put the bottle away; then, yawning, glanced about the room at the cats and dogs in their cages. The yawn stopped abruptly and he felt an involuntary shiver in his spine, for all the dogs and cats lay motionless in their cages, paws crossed, staring blankly into space. Clark watched them for almost a full minute, and none of them moved. Then, as if by mutual agreement, they suddenly stirred, whining, or pawing at the cages, or curling up to sleep, each behaving in its own ordinary way. Feeling numb, Clark reached out to quiet a crying puppy. He must have been dreaming on his feet. He really was going to have to get more sleep. . . .

The door squeaked open, then slammed, and Anny burst into the room. "Anny!" he said. "What are you doing out of bed?" Then he saw the little animal that she was holding, clutched tightly against her coat.

"Is hurt," she whispered.

"Where did you find that?" He peered closer—he'd never seen a miniature horse so small.

She pointed. "Outside."

"Anny, don't you know you're not supposed to go outside at night?"

She hung her head and nodded.

"Then why did you go out?"

"Ace went out." She looked at him pleadingly. "I had to find him."

Clark sighed. "And you found this little beast instead."

Anny nodded and said, "Can't find Ace." She clutched the little horse tighter and a tear slipped down her cheek. Clark gently pulled the horse out of her arms and laid it on the examining table; it struggled, trying to get away.

"Anny," he said, "I'm sure Ace will come back. Cats wander sometimes, you know, and they usually do come back. Come here now. I need you to hold the little horse for a minute. Okay? Come on, now."

Anny sniffed, rubbed the tears off her face, and reached for the horse, petting it gently. It quieted under her hands. Clark examined it quickly, finding no significant injuries except for the broken forelimb, but he puzzled for a moment over the hooves, each of which had a pair of extraneous digits dangling behind it. He had a vague memory of learning about it in school—polydactylism, or something like that; a birth deformity. He'd occasionally seen cats with six or seven toes on each paw; this must be the same sort of thing.

"Circus horse," Anny said suddenly.

"What?"

"It ran away, Granpa. From the circus. All the animals, they ran away, but they all went back. Except this one."

Clark remembered his daughter talking about the circus, saying that she planned to take Anny to see it. They'd had an argument about it. He said, "Anny, do you mean you saw the circus? Where?"

She pointed west, in the direction of young Davidson's property. Clark frowned. Davidson had a big empty pasture near the main road, which he would rent to anyone who paid him enough money; it was not surprising that a small traveling circus might choose to set up there. It frightened him to think of Anny going that far in the dark, but she was so miserable about Ace that he hadn't the heart to scold her. That blasted cat! He hoped—guiltily—that it would never come back.

He looked back at the little horse; a miniature circus horse, and a freak miniature horse at that. He'd have to take it back tomorrow and collect as much money as he could, in cash. The very thought of dealing with a circus made him uneasy; he supposed there was nothing wrong with most of them, but the last one he had encountered had been a shoestring operation where he'd had to deal with multiple cases of animal abuse. He remembered the sick smell of the cages, the deformed animals in the freak show—the two-headed lamb that was already dead, the eyeless dog, the calf that staggered about on its knees, unable to get up—and worse, the humans of the freak show who had stood nearby, watching him.

But that had been many years ago. The little horse on the table was deformed, but it had not been abused; aside from its injury it was in good health. All Clark needed to worry about was ensuring that he got paid for his work.

He manipulated the bones experimentally; it seemed to be a simple fracture, easy enough to reduce and cast, but he'd better take some films to be sure. And he'd have to be careful with the anesthetic dose: the little horse couldn't weigh more than fifteen pounds. It wouldn't take much. Calculating dosages in his head, he pulled off the horse's plastic collar and shoved it aside, exposing the jugular vein. It was a tiny vein; it would be as hard to hit as a cat's. Clark wondered if he would ever get to bed.

Anny fell asleep in a corner, her head pillowed on a dog-blanket, while Granpa put on the cast. She didn't wake up until the cast was finished. She sat up, rubbing her eyes, peering at the tiny horse which slumbered peacefully on the table, at Granpa sitting on a stool beside it, waiting for the cast to harden. Had she heard something? Sleepily she wandered out of the exam room and into the waiting room. She heard a faint meow at the door.

"*Ace!*" Anny dashed to the door, yanked it open. Ace walked casually into the room and she hugged him in delight, then sat back happily and watched his awkward attempts to wash his tail. It was so good to have him back! She picked him up and put him in her lap, and he purred noisily.

"Excuse me."

Anny looked up, startled by the strange voice, and saw the girl—one of the girls from the circus tent! Anny grabbed Ace and ran out of the room, shouting, "Granpa! Granpa!"

"Who did you say?" Clark said. Anny was so excited, she wasn't making much sense.

"The girl!" Anny said. "The circus girl."

"Ah," Clark said. "Thanks, Anny. I wonder if she brought any money with her?" He tapped the cast, nodded absently, and placed the sleeping horse safely in a cage; it wouldn't do for it to roll off the table and break another leg. Then, whistling to himself, he strolled into the waiting room.

A girl in vivid dark blue coveralls stood uneasily in the middle of the room, shifting from foot to foot. Her hair was long, straight and silky black, glittering with multifaceted jewels. She held a little metal box that looked like a cassette player, the sort that joggers carried.

"What can I do for you?" Clark said.

She hesitated, glancing over his shoulder at the doorway where Anny crouched half-hidden, then said, "I'm Huong O'Brien, and I—um, we've lost an animal. About like so, a little horse." She measured the size with her hands. "I've managed to trace its collar to here—do you have it?"

Clark nodded solemnly. "Yes, my granddaughter found it. It's been injured—a broken leg—but I've got it casted and it should be just fine, given a little time."

Clark saw Huong's lovely face fill with relief. "Thank goodness," she whispered. "First thing that's gone right all day."

She followed him into the exam room, and Clark saw that Anny, with Ace clutched in her arms, had backed into a corner behind a dog cage without taking her eyes off Huong. Clark took the little horse out of the cage and put it back on the table: it was starting to wake up. Huong stroked the horse and brushed her fingers against the cast, frowning a little.

"How'd you lose the little guy?" Clark asked.

"Oh, well, it's been one of those days. The machine malfunctioned and the whole collection got loose, and when we activated the collars they were *all* supposed to come back, not all but one." She sighed, smoothing the horse's fluffy mane. "Poor little beast. It must have been trying to come back—it just couldn't manage." She looked up at Clark. "Thank you so much for finding it, and all. If I can do anything for you—"

"There's a charge for the treatment, of course," Clark said smoothly.

"A charge?"

"Yes—it'll come to fifty dollars. Just tell your manager at the circus tomorrow, and as soon as he pays the bill you can come and get the horse."

"I'm not sure I—" Huong broke off and sat down on a stool. She tugged nervously at her long hair, muttering to herself—something about studying zoology, not sociology or history. "Look," she said finally. "I don't have any money, and I can't wait until tomorrow. Surely there's something I could do for you, something that would be the equivalent of the payment you need?"

Clark stared open-mouthed, wondering if she meant what he thought she meant. Surely not. But one never knew; circus performers were a very strange lot. He noticed that Anny had crept out of the corner and was watching Huong intently, apparently fascinated by her. Huong caught the girl's glance and stared back. "I don't think—" Clark started.

Huong suddenly jumped up, went to Anny, and knelt in front of her. Anny stood very still, hardly breathing, as Huong touched her forehead and smoothed her wispy blond hair. When Huong moved her hand away, Anny reached out in turn, timidly touching one of the crystal jewels in Huong's hair. Huong smiled, then turned to Clark.

"What's the matter with her?" Huong said.

"Hydrocephalus," Clark said. "Not that it's any of your business."

"Hydrocephalus? Brain cells . . . destroyed?" Huong shivered, looking at Anny with pity. "I can repair the damage," she said. "Would that be payment enough?"

"What the hell are you talking about?" Clark whispered.

"I can repair it. Regenerate the brain. Let me take her back—"

"Get out of here," Clark said tightly. God, what an idiot she

must think he was, if she thought he'd fall for something like
that! He was suddenly almost blind with fury; the only thing
that kept his temper from exploding was Anny's presence.

"You don't understand."

"I do understand, and you're not laying a hand on my
granddaughter." Clark caught Anny's arm, pulled her away
from Huong. "You know she can't be healed. What would you
do with her, put her in your freak show? With your freak horse?
Get out, now, and leave her alone."

Huong stared at him, her eyes huge. "I'm sorry," she
whispered. "I—I don't know the customs—" Distraught, she
backed away from Clark, fumbling in her hair to undo a clasp,
and pulled the string of shimmering jewels out of her hair. She
held them out to Clark and said, "Please. I have to go, and I
have to take the horse. Please take these in payment."

Clark started to shake his head, but then he saw the way
Anny was staring at the jewels, her mouth open, her eyes
shining. "All right," Clark muttered.

Huong slowly dropped the glittering pieces, and Anny
leaned forward to catch them, both hands cupped beneath
Huong's. Then Huong reached for the little horse on the table.

"Wait," Anny said softly. Clark stared in shock. Anny had
put the jewels on the floor and had picked up Ace. She was
holding the cat out to Huong.

Huong hesitated, looking at Clark as if for permission to take
the cat. He swallowed hard, blinking, wondering if he was
dreaming again. What had gotten into Anny? Clark was more
than glad for a chance to get rid of the cat, but he'd never
imagined that Anny would allow it to be taken from her.

"Anny, you really want her to take Ace?"

She nodded solemnly.

"Think about what you're doing! You can't change your
mind."

Anny nodded again, and firmly pushed Ace into Huong's
hands.

"Well, okay then," Clark said feebly. He felt badly rattled.
He watched as Huong tucked the cat under one arm, the little
horse under the other. She glanced from Anny to Clark, her
head tilted quizzically as if she were about to say something—

but she said nothing. With a last look at Anny, she gave her head a quick shake and hurried out the door.

In the morning Clark woke tired and irritable, with the memory of Huong O'Brien giving him the chills. He stumbled down the hall to Anny's room and opened the door. She was asleep, hugging her pillow, and a gray cat was snuggled in a blissful ball beside her. Clark blinked and poked the cat, which looked up at him and glared with malevolent intelligence. Clearly it was not Ace.

Gently he shook Anny awake. "Where'd you get this cat?"

She looked puzzled. "It's Ace."

"No it isn't. Look at it."

She pushed herself up on one elbow and stroked the cat's perfectly ordinary gray head. "He's all better, Granpa," she said, and rolled over and went back to sleep.

Clark stared at the cat, which stared back at him, *all better*, and he shivered. Every second he felt colder, with a dreadful fear building, and he got up and went to the clinic, almost running by the time he got there, and frantically he began to pull books off the shelves.

An hour later, when Anny woke and went to look for her Granpa, she found him sprawled at his desk in the clinic, crying. She had never seen him cry before. There was a sloppy pile of books on his desk. Anny moved closer to look at them. The top book was open to a picture of the little horse she had found last night, and the plastic collar the horse had worn was draped atop the open book. Anny picked up the collar and looked at it. There were letters on it; she struggled to read them, but she would never know what they meant.

Oligocene Field Trip: Cambridge University; March 14, 2076. Student: Huong O'Brien. Specimen: Miohippus.

Riding the Nightmare
by
Lisa Tuttle

Lisa Tuttle made her first sale in 1972 to the anthology Clarion
II, *after having attended the Clarion workshop, and by 1974
had won the John W. Campbell Award for Best New Writer of
the Year. She has gone on to become one of the most respected
writers of her generation, winning the Nebula Award in
1981—which she refused to accept—and publishing widely in
markets such as* Interzone, The Magazine of Fantasy and
Science Fiction, The Twilight Zone Magazine, Analog, Other
Edens, Zenith, *and* Pulphouse, *and in horror anthologies such
as* Alien Sex, Night Visions, *and* Women of Darkness. *Her
short work has been collected in* A Nest of Nightmares *and* A
Spaceship Built of Stone. *Her other books include a novel in
collaboration with George R.R. Martin,* Windhaven, *the solo
novels* Familiar Spirit, Gabriel, *and* Lost Future, *the nonfiction
works* Heroines *and* Encyclopaedia of Feminism, *and, as
editor,* Skin of the Soul: New Horror Stories by Women. *Her
most recent book is a new collection of her short work,*
Memories of the Body: Tales of Desire and Transformation.
*Born in Texas, she moved to Great Britain in 1980, and now
lives with her family in Scotland.*

*Here she offers us a chance to ride the Nightmare, but it's an
offer you'd better refuse . . . if you can.*

*   *   *

Twilight, *l'heure bleue:* Tess O'Neal sat on the balcony of her
sixth-floor apartment and looked out at the soft, suburban
sprawl of New Orleans, a blur of green trees and multicoloured
houses, with the jewels of lights just winking on. It was a time
of day which made her nostalgic and gently melancholy,
feelings she usually enjoyed. But not now. For once she wished
she were not alone with the evening.

Gordon had cancelled their date. No great disaster—he'd
said they could have all day Sunday together—but the change
of plans struck Tess as ominous, and she questioned him.

"Is something wrong?"

He hesitated. Maybe he was only reacting to the sharp note in her voice. "Of course not. Jude . . . made some plans, and it would spoil things if I went out. She sends her apologies."

There was nothing odd in that. Jude was Gordon's wife and also Tess's friend, a situation they were all comfortable with. But Jude was slightly scatter-brained, and when she confused dates, it was Tess who had to take second place. Usually, Tess did not mind. Now she did.

"We'll talk on Sunday," Gordon said.

Tess didn't want to talk. She didn't want explanations. She wanted Gordon's body on hers, making her believe that nothing had changed, nothing would ever change between them.

They're in it together. Him and his wife. And I'm left out in the cold.

She looked up at the darkening sky. As blue as the nightmare's eye, she thought, and shivered. She got up and went inside, suddenly feeling too vulnerable in the open air.

She had never told Gordon about the nightmare. He admired her as a competent, sophisticated, independent woman. How could she talk to him about childhood fears? Worse, how could she tell him that this was one childhood fear which hadn't stayed in childhood but had come after her?

As she turned to lock the sliding glass door behind her, Tess froze.

The mare's long head was there, resting on the balcony rail as if on a stable door, the long mane waving slightly in the breeze, the blueish eye fixed commandingly on her.

Tess stumbled backward, and the vision, broken, vanished.

There was nothing outside that should not be, nothing but sky and city and her own dark reflection in the glass.

"Snap out of it, O'Neal," she said aloud. Bad enough to dream the nightmare, but if she was going to start seeing it with her eyes open, she really needed help.

For a moment she thought of phoning Gordon. But what could she say? Not only would it go against the rules to phone him after he'd said they could not meet, but it would go against everything he knew and expected of her if she began babbling about a nightmare. She simply wanted his presence, the way, as a child, she had wanted her father to put his arms around her and tell her not to cry. But she was a grown woman now. She didn't need anyone else to tell her what was real and what was not; she knew that the best way to banish fears and depression was by working, not brooding.

She poured herself a Coke and settled at her desk with a stack of transcripts. She was a doctoral candidate in linguistics, working on a thesis examining the differences in language use between men and women. It was a subject of which, by now, she was thoroughly sick. She wondered sometimes if she would ever be able to speak unselfconsciously again, without monitoring her own speech patterns to edit out the stray, feminine modifiers and apologies.

The window was open. Through it, she could see the black and windy sky and there, running on the wind, was the creamy white mare with tumbling mane and rolling blue eyes. Around her neck hung a shining crescent moon, the golden *lunula* strung on a white and scarlet cord. And Tess was on her feet, walking toward the window as if hypnotized. It was then that she became aware of herself, and knew she was dreaming, and that she must break the dream. With a great effort of will, she flung herself backwards, towards the place where she knew her bed would be, tossing her head as she strained to open her eyes.

And woke with a start to find herself still at her desk. She must have put her head down for a moment. Her watch showed it was past midnight. Tess got up, her heart beating unpleasantly fast, and glanced toward the sliding glass door. That it was not the window of her dream made no difference. The window in her dream was always the bedroom window of her childhood, the scene always the same as the first time the nightmare had come for her. There was no horse outside on the balcony, or in the sky beyond. There was no horse except in her mind.

Tess went to bed, knowing the nightmare would not come again. Never twice in one night, and she had succeeded in refusing the first visit. Nevertheless, she slept badly, with confused dreams of quarrelling with Gordon as she never quarrelled with him in life, dreams in which Gordon became her father and announced his intended marriage to Jude, and

Tess wept and argued and wept and woke in the morning feeling exhausted.

Gordon arrived on Sunday with champagne, flowers, and a shopping bag full of gourmet treats for an indoor picnic. He gave off a glow of happiness and well-being which at once put Tess on the defensive, for his happiness had nothing to do with her.

He kissed her and looked at her tenderly—so tenderly that her stomach turned over with dread. He was looking at her with affection and pity, she thought—not with desire.

"What is it?" she asked sharply, pulling away from him. "What's happened?"

He was surprised. "Nothing," he said. Then: "Nothing bad, I promise. But I'll tell you all about it. Why don't we have something to eat first? I've brought—"

"I couldn't eat with something hanging over me, wondering . . ."

"I told you, it's nothing bad, nothing to worry about." He frowned. "Are you getting your period?"

"I'm *not* getting my period; I'm *not* being irrational—" She stopped and swallowed and sighed, forcing herself to relax. "All right, I am being irrational. I've been sleeping badly. And there's this nightmare—the same nightmare I had as a kid, just before my mother died."

"Poor baby," he said, holding her close. He sounded protective but also amused. "Nightmares. That doesn't sound like my Tess."

"It's not that I'm superstitious—"

"Of course not."

"But I've been feeling all week that something bad was about to happen, something to change my whole life. And with the nightmare—I hadn't seen it since just before my mother died. To have it come now, and then when you said we'd talk—"

"It isn't bad, I promise you. But I won't keep you in suspense. Let's just have a drink first, all right?"

"Sure."

He turned away from her to open the champagne, and she stared at him, drinking in the details as if she might not see him again for a very long time: the curls at the back of his neck, the crisp, black beard, his gentle, rather small hands, skilled at so many things. She felt what it would be to lose him, to lose the right to touch him, never again to have him turn and smile at her.

But why think that? Why should she lose him? How could she, when he had never been "hers" in any traditional sense, nor did she want him to be. She liked her freedom, both physical and emotional. She liked living alone, yet she wanted a lover, someone she could count on who would not make too many demands of her. In Gordon she had found precisely the mixture of distance and intimacy which she needed. It had worked well for nearly three years, so why did she imagine losing him? She trusted Gordon, believed in his honesty and his love for her. She didn't think there was another woman, and she knew he hadn't grown tired of her. She didn't believe he had changed. But Jude might.

Gordon handed her a long-stemmed glass full of champagne, and after they had toasted one another, and sipped, he said, "Jude's pregnant. She found out for sure last week."

Tess stared at him, feeling nothing at all.

He said quickly, "It wasn't planned. I wasn't keeping anything from you. Jude and I, we haven't even—hadn't even—discussed having children. It just never came up. But now that it's happened . . . Jude really likes the idea of having a baby and . . ."

"Who's the father?"

She felt him withdraw. "That's not worthy of you, Tess."

"Why? It seems like a reasonable question, considering—"

"Considering that Jude hasn't been involved with anyone since Morty went back to New York? I thought you and Jude were friends. What do you two talk about over your lunches?"

The brief, mean triumph she had felt was gone, replaced by anguish. "Not our sex lives," she said. "Look, you've got an open marriage, you tell me it was an accident. I'm sorry, I didn't know you'd take it that way. I was just trying to find out what—forget I asked."

"I will." He turned away and began to set out the food he had brought onto plates. The champagne was harsh in her mouth as

Tess watched his so-familiar, economical movements, and wanted to touch his back where the blue cloth of his shirt stretched a little too tightly.

She drew a deep breath and said, "Congratulations. I should have said that first of all. How does it feel, knowing you're going to be a father?"

He looked around, still cautious, and then smiled. "I'm not sure. It doesn't seem real yet. I guess I'll get used to it."

"I guess it'll change things," she said. "For you and me."

He went to her and took her in his arms. "I don't want it to."

"But it's bound to."

"In practical ways, maybe. We might have less time together, but we'll manage somehow. Jude and I were never a traditional couple, and we aren't going to be traditional parents, either. I'll still need you—I'm not going to stop loving you." He said it so fiercely that she smiled, and pressed her face against his chest to hide it. "Do you believe me? Nothing can change the way I feel about you. I love you. That's not going to change. Do you believe me?"

She didn't say anything. He forced her head up off his chest and made her look at him. "Do you believe me?" He kissed her when she wouldn't reply, then kissed her again, more deeply, and then they were kissing passionately, and she was pulling him onto the floor, and they made love, their bodies making the promises they both wanted.

After Gordon had left that night, the nightmare came again.

Tess found herself standing beside the high, narrow bed she'd slept in as a child, facing the open window. The pale curtains billowed like sails. Outside, galloping in place like a rocking horse, moving and yet stationary, was the blue-eyed, cream-coloured mare.

With part of her mind Tess knew that she could refuse this visit. She could turn her head, and wrench her eyes open, and find herself, heart pounding, safe in her bed.

Instead, she let herself go into the dream. She took a step forward. She felt alert and hypersensitive, as if it were the true state of waking. She was aware of her own body as she usually never was in life or in a dream, conscious of her nakedness as the breeze from the open window caressed it, and feeling the slight bounce of her breasts and the rough weave of the carpet beneath her feet as she walked towards the window.

She clambered onto the window-sill and, with total confidence, leaped out, knowing that the horse would catch her.

She landed easily and securely on the mare's back, feeling the scratch and prickle of the horsehair on her inner thighs. Her arms went around the high, arched neck and she pressed her face against it, breathing in the rough, salty, smoky scent of horseflesh. She felt the pull and play of muscle and bone beneath her and in her legs as the mare began to gallop. Tess looked down at the horse's legs, seeing how they braced and pounded against the air. She felt a slight shock, then, for where there should have been a hoof, she saw instead five toes. Tess frowned, and leaned further as she stared through the darkness, trying to see.

But they were her own hooves divided into five toes—they had always been so since the night of her creation. The thinly-beaten gold of the *lunula* on its silken chain bounced against the solid muscle of her chest as she loped through the sky.

Some unquestioned instinct took her to the right house. Above it, she caught a crosswind and, tucking her forelegs in close to her chest, glided spirally down until all four feet could be firmly planted on the earth. This was a single-storey house she visited tonight. She turned her head and, at a glance, the window swung open, the screen which had covered it a moment earlier now vanished. The mare took one delicate step closer and put her head through the window into the bedroom.

The bed, with a man and woman sleeping in it, was directly beneath the window. She breathed gently upon the woman's sleeping face and then drew back her head and waited.

The woman opened her eyes and looked into the mare's blue gaze. She seemed confused but not frightened, and after a moment she sat up slowly, moving cautiously as if for fear of alarming the horse. The horse was not alarmed. She suffered the woman to stroke her nose and pat her face before she backed away, pulling her head out of the house. She had timed it perfectly. The woman came after her as if drawn on a rope, leaning out the window and making soft, affectionate noises. The mare moved as if uneasy, still backing, and then, abruptly flirtatious, offered her back, an invitation to the woman to mount.

The woman understood at once and did not hesitate. From the window ledge she slipped onto the mare's back in a smooth, fluid movement, as if she had done this every night of her life.

Feeling her rider in place, legs clasped firmly on her sides, the mare leaped skyward with more speed than grace. She felt the woman gasp as she was flung forward, and felt the woman's hands knot in her mane. She was obviously an experienced rider, not one it would be easy to throw. But the mare did not wish to throw her, merely to give her a very rough ride.

High over the sleeping city galloped the nightmare, rising at impossibly steep angles, shying at invisible barriers, and now and then tucking her legs beneath her to drop like a stone. The gasps and cries from her rider soon ceased. The woman, concentrating on clinging for her life, could have had no energy to spare for fear.

Not until dawn did the nightmare return the woman, leaping through the bedroom window in defiance of logic and throwing her onto the motionless safety of her bed, beside her still-sleeping husband.

When Tess woke a few hours later she was stiff and sore, as if she had been dancing, or running, all night. She got up slowly, wincing, and aware of a much worse emotional pain waiting for her, like the anticipation of bad news. The nightmare had come for her, and this time she had gone with it—she was certain of that much. But where had it taken her? What had she done?

In the bathroom, as she waited for the shower to heat up, racking her sleepy brain for some memory of the night before, Tess caught a glimpse in the mirror of something on her back, at waist level. She turned, presenting her back to the glass, and then craned her neck around, slowly against the stiffness, to look at her reflection.

She stared at the bloodstains. Stared and stared at the saddle of blood across her back.

She washed it off, of course, with plenty of hot water and

soap, and tried not to think about it too hard. That was exactly what she had done the last time this had happened: when she was nine years old, on the morning after the night her mother had miscarried; on the morning of the day her mother had died.

All day Tess fought against the urge to phone Gordon. All day she was like a sleep-walker as she taught a class, supervised studies, stared at meaningless words in the library, and avoided telephones.

She thought, as she had thought before, that she should see a psychiatrist. But how could a psychiatrist help her? She *knew* she could not, by all the rules of reason and logic, have caused her mother's death. She knew she felt guilty because she had not wanted the little sister or brother her parents had planned, and on some level she believed that her desire, expressed in the nightmare, had been responsible for the miscarriage and thus—although indirectly and unintentionally—for her mother's death. She didn't need a psychiatrist to tell her all that. She had figured it out for herself, some time in her teens. And yet, figuring it out hadn't ended the feeling of guilt. That was why the very thought of the nightmare was so frightening to her.

If Jude is all right, she thought, if nothing has happened to her, then I'll know it was just a crazy dream and I'll see a psychiatrist.

Gordon telephoned the next day, finally. Jude was all right, he said, although Tess had not asked. Jude was just fine. Only—she'd lost the child. But miscarriage at this early stage was apparently relatively common. The doctors said she was physically healthy and strong and would have no problem carrying another child to term. Only—although she was physically all right, Jude was pretty upset. She had taken the whole thing badly, and in a way he'd never expected. She was saying some pretty strange things—

"What sort of things?" She clutched the phone as if it were his arm, trying to force him to speak.

"I need to see you, Tess. I need to talk to you. Could we meet for lunch?"

"Tomorrow?"

"Better make it Friday."

"Just lunch?" She was pressing him as she never did, unable to hide her desperation.

"I can't leave Jude for long. She needs me now. It'll have to be just lunch. The Italian place?"

Tess felt a wave of pure hatred for Jude. She wanted to tell Gordon that she needed him just as much, or more than, his wife did; that she was in far more trouble than Jude with her mere, commonplace miscarriage.

"That's fine," she said, and made her voice throb with sympathy as she told Gordon how sorry she was to hear about Jude. "Let me know if there's anything at all I can do—tell her that."

"I'll see you on Friday," he said.

Gordon didn't waste any time on Friday. As soon as they had ordered, he came right to the point.

"This has affected Jude much more than I could have dreamed. I'd hardly come to terms with the idea that she was pregnant, and she's responding as if she'd lost an actual baby instead of only . . . I've told her we'll start another just as soon as we can, but she seems to think she's doomed to lose that one, too." He had been looking into her eyes as he spoke, but now he dropped his gaze to the white tablecloth. "Maybe Jude has always been a little unstable, I don't know. Probably it's something hormonal, and she'll get back to normal soon. But whatever . . . it seems to have affected her mind. And she's got this crazy idea that the miscarriage is somehow *your* fault." He looked up with a grimace, to see how she responded.

Tess said quietly, "I'm sorry."

"Maybe she's always been jealous of you on some level—no, I can't believe that. It's the shock and the grief, and she's fixed on you . . . I don't know why. I'm sure she'll get over it. But right now there's no reasoning with her. She won't even consider the idea of seeing you. Don't try to call her, and—" He sighed deeply. "She doesn't want me to see you, either. She wanted me to tell you, today, that it's all over."

"Just like that."

"Oh, Tess." He looked at her across the table, obviously pained. She noticed for the first time the small lines that had appeared around his eyes. "Tess, you know I love you. It's not that I love Jude any more than I love you. I'd never agree to choose between you."

"That's exactly what you're doing."

"I'm not. It's not forever. But Jude is my wife. I have a responsibility to her. You've always known that. She can't cope right now, that's all. I've got to go along with her. But this isn't the real Jude—she's not acting like herself at all."

"Of course she is," said Tess. "She's always been erratic and illogical and acted on emotion."

"If you saw her, if you tried to talk to her, you'd realize. She just won't—or can't—listen to reason. But once she's had time to recover, I know she'll see how ridiculous she was. And once she's pregnant again, she'll be back to normal, I'm certain."

Tess realized she wasn't going to be able to eat her lunch. Her stomach was as tight as a fist.

Gordon said, "This won't last forever, I promise. But for now, we're just going to have to stop seeing each other."

No apologies, no softening of the blow. He was speaking to her man to man, Tess thought. She wondered what he would do if she burst into tears or began shouting at him.

"Why are you smiling?" he asked.

"I didn't know I was. Do we have to stop all contact with each other? Do I pretend you've dropped off the face of the earth, or what?"

"I'll phone you. I'll keep in touch. And I'll let you know if anything changes—when something changes."

Tess looked at her watch. "I have to go back and supervise some tests."

"I'll walk you—"

"No, stay, finish your food," she said. "Don't get up." She had suddenly imagined herself clinging to him on a street corner, begging him not to leave her. She didn't want to risk that, yet she could not kiss him casually, as if she would be seeing him again in a few hours or days. As she came around the table, she put her hand on his face for just a moment, then left without looking back.

As a child, Tess had been mad about horses, going through the traditional girlish phase of reading, talking, drawing and dreaming of them, begging for the impossible, a horse of her own. For her ninth birthday her parents had enrolled her for riding lessons. For half a year she had been learning to ride, but after her mother's death Tess had refused to have anything more to do with horses, even had a kind of horror of them. She had only one memento from that phase of her life: the blue-glazed, ceramic head of a horse. In her youth she'd kept it hidden away, but now she took pleasure in it again, in its beauty, the sweeping arch of the sculpted neck and the deep, mottled colour. It was a beautiful object, nothing like the nightmare.

Tess sat alone in her apartment sipping bourbon and Coke and gazing at the horse head, now and again lifting it to touch its coolness to her flushed cheek.

You didn't kill your mother, she told herself. Wishing the baby would not be born is not the same thing as *making* it not be born. You weren't—aren't—responsible for your dreams. And dreams don't kill.

Outside, the day blued towards night and Tess went on drinking. She felt more helpless and alone than she had ever before felt as an adult, as if the power to rule her own life had been taken from her. She was controlled, she thought, by the emotions of others: by Jude's fear, by Gordon's sense of responsibility, by her own childish guilt.

But Tess did not allow herself to sink into despair. The next morning, although hungover and sad, she knew that life must go on. She was accustomed, after all, to being alone and to taking care of herself. She knew how to shut out other thoughts while she worked, and she made an effort to schedule activities for her non-working hours so that dinner out, or a film, or drinks with friends carried her safely through the dangerous, melancholy hour of blue.

Over the next six weeks, Gordon spoke to her briefly three times. Jude seemed to be getting better, he said, but she was still adamant in her feelings towards Tess. Tess could never think of anything to say to this, and the silence stretched between them, and then Gordon stopped calling. After three months, Tess began to believe that it was truly over between them. And then Gordon came to see her.

He looked thin and unhappy. At the sight of him, Tess forgot her own misery and only wanted to comfort him. She poured him a drink and hovered over him, touching his hair shyly. He caught her hand and pulled her down beside him on the couch, and began to kiss and caress her rather clumsily. She was helping him undress when she realized he was crying.

"Gordon! Darling, what's wrong?" She was shocked by his tears. She tried to hold him, to let him cry, but understood he didn't want that. After a minute he blew his nose and shook his head hard, repudiating the tears.

"Jude and I," he began. Then, after a pause, "Jude's left me."

Tess felt a shocking sense of triumph, which she repressed at once. She waited, saying nothing.

"It's been hell," he said. "Ever since the miscarriage. That crazy idea she had, that you were somehow responsible for it. She said it was because you didn't mind sharing me with her, but that a baby would have changed things—you would have been left out of the cosy family group. I told her that you weren't like that, you weren't jealous, but she just laughed at me, and said men didn't understand."

She must go carefully here, Tess thought. She had to admit her responsibility, and not let Gordon blame Jude too much, but she didn't want Gordon thinking she was mad.

"Gordon," she said. "I *was* jealous—and I was very afraid that once you were a father things would change and I'd be left out in the cold."

He dismissed her confession with a grimace and a wave of his hand. "So what? That doesn't make any difference. Even if you'd wanted her to have a miscarriage you didn't make it happen. You couldn't. Jude seems to think that you wished it on her, like you were some kind of a witch. She's crazy, that's what it comes down to."

"She might come back."

"No. It's over. We'd talked about a trial separation, and we started seeing a marriage counsellor. It made it worse. All sorts of things came up, things I hadn't thought were problems. And then she found somebody else, she's gone off with somebody else. She won't be with him for long, but she won't come back."

Tess had thought for a long time that the break-up of Gordon and Jude would inevitably lead to the break-up between Gordon and herself, and so for the next few months she was tense, full of an unexamined anxiety, waiting for this to happen. Gordon, too, was uneasy, unanchored without his wife. Unlike Tess, he did not enjoy living alone, but he made a great effort to ration his time with Tess, not to impose upon her. They tried to go on as they always had, ignoring the fact that Jude was no longer there to limit the time they spent together. But when Tess finished her doctorate, they had to admit to the inevitability of some major, permanent change in their relationship. Tess could stay on in New Orleans, teaching English as a foreign language and scraping a living somehow, but that wasn't what she wanted. It wasn't what she had worked and studied for, and so she tried to ignore the feeling of dread that lodged in her stomach as she sent out her CV and searched in earnest for a university which might hire her. She had always known this time would come. She didn't talk about it to Gordon. Why should she? It was her life, her career, her responsibility. She would make her plans, and then she would tell him.

An offer came from a university in upstate New York. It wasn't brilliant, but it was better than she'd expected: a heavy teaching schedule, but with a chance of continuing her own research.

She told Gordon about it over dinner in a Mexican restaurant.

"It sounds good, just right for you," he said, nodding.

"It's not perfect. And it probably won't last. I can't count on more than a year."

"You're good," he said. "They'll see that. You'll get tenure."

"Maybe I won't want it. I might hate it there."

"Don't be silly." He looked so calm and unmoved that Tess felt herself begin to panic. Didn't he care? Could he really let her go so easily? She crunched down hard on a tortilla chip and almost missed his next words. ". . . scout around," he was saying. "If I can't find anything in Watertown, there must be other cities close enough that we could at least have weekends together."

She stared, disbelieving. "You'd quit your job? You'd move across the country just because I'm . . ."

"Why not?"

"Your job . . ."

"I'm not in love with my job," he said.

Tess looked into his eyes and felt herself falling. She said, "Upstate New York is not the most exciting place—"

"They need accountants there just like everywhere else," he said. "I'll find a job. I'm good. Don't you believe me?" He grinned at her with that easy arrogance she'd always found paradoxically both irritating and attractive.

"Are you sure?" she asked.

"I'm sure about this: I'm not letting you go without a fight. If you're not sure about me, better say so now, and we can start fighting." He grinned again, and beneath the table, gripped her knees between his. "But I'm going to win."

Six months later they were living together in a small, rented house in Watertown, New York. But although living together, they saw less of each other than they had in New Orleans. Unable to find a job actually in Watertown, Gordon spent at least three hours on the road every day, travelling to and from work. He left in the mornings while Tess still slept, and returned, exhausted, in time for a later dinner and then bed. It was a very different life they led from the one they'd known in New Orleans. They had left behind all those restaurant meals, the easy socializing in French Quarter bars, the flirtations with other people, the long, sultry evenings of doing very little in the open air. The days this far north were short, the nights long and cold. Because Tess didn't like to cook, and Gordon had time for it only on the weekends, they ate a lot of frozen convenience foods, omelettes, and sandwiches. They watched a lot of television, complaining about it and apologizing to each other. They planned to take up hobbies, learn sports, join local organizations, but when the weekends came almost always they spent the two days at home, in bed, together.

Her own happiness surprised Tess. She had always believed that she would feel suffocated if she lived with a man, but now whenever Gordon was out of the house she missed him. Being with him, whether talking, making love, or simply staring like two zombies at the flickering screen, was all she wanted when she wasn't working. She couldn't believe that she had imagined herself content with so little for so long—to have shared

Gordon with another woman without jealousy. She knew she would be jealous now, if Gordon had another lover, but she also knew she had nothing to worry about. She had changed, and so had he. When he asked her to marry him she didn't even hesitate. She knew what she wanted.

Within four months of the marriage Tess was pregnant.

It wasn't planned—and yet it wasn't an accident, either. She had been careful for too many years to make such a simple mistake, and in Gordon's silence was his part of the responsibility. Without a word spoken, in one shared moment, they had decided. At least, they had decided not to decide, to leave it to fate for once. And afterwards Tess was terrified, waking in the middle of the night to brood on the mistake she was making, wondering, almost until the very last month, if she couldn't manage to have an abortion, after all.

Gordon did everything he could to make things easier for her. Since he couldn't actually have the baby for her, he devoted himself to her comfort. And except for the physical unpleasantness of being pregnant, and the middle of the night terrors, Tess sometimes thought, as she basked in the steady glow of Gordon's attentive love, that this might be the happiest time of her life.

In the months before the baby was born they decided that Gordon's continuing to commute to work wouldn't be possible. Instead, he would set up on his own as an accountant, and work from home. It might be difficult for the first few years, but Gordon had a few investments here and there, and at a pinch they could scrape by on Tess's salary. Gordon said, with his usual self-confidence, that he could make far more money self-employed than anyone ever did as an employee, and Tess believed him. Things would work out.

Her labour was long and difficult. When at last the baby was placed in her arms Tess looked down at it, feeling exhausted and detached, wondering what this little creature had to do with her. She was glad when Gordon took it away from her. Lying back against the pillows she watched her husband.

His face changed, became softer. Tess recognized that rapturous, melting expression because she had seen it occasionally, during sex. She had never seen him look at anyone else like that. She burst into tears.

Gordon was beside her immediately, pushing the baby at her. But she didn't want the baby. She only wanted Gordon, although she couldn't stop crying long enough to tell him. He held her as she held the baby, and gradually his presence calmed her. After all, the baby was *theirs*. She and Gordon belonged to each other more certainly now than ever before. No longer merely a couple, they were now a family. She knew she should be happy.

She tried to be happy, and sometimes she was, but this baby girl, called Lexi (short for Alexandra), made her feel not only love, but also fear and frustration and pain. Motherhood was not as instinctive as she had believed it would be, for Gordon was clearly better at it than she was, despite her physical equipment. Breast-feeding, which Tess had confidently expected to enjoy, was a disaster. No one had told her, and she had never dreamed, that it would *hurt*. And her suffering was in vain. Lexi didn't thrive until they put her on the bottle. Watching Gordon giving Lexi her late-night feed while she was meant to be sleeping, Tess tried not to feel left out.

It was a relief, in a way, to be able to go back to work after six weeks: back to her own interests, to her students and colleagues, doing the things she knew she was good at. But it wasn't quite the same, for she missed Lexi when she wasn't around. Always, now, she felt a worrying tug of absence. For all the problems, she couldn't wish Lexi away. She only wished that loving Lexi could be as simple and straightforward as loving Gordon. If only she could explain herself to Lexi, she thought, and Lexi explain herself to Tess—if only they shared a language.

When she said this to Gordon one evening after Lexi had been put to bed, he laughed.

"She'll be talking soon enough, and then it'll be why? why? why? all the time, and demanding toys and candy and clothes. Right now, life is simple. She cries when she wants to have her diaper changed, or she wants to be fed, or she wants to be burped or cuddled. Then she's happy."

"But you have to figure out what she wants," Tess said. "She can't tell you—that's my point. And if you do the wrong thing, she just goes on crying and getting more and more unhappy. I'm no more complex than Lexi, really. I have the same sorts of needs. But I can tell you what I want. If I started crying now, you'd probably think I wanted my dinner. But what I really want is a cuddle."

He looked at her, tenderly, and left his chair to join her on the couch. He kissed her affectionately.

She kissed him more demandingly, but he didn't respond.

"You'll have to do better than that," she said. "Or I'll start crying."

"I was thinking about dinner."

"Forget about dinner. Why don't you check to see if my diapers need changing?"

He laughed. Maybe he laughed too loudly, because a moment later, like a response, came Lexi's wail.

"Leave her," said Tess. "She'll fall back to sleep."

They sat tensely, holding each other, waiting for this to happen. Lexi's cries became louder and more urgent.

Tess sighed. The moment had passed away. "I'll go," she said. "You fix dinner."

Time alone with Gordon was what Tess missed most. Their desires, and the opportunity to make love, seldom meshed. As Lexi approached her first birthday she seemed to spend even more time awake and demanding attention. This affected not only her parents' relationship, but also Gordon's fledgling business. He was floundering, distracted by the demands of fatherhood, unable to put the time and energy he needed into building up a list of clients. Time was all he needed, Tess thought, and he must have that time. She thought it all through before approaching him about it, but she was certain that he would agree with her. He would be reasonable, as he always was. She didn't expect an argument.

"Day-care!" he repeated, pronouncing it like an obscenity. "Leave Lexi in some crummy nursery? Are you kidding?"

"Why are you sure it would be crummy? I'm not proposing we look for the cheapest place we can find. Of course we'll look around and see what's available, and choose the best we can afford."

"But why?"

"Because there's no way we can afford a full-time babysitter, you know that."

"We don't need a full-time babysitter. We've got me."

"That's what I mean. You're not being paid to look after Lexi, but while you're taking care of her you can't make a living."

He stared at her. She couldn't read his expression; he was miles away from her. "I see. I've had my chance, and I've failed, so now I have to get a real job."

"No!" She clutched his hand, then lowered her voice. "For heaven's sake, Gordon, I'm not criticizing you. And I'm not saying you should go to work for some company . . . I believe in you. Everything you said about being able to make a lot of money in a few years, I'm sure that's true. I know you'll make a success of it. Only . . . you need time. You can't be out meeting people, or writing letters, or balancing books if you have to keep breaking off to get Lexi her rattle. Your work needs attention just as much as she does . . . you have to be able to really commit yourself to it."

"You're right," he said in his usual, reasonable tone. He sighed, and Tess's heart lifted as he said, "I've been thinking about it a lot, and coming to the same conclusion. Well, not quite the same conclusion. You're right that I can't get much work done while I'm looking after Lexi. Weekends aren't enough. But why do we have to pay someone else to look after Lexi? We can manage ourselves—we just need to be a little more flexible. We could divide up the week between us. You don't have classes on Tuesdays and Thursdays. If you stayed home then, and took responsibility for the weekends, too— why are you shaking your head?"

"Just because I don't have classes on Tuesdays and Thursdays doesn't mean I don't have work to do. I have to be around to supervise, to advise, and there's my research. When am I ever going to get my book written if I don't have some time to myself? We can't manage by ourselves. There's no shame in that. It's why day-care centres exist. We both have to make a living, and for that we need—"

"What about what Lexi needs?"

"Gordon, she'll have plenty of attention, we're not going to deprive her of anything."

"We're going to deprive ourselves, though." He was almost vibrating with intensity. "Look, one of the greatest experiences in the world is bringing up a child. Teaching her, watching her change and grow every day. I don't want to miss out on that. Maybe in a couple of years, but not now. We can manage. So what if we're not rich? There are things more important than money and careers. If you spent more time with her yourself you'd know what I mean."

"You think I don't spend enough time with her?" Tess said quietly.

"I didn't say that."

"But it's what you think. You think I'm selfish, or that my job is more important to me. It's not that. I love Lexi very much. I love her as much as you do. But I won't—I can't—let her absorb me. I miss her whenever I'm away from her, but I know I can't let my whole life revolve around her. You can't hold on to her forever. Eventually she'll have to grow up and leave us."

"For God's sake, she's not even a year old! You're talking like I'm trying to stop her from going to college or something."

"She may be a baby, but she's still a person. She has a life apart from you and me—she has to. And so do we. Not just individually, but as a couple. Or aren't we a couple anymore? Are we only Lexi's parents? I *miss* you, Gordon; I feel like—" She stopped, because if she said anything more she knew she would be crying.

"Let's go to bed," Gordon said, not looking at her. "Let's not argue. We'll talk about it later."

They went to bed and made love and, for a little while, Tess felt they had reached an understanding, had confirmed the love they still had for each other.

But then the nightmare came.

Lying in bed, drowsily aware of Gordon's close, sleeping warmth, Tess heard the window fly open. When she opened her eyes she saw, as she had known she would, the familiar, bone-white head of the mare staring in at her, waiting for her.

Her heart sank. I won't move, she thought. I won't go. I will

wake myself. But she struggled in vain to open her eyes, or to
close them, or even to turn her head so that the creature would
be out of her sight. She felt the bitter chill of the winter night
flooding the bedroom, and she began to shiver. I must close the
window, she thought, and as she thought that, she realized she
was getting up, and walking toward the creature who had come
for her.

Tess stared at the horse, recognizing the invitation in the toss
of the pale head. She tried to refuse it. I don't wish anyone any
harm, she thought. I love my daughter. I love my husband. I
don't want you. Go away.

But she could not wake, or speak, or do anything but walk in
slow, somnambulist fashion towards the window, outside of
which the nightmare ran in place on the wind.

I don't want to hurt anyone—I won't! Oh, please, let me
wake!

But it was her own body which carried her, despite her
mental protests, to the window and onto the sill. And as she
struggled against the dream, almost crying with frustration, she
flung herself through the open window, into the cold night,
upon the nightmare's back.

And then she was clinging desperately to the creature's neck,
feeling herself slipping on its icy back, as it mounted the sky.
The ride was nothing like the last one. She was terrified, and
she knew she was in imminent danger of falling, if not of being
thrown. Whatever she had once known of riding had vanished.
The muscles in her thighs ached, and the cold had numbed her
fingers. She didn't think she would be able to hang on for very
long, particularly not if the mare continued to leap and swerve
and climb so madly. Closing her eyes, Tess tried to relax, to let
instinct take over. She pressed her cheek against the mare's
neck and breathed in the smell of blood. Choking back her
revulsion, she struggled to sit upright, despite the pressure of
the wind. Neck muscles knotted and moved within her embrace, and the mare's long head turned back, one wild eye
rolling to look at her.

Tess felt herself slipping, sliding inexorably down. Unless
the mare slowed her pace she would fall, she thought. She
struggled to keep her grip on the creature's twisting neck, and

because she still could not speak, sent one final, pleading look at the mare to ask for mercy. And just before the nightmare threw her, their eyes met, and Tess understood. Within the nightmare's eye she saw her daughter's cold, blue gaze: judgemental, selfish, pitiless.

Wild, Wild Horses
by
Howard Waldrop

*Half-man and half-horse, the centaur is one of the few mythical
creatures usually considered to be more human than beast. It's
doubtful, for instance, that anyone would ask a sphinx or a
griffin to tea, but centaurs, who had their own civilization and
customs, were often admitted into human society. In spite of the
rude and barbarous side of their natures (which was likely to
emerge, with disastrous results, if you were unwise enough to
get them drunk), centaurs were often portrayed as seers and
sages, and the wisest of them, Chiron, was the teacher of
Achilles, Aesculapius, and many of the other heroes of Greek
mythology. So distinguished was Chiron, in fact, that when he
died, Zeus raised him to the heavens as the constellation
Sagittarius. Before that, however, he may have had one or two
final adventures, as the sly and erudite story that follows
vividly demonstrates . . .*

*Howard Waldrop is widely considered to be one of the best
short-story writers in the business, and his famous story "The
Ugly Chickens" won both the Nebula and the World fantasy
awards in 1981. His work has been gathered in three collec-
tions:* Howard Who?, All About Strange Monsters of the
Recent Past: Neat Stories by Howard Waldrop, *and* Night of
the Cooters: More Neat Stories by Howard Waldrop, *with more
collections in the works. Waldrop is also the author of the novel*
The Texas-Israeli War: 1999, *in collaboration with Jake
Saunders, and of two solo novels,* Them Bones *and* A Dozen
Tough Jobs. *He is at work on a new novel, tentatively entitled*
The Moon World. *Waldrop lives in Austin, Texas.*

* * *

Up on the platform, Ambrose was preaching against the
heathen, in Latin, to a crowd largely pagan who spoke only
Greek.

The spectacle of a man wailing, cajoling, pleading and crying in another tongue had drawn a large gathering. "Go it, Roman!" some yelled encouragingly.

The man on the raised boards at the edge of the marketplace redoubled his efforts, becoming a fountain of tears, a blur of gesticulations, now here, now there. Such preaching they hadn't seen since the old days when the Christians had been an outlawed sect.

Then another man in the crowd yelled at the onlookers in Greek. "Listen not to him!" he said. "He's a patripassionist. He believes God Himself came down and took part in the suffering of Jesus Christ on the Cross! He denies the accepted Trinity of Father, Son, Holy Ghost! Come across the creek and hear the True Word, spoken by followers of the True Church. And in a language you can understand!"

With a snarl, Ambrose flung himself over the railing and onto the other Christian. There was a great flurry of dust, growling and coughs as they tore at each other's faces and clothing. The crowd egged them on; this was better than preaching anytime.

"What's all this, then?" asked an ædile, on his morning inspection of the roadways. He began beating with his staff of office at the center of the struggle until, with yelps of pain, the two men separated.

"Heretic!" shouted the second Christian.

"Whining Nicean dog!" yelled Ambrose.

With his staff the ædile rapped Ambrose smartly on the head and poked the second man in the ribs in one smooth motion. Two of the local military reservists hurried up through the crowd.

"What's this, your honor?" they asked, grabbing the two panting men.

"Christians," he said. "Since the new emperor Julian let all the exiles and fragmented bishops return, there's been nothing but trouble, trouble, trouble with them. It would be fine if they killed each other in private, but they endanger decent gods-fearing folk with their idiotic schisms. They cause commotion in the reopened temples and trouble at public ceremonies."

"Quite right," said the reservists, who both wore fish

symbols on chains around their necks. They each punched and slapped the man they held a few times for effect.

"Don't think it doesn't do my heart glad to see officers carrying out their civic duties in spite of their personal convictions," said the ædile. "There's hope for this empire yet."

"Sorry you had to deal with this, sir. We'll take care of them," said one of the reservists, saluting with his forearm across his chest.

The crowd, grumbling, dispersed. The minor official continued on his way toward the rededicated Temple of Mars.

The four talked among themselves a moment, then the two policemen and the second Christian grabbed Ambrose and frog-walked him up a narrow alleyway.

The marketplace returned to its deadly dull normality.

P. Renatus Vegetius had been on his way to the house of his retired military friend Aurem Præbens when the fight had broken out just in front of him.

He shook his head. Surely the new emperor knew what would happen when he allowed all the exiled misfits and disgruntled Christians back. There was already talk that Julian was helping the Jews rebuild their temple in Jerusalem, that he would take state funds away from the Christian churches, that he would renew the imperial office of Pontifex Maximus.

This small town, Smyrnea, fifty miles from Byzantium where the new emperor sat after his march from Germany, was supposed to have the Emperor's ear. It was in this town he had spent his childhood and youth in exile, watched over by the old emperor's spies, before going to Rome and Athens to study in his young manhood. Well, only time would tell what would happen with Julian's plans to revitalize the increasingly disparate eastern and western provinces.

Statecraft for the statesmen, thought Vegetius. He was on his way to Præbens' house to consult manuscripts in the library there so he could put the finishing touches on his work, *de re militaria,* a training manual to be read to officers in the army. It lacked only a section on impediments and baggage-train convoy duties, of which Præbens had once written copious notes while accompanying Constantine on one of his eastward marches.

P. Renatus Vegetius had himself never been in the army. He had held minor offices (he had once been ædile of this very town, twenty years before, but that was when the job consisted of little more than seeing that the streets were swept; the Christians, after their big meeting at Nicea having brought pressure on Constantine and his sons to close down all the temples and call off public spectacles). Not like today where an ædile got real respect; a broad-shouldered job fitting for a man. Still, Vegetius was glad the present troubles hadn't happened in his times.

Across the street, hurrying toward him, was Decius Muccinus, nomenclator to his friend Præbens. He was moving faster than Vegetius had ever seen him do, almost at a flat run. Unseemly in a slave, even one his master had promised freedom in six months. He was a young man with a beard of the Greek cut.

"Salve, Muccinus!" said Vegetius.

The slave jerked to a stop. "Sir," he said, "forgive me. I was hurrying to your house, sent by my master to fetch you. Astonishing news, if true, which I am forbidden to tell."

"Well, well," said Renatus Vegetius, hurrying with the young man toward Præbens' town home. "Surely you can tell me something?"

"Only that you will be highly pleased." He leaned toward Vegetius, whispering. "Approaching: Singultus Correptus and Sternuus Maximus. Correptus' wife is Livia, Maximus' son is due for a promotion in the army."

"Salve, Singultus! Sternuus!" said Vegetius, stopping to shake their wrists. "How's the lovely Livia, Singultus? And Sternuus, that son of yours had done alright for himself, hasn't he?"

After a further exchange of pleasantries they hurried on. "Thank you, Muccinus," said Vegetius. "You needn't have done that for me."

"Old habits die hard," said the slave.

"Great news, great news!" said Aurem Præbens. "One of your dreams come true! (And I'm not talking about that damned book of veterinary you want to write.) Sharpen up your javelin, you old fart! A lion's been seen here in Thracia itself. Less than twenty miles away!" He waved a letter around. "Someone, anonymous, says I and my friends should know before the news becomes general!"

There had supposedly been no lions this side of the Pontus Euxinus since the end of the Republic four hundred years before. One of Vegetius' secret wishes was to hunt lions from a chariot in the old style and to write a treatise on the subject. He had been planning a trip to Libya the year after next (gods willing) once he had finished this book, and the one on the diseases of mules and horses, to engage in such a hunt. But here, now, in Thracia!

"I've called on Morus Matutinus (who served in Africa) and Phoebus Siccus (who owns an old hunting chariot) and have sent for three teams of swift coursers for our use!" said Præbens. "How does that grab your testicles?"

Aurem Præbens was beaming. Vegetius was beside himself. Sometimes the gods were kind.

Sometimes they weren't. The party had been out for two days; thirty men and slaves, twenty horses, two impedimenta wagons and fifty yelping, fighting dogs.

As a scent they had brought with them a lion's skin that had hung on one wall of Morus Matutinus' atrium. By the second day of the dogs milling around and biting each other in uncontained excitement, the slaves were betting among themselves that the hounds would soon strike a trail and follow it the twenty miles straight back to Matutinus' house.

Phoebus Siccus, an old, old wrinkled man, was decked out in his armor from fifty years before. He could turn completely around in the worn leather and metal breastplate before it began to move with him.

"Either these are the sorriest dogs I've ever seen, or there's no lion closer than Mesopotamia. Who the Dis' idea was this, anyway?" asked Siccus through his lips which looked like two broken flints.

The dogs had run up a wisent, two scrawny deer and an ass in forty-eight hours. Each time the houndsmen would kick them howling away from the cornered animals and then stick their noses back in the lion's skin.

"I'm going over to the brook yonder," said Renatus Vegetius. He mounted his horse.

"May I go with him, master?" asked Decius Muccinus. "I should like a swim."

"The last thing I need out here," said Præbens, "is a nomenclator. The guys who own these hounds all answer to 'Hey, shithead!' " He turned to Vegetius. "Sorry. I wanted this hunt for you. We'll take the dogs back north, then home. Follow the wagon tracks. If you miss the lion, though, you'll hate yourself."

"If I don't cool off, I will die," said Vegetius. "Good hunting."

"Hah! I'm going to find out who sent that letter and turn the dogs on his butt," said Præbens.

It was a stream straight out of Hesiod, pure, pebbled and cold. Vegetius sat on a rock with his swollen feet in the gurgling water. Muccinus, who had stripped naked and swam back and forth a few times, was now asleep on the grass. Upstream tall rushes grew; to each side of the stream banks lifted up and hung over, shading the western side of the waters in this early afternoon.

Their two horses stopped their grazing. One backed up whinnying, its eyes growing wider.

"What is it?" he asked the horse, reaching out to calm it. Then his blood froze. *Oh gods,* he thought, looking upstream and scrambling for his javelin, *what if the lion's found us?*

He kicked Muccinus with his bare foot.

"Mmmph?" asked the slave, rolling over. Then he jumped up, seeing Vegetius trying to put his sandals on over his head. He pulled a dagger from his lump of clothing on the ground.

"What? What?"

They looked upstream. Something moved along the tall rushes. The green fronds parted.

The oldest man they had ever seen stood at the edge of the reeds, naked from the waist up. He might as well have been clothed; his hair and beard were pure white and hung in waves down his back and chest. He looked like a white haystack from which a face stuck out. They couldn't tell if the hair reached the ground as the reeds covered all below his waist.

In his hand he held a thin tapered pole to which was attached a light line, gossamer in the sun, probably of plaited horsehair. At the end of the line was a hook with a tuft of red and white yarn tied to it. He waved the pole back and forth a few times and flipped the line into the water.

There was a splash as something rose to the lure. The line tightened, the pole bent, and the old man heaved up and back.

A two-pound grayling, blue and purple-spotted in the sunlight, its dorsal fin like a battle flag, flew out of the water at the end of the line and landed flapping back in the reeds.

The old man bent out of sight to pick it up.

"Well done, sir," said Vegetius. The old man looked up. "I'd be careful though. There's supposed to be a lion about!"

The old man looked at them, his face breaking out into a smile. He flipped the line back out; soon he was fast to another grayling, this one larger, and pulled it in.

"I said, there's a lion about!" yelled Vegetius, cupping his hands.

"Nonchalant bastard," said Muccinus. "Or maybe deaf as a post."

The old man shouldered the pole and the brace of grayling and went through the reeds on his way upstream.

"I saw no houses about," said Muccinus. "Wonder where he came from?"

"Who knows?" said Vegetius.

The sun was still hot, so they followed the shady side of the brook upstream for a mile or so.

They came upon the cave around a bend. Outside were hung drying wild onions, radishes, garlics. There was a rack out in the sun on which split fish curled.

Fungi and mushrooms grew in the shady spots.

"Quite homey," said Muccinus. "Hello the cave!"

There was no answer.

"He has frequent visitors," said Vegetius, pointing to the ground outside the cave opening. It was churned with innumerable hoof prints. "Either he's a companionable old cuss, or he's popular because those aren't regular mushrooms."

"Hello," Renatus continued, dismounting. He tied his horse's reins to a root which grew from the cliff wall. The horse was nervous again.

Inside, the cave was cluttered with thousands and thousands of scrolls, book boxes, clay tablets and slates.

"Muccinus," he said. "Look at *this*!"

They walked in. Amid the clutter was a chest-high table; at one corner of the room a pile of mashed-down straw. There were no chairs, only piles and piles of scrolls and books in a dozen languages.

Decius Muccinus poked around in the stacks. "Greek. The curved writing of Ind. Latin. The old triangle writing. Who could read this stuff? What's it doing *here*?"

Renatus Vegetius went to the high table. There were several closed scroll tubes there. One was open. On the table, by itself, was a single page, cut evidently from a lengthy work, headed, as it was, Book 19 in Greek, and at the top, the title . . .

If Iupiter Ammon had pulled P. Renatus Vegetius up to the top of Mount Olympus and said to him: *Go anywhere, mortal, and get your heart's content; anywhere in time and anywhere in the world: it is yours,* Vegetius would have in the next instant been back in this cave with his hand on this piece of paper.

It was the *Hippiatrika*, the lost book of veterinary medicine. It was as old as time, older than Homer. When he had read Pelagonius' *Ars Veterinaria,* Vegetius remembered the author's railing at the fates which had lost the book to the ken of man since the Trojan War. Pelagonius wailed for the lost knowledge it was supposed to contain.

And here Vegetius had in his hand a page of it. He read the first paragraph and knew, with all his mind and heart, that this was *it*.

Their horses whickered outside. Then their hooves clattered. The horses ran by, blurs. Vegetius had only his short sword with him—the javelin had been in the saddle boot. Muccinus once again drew the dagger forbidden to slaves.

They heard another clatter of hooves. At least it wasn't the lion. "Hello! Hello!" they both shouted.

"I know you're in there. No need to yell," said a voice, an old man's voice, older even than that of Phoebus Siccus.

Then the old man came into the cave, followed by the horse.

No.

The old man and the horse came in together.

No.

The old man was the horse.

"Finding anything interesting to read?" he asked, looking from one to the other, then settling his gaze on Vegetius.

Somewhere down his back his hair turned into a brittle white mane. He was white and grey from the top of his head to his hooves. A black leg lifted, clacked to the floor.

It was easier, thought Vegetius, if you only looked at the front half.

"The *Hippiatrika*?" he asked. "Where did you get it?"

The centaur looked toward the table. A mixture of warm animal and human body odour came to Vegetius' nose, like sweaty men on a wet horsehide triclinium. More than anything it convinced him that the encounter he was having was real.

"I wrote it," said the centaur.

Vegetius nearly fainted.

"I think your master needs some water," said the centaur to Muccinus. "There's a cup outside. And please don't run away."

"He's . . . he's not . . . my master," said Muccinus. "And I need some too."

Vegetius held onto a table leg until the slave returned with the cup. As he stood woozily, he noticed that the hooves of the centaur were in bad shape. One leg, the right front, was thinner than the others, with a knot on it as if it had been broken once. What chest Renatus could see through the drapery of white hair looked thin and mottled. Vegetius took the cup and drank.

"Chiron," he said to the centaur. Chiron, the teacher of Hercules and Asclepius, the only centaur able to read and write. The only one ever to be married to a human woman; the only centaur able to drink wine without becoming a raging animal. Chiron, author of the *Hippiatrika*.

"You must be P. Renatus Vegetius," said the horse-man.

"How did you know my name?"

The centaur laughed, his long hair flying.

"How goes the lion hunt?"

"The letter was your doing?"

"Somewhat. I wanted to meet you. I read a copy of your *Histories*."

"And you knew I would come to hunt a lion?"

"After your rhapsode on lion-hunting in the chapter on Egypt? And in your argument, you said you would someday write a treatise on warfare, and a book amplifying Pelagonius' *Ars Veterinaria*? To read a man is sometimes to know all you need," said Chiron.

"Vegetius," said Decius Muccinus. "You're . . . talking literature . . . with . . . a . . . centaur."

"One with a purpose," said Chiron.

"What's that?" asked Vegetius.

"I have something you desire. The *Hippiatrika*. The whole manuscript." Vegetius looked wildly around. "It's in a safe place. Don't worry. Help me, and it, and all these other works, are yours."

"What do you wish?"

"I'm old. I want to return to my homeland to die. You can help me."

"Your homeland? Scythia? Ind? Africa?" asked Vegetius, following the best authorities as to the homeland of the centaurs.

"Take me to the Pillars of Hercules," said Chiron. "Then I can be home in a few days."

"The Pillars of Hercules! That's at the western edge of the Empire! That's where the Greeks once sent an expedition to see if the sun hissed as it went down in the ocean! We're in the East. How am I supposed to get a centaur from one end of the civilized world to the other?"

"You're an intelligent man," said Chiron. "If you can't conceive of getting me across the Empire, think what it would be like for me, alone. When I was young and strong, I might have done it. I could outrun any horse when I had to. But no longer. I wouldn't be gone fifty miles before some rich man would have me hunted down for his menagerie. The fact that

I'm a rational being, and can think and speak, would appeal to him not at all. I'd end my days in a cage, in Thracia."

He looked at Vegetius.

"I can't believe this," said Decius Muccinus.

"I'm the last one," said Chiron. "And you get the *Hippiatrika*. It is all you think it to be. Just get me home, Renatus Vegetius. I ask no more."

"I wouldn't know how to begin," said Vegetius.

"Nemo Prorsus," said Muccinus.

"What?"

"Nemo Prorsus. A very clever man in Cyzicus. If you want to go through with this, I mean," said Muccinus. "He's done everything, been everywhere. All it takes is money. Vast amounts."

Chiron turned his eyes to Vegetius. "Please?"

"Done," said Vegetius, crossing his wrists three times and spitting, "and done!"

In the week following, after he had sent for Prorsus, Vegetius went to Aurem Praebens. He found him dictating to Muccinus.

"I'd like to buy Decius from you," said Vegetius.

"What!?" screamed Muccinus. "After what I've gone through! I'm to be freed in—"

"Quiet, slave," said Aurem.

"I—"

"Just what did you have in mind?" asked Praebens.

"You're to free him in six months. Sell him to me, now. I'll free him when I return from my—researches in Alexandria." (This was the cover story.) "You know everyone in this one-horse town, anyway. I'll need someone quick with me, a nomenclator, one who can read and write. And I trust no one more than your Decius Muccinus."

Decius was glowering at him.

"Besides," said Vegetius, "sell him to *me*, and it won't be *you* who has to pay the five percent manumission tax!"

"Decius, you've been like a son to me, but business is business," said Praebens to the slave. Then to Vegetius, "Three thousand sesterces."

"Three thousand? I'm going to have him read to me, not sleep with me!"

"I'm worth four thousand if I'm worth a talent," said Decius, his feelings hurt.

"Three thousand five hundred," said Præbens.

"Three thousand five hundred? Can he fly, too?"

"Three thousand eight hundred and not a denarius less!"

"What, does a whole family come with him, eight strong boys?" asked Vegetius.

"Four thousand," said Præbens.

"Done!"

"Done," said Præbens, crossing his wrists three times and spitting, "and done!"

Decius was smiling as they had him write up his own bill of sale.

They decided to move Chiron nearer town as they received word Nemo Prorsus was on his way across the Hellespont. Vegetius and Muccinus went out to help him close up his cave, stacking stones across the entrance all one afternoon.

He was to stay in one of the outbuildings in an olive grove owned by Vegetius' uncle, Verbius Mellarius the rhetorician.

"Excuse me," said Chiron. He backed up, lifting his tail and dropping a pile of road apples on the path. "I usually don't do that so close to home, but I'm leaving. And my stomach's not what it used to be."

After they sealed the cavern off fairly well, they began to ride downstream as the sun went down. Chiron took a long last look back.

"If these were the olden days," he said, "I'd ask one of the Cyclops to keep an eye on the place for me."

A few minutes later, Decius Muccinus looked at Chiron and began to laugh.

"So this is the famous Mr. Chiron, eh?" said Nemo Prorsus, a squat thick man with a Greek beard. He wore trousers in the eastern fashion and a leather tunic covered with brass spikes. He was bald as a melon. "Glad to meet a real centaur. I once fixed up a mermaid and sold it to the Prince of Parsi, but this is the closest I ever come to a real mythical creature."

"I'm no myth," said Chiron.

"Think you can do it, Nemo?" asked Decius.

"That's *Mister* Nemo to you, slave boy!" He studied a moment. "Yeah. But it's gonna take all your master's money. Have him give it all to me."

"Why are you talking about me in the third person?" asked Vegetius.

"I didn't start this," said Nemo Prorsus. "Yeah, gov, I can do it, but you'll have to give me near all your money and go along with everything I say. Whatever's left over we can split. Bargain?"

"Done," said Vegetius, sighing.

"Done," said Prorsus, crossing his wrists three times and spitting, "and done."

"It'll take about three days to get everything cooking. I suggest we all lay pretty low," said Prorsus.

"There's one thing I'd like to do before we leave. If Vegetius is paying," said Chiron.

"I suppose I am," said Vegetius, sighing again.

"I'd like to visit a lupercalia."

"Sonofabitch!" said Prorsus. "You're what, a million years old or somethin'? A lupercalia, no less!"

"I used to go all five ways when I was young," said Chiron. "But that was long, long ago. I'd like to go, just once, again."

"Sonofabitch!" said Nemo Prorsus. "Come on, Mr. Vegetius! Let's give the old guy a real treat. I know a place, way out in the sticks, where nobody cares what comes and goes. No offense, Mr. Chiron!"

"None taken."

So in the early morning hours they took him to a brothel by the back ways, and then into a stable by the front door, then back to the brothel again. Several of the women had several rides. Everyone became drunk and agreeable, the night became a warm blur. The women covered Chiron with flowers and sequins; one, a Greek girl named Chiote, poured libations of wine and perfumed oils in his hair and mane.

The next day no one at the lupercalia remembered much of

what happened, or whether it had or that they only dreamed it; some illusion caused by the edicts of the new Emperor, perhaps some psychic slippage to an earlier, simpler time.

"Well," said Prorsus, when he woke up with matted eyebrows and a dry mouth in the olive grove the next morning. "Time to get to work. Shell out the loot."

First he bought sixteen horses.

Then he found eight old men, solitary worshippers of Bacchus, and asked them if they could ride a horse in a straight line. Then he made them prove it. He promised them all the wine they could drink each night as long as they could ride the next morning, and free passage back to Byzantium, if they chose it, or could remember where they were from, or why they should go back whenever they got wherever it was.

"But . . . but . . ." said Vegetius. "The money!"

"An empty purse contains nothing but the seeds of failure," said Prorsus. "We made a bargain. Your centaur wants home. He's giving you something in return. You're giving me something—your complete trust and your cash. True?"

"Well, yes."

"Then let me do my job," said Prorsus, and pulled more sesterces out of the bag.

Then he went out and bought an elephant with one tusk.

He had draped two white blankets over the pachyderm's sides, tied on with rope. Prorsus took a paint brush, and in a fairly good hand painted:

VIDE ELEPHANTOS HANNIBALENSIS

on each side with an arrow pointing backwards.

"Not very good Latin," said Vegetius.

"Good enough for these garlic-eating yahoos!" said Prorsus. "The first rule is, when you're hiding a marvel, give them something else to gawk at!" He put down the paint brush.

"Besides," he said. "Anyone who thinks he's going to see some six hundred-year-old elephants deserves to miss a centaur or two."

He winked and left to see about the Imperial Post Road permits.

"Here goes nothing," said Muccinus, naked and sitting on the elephant's head.

It was the first morning of the westward trip. They were nearing the first village on the road toward Phillippi and Dyrrhachium.

"Put your lungs in it, you old farts!" yelled Prorsus from his blue-painted horse up ahead.

The eight old men sat up as straight as they could on their horses. Two of them had bagpipes, two had trumpets, two serpentines which curved around them to rest on the backs of their saddles, and the other two flailed away at drums.

It wasn't music, it was an atrocious noise. The elephant almost ran off the road. Muccinus steered it back by kicking it behind its right ear.

Vegetius, wincing, could imagine Apollo, Orpheus, and Harmonia throwing themselves off Olympus in suicide at what was being done in their name.

All the people ran out of their houses, stood in the road, made way for them.

They began to cheer and yell as the blatting entourage came even with them. Prorsus, wearing a headdress of purple ostrich feathers, gave them a sweeping blessing with his arms.

All eyes were on the elephant. It trumpeted, drowning out the cacophony ahead of it for a second or two. It drew even with the middle of the village. Heads turned back toward Byzantium, peering. Most of the villagers were still looking that way when the noisy column drew out of sight around a curve in the post road.

None had noticed that in the middle of the eight old mounted men was another old man, his hair and beard now cut short, his hair combed to hide his pointed ears, who played no instrument and looked neither left nor right.

At one town, Vegetius saw Prorsus proved right. It happened on the edge of a large crowd where he rode. As they drew even with the applause, a child pointed to the mounted musicians.

"Look Mater," said the girl, "that man in the middle is half-horsey."

The woman picked the child up by the hair and shook her.

"Learn not to lie, Portia," said her mother, never taking her eyes off the elephant.

"I can't believe it," said Vegetius. "Two and a half months gone by, halfway to the Pillars, and no troubles!"

"These is strange times," said Prorsus, putting more wood on the fire. "Nobody knows what to expect with a new Emperor sittin' on the throne like it was a pot. They don't know which way to jump. They're all just waiting for the other caliga to drop." They were camped off the road near Aquilia in Noricum. The old men were already drunk or asleep. Chiron lay nearby, his human part asleep on a flat rock, his equine body folded under him. Now and then a long low sound came from his chest.

"This trip's been pretty easy. Company's better, anyway," said Prorsus. "I've had some tough jobs, with real scuzzes to work with. I once stole a quinquireme from Ephesus and sold it a week later in Sardis, and nobody ever saw it."

"Wait a minute," said Decius. "Sardis is overland from Ephesus. There aren't any rivers or canals connecting them!"

"It was for a bet," said Prorsus. "Some jobs is just easier than others, I guess."

So it went through Mutina and Trebia in Gallo Cisalpina, Dertona in Liguria, where the roads often became crowded, and missing entirely the dead backwater of Italia itself, through Augusta Taurinorem, Massilia and Narbo Martius in Narbonensis, down the long chest of Tarraconensis, past Novo Carthago on the shore of the Mare Internum, and along the coast roads, passing south of Hispalia in Baetica to the Gates of Hercules.

They were on a hill overlooking a small seaport. Across to the southwest was Mauretania, emblazoned with the sunset.

"We're here," said Vegetius to Chiron. "Now let's get you home."

"We'll have to hire a ship."

"So it is Africa we go to!" said Decius Muccinus.

"Not really," said Chiron.

"Then for the god's sakes, where?" asked Vegetius.

"Out there," said Chiron, pointing to the sunset.

"What! There's nothing out there!"

"There's another land. The land centaurs come from. And horses."

"How the Dis did you get here? You didn't have ships!"

"We walked. It was colder then. The ocean was lower then, and more land stuck out. Of course, we came the other way, through Asia. I'm taking you by a short cut."

Whistling a tune, Prorsus started down the hill.

"Where are you going?" asked Vegetius, beside himself.

"To find passage back for the drunks and to find a boat that'll get him home," he said, jerking his thumb toward the centaur.

"What! What!"

"He hasn't lied to you yet, has he?" asked Prorsus, over his shoulder.

Vegetius ran down to a cork tree and gnawed at the bark, tears streaming down his face. After a while, he felt better.

"Sorry," he said to Chiron. "It's been such a long trip. I thought it almost over."

Chiron put his hands on Vegetius' shoulders. "Soon," he said. "Soon, you'll have the book. Soon I'll be home. It had to be this way. If I would have told you in Smyrnea, you would not have come. And you would have remained a bitter old man the rest of your life. And I would die in Thracia, so far from my homeland."

"I'm just tired."

"I, too," said Chiron. "More than you know. Let's make camp. No more masquerades. No more processions. Let the world gape. I'm going home."

They boarded a ship next midnight and set sail westward. Prorsus had sold the elephant to a merchantman captain returning to Nyzantium in exchange for passage for the old men. They had said their goodbyes the evening before boarding.

When dawn broke on the ship in the Mare Atlanticum, it

became very quiet. The crew saw the centaur and kept its distance.

"When do we put north or south?" asked the bosun, expecting a turn starboard toward Hibernia, or port to the Wild Dog Islands.

"We don't," said the captain. He reached into the poop cabin and pulled out a bag half his size.

He kicked at it.

It jangled.

"Hear that?" asked the captain. "The bag talks!"

"That it does," said the bosun.

"What does it say?"

"It says west by northwest by the stars, sir!"

"Just what it said to me."

For two weeks the sea had been still and flat as a sheet of lead, without a cloud in the sky.

The sail was furled. The sailors' hands were raw with rowing toward the westering sun.

"It used to be much easier to sail there for a while, or so I'm told," said Chiron. "There used to be a big island out here in the middle, though they charged an arm and a leg for a port call."

During the last week they had lightened the load as much as possible. Now there was nothing left but food, water, the money bags and some extra canvas on board. Still the hours of flat calm dragged by.

Vegetius, Prorsus and Muccinus took turns at the oars, and Chiron stood helm though there was very little need to steer.

The sun came up abaft them every morning, and set before them each evening, and it seemed they had moved not at all.

They awoke to find themselves, the captain and bosun at one end of the vessel and the crew at the other. No one was rowing. The oars were shipped.

"Well," said the captain. "What is it?"

One of the men stepped forward. "We've been without wind for seventeen days now. We row all day and night. We get nowhere."

"There's nothing for it but to put our backs in and hope for wind," said the captain.

"We could turn back." There were grumbles behind him from the others.

There was a consultation with the passengers. "Out of the question," said the captain. "We're more than halfway there."

"Says who?" yelled someone.

"Say I, and I'm captain."

"Well, then," said the crew's leader. "We could lighten the load."

"What's that?" asked Prorsus, suddenly taking an interest in the proceedings.

"You know what I mean, governor," said the crewman, nodding his head sideways. "Why don't we put the horsey over the side?"

"Quite right!" said Prorsus. He grabbed the sailor by crotch and tunic and pitched him over the railing. The man coughed and floundered in the glassy water.

"Next!" said Prorsus. "I figure three more make up for my friend Chiron here." He opened his arms in a wrestler's invitation. "Weight's weight."

No one came forward.

"Toss him a line," said Prorsus.

They pulled the wet and straggling sailor back aboard.

"Do we understand each other?" Prorsus asked the assembled sailors.

"Aye aye!" they said in one voice.

As if by some propitiatory magic, a dancing line of water moved toward them from the east. It caught up to and passed the ship. The frill of mane on Chiron's back fluttered and a cool breeze blew into Vegetius' right ear.

"Well, hell and damn!" yelled the captain to the crew. "Don't you know wind when you feel it? Unfurl the fonkin' sail!"

The canvas came down and filled, the ship groaned and jerked ahead, bearing them away from the morning sun. The sailors, among them the wet one, joined in "Old Neptune's Song."

They lowered the gangplank, and Chiron went down into the surf and onto the sandbar in the river estuary.

The shoreline was broken by trees and clearings. Here and there shaggy humped shapes grazed, some few stopping to watch, then returning to their forage. They looked like wisents only they had smaller horns.

Chiron turned to the ship.

"Fishing should be good all up the shore," he said. "Won't take long to replenish your stores. Good water, too. Follow the warm water north, then follow east when it turns. You'll end up in Britannia or Hibernia. You know them, captain?"

"I'm half tindigger," he said. "I paint myself blue once a year when the mood overcomes me."

Chiron laughed, then coughed, a hard wracking series of them. He leaned the upper half of his body against a tree, steadying himself with his right hand. Then he straightened and turned to walk away.

"Goodbye. Goodbye, horsey. So long Mr. Chiron," they all yelled from the ship.

"Wait! Wait! The *Hippiatrika*!?" yelled Vegetius.

Chiron turned. "In the cave. On the table. The two unopened scroll tubes. Thank you, Renatus Vegetius. I will remember you always."

He turned then, lifted his tail, his regrown hair and beard streaming in the wind like a white banner, and broke, for a few paces, into a canter, and disappeared through the nearest stand of trees, heading westward.

A yell of exultation and homecoming, of surrender and defiance rose up, startling some of the browsing creatures. Then it, too, like the drumming hoofbeats, echoed and died away westward.

"Back water and up sail, you sea hogs!" hollered the captain.

In the three years of life remaining to him, P. Renatus Vegetius returned home, retrieved the books in the cave, and incorporated the *Hippiatrika* into his great work on the diseases of mules, horses and cattle, the *Mulomedicina*.

Decius Muccinus, free and married, had twin sons whom they named Aurem and Renatus.

Nemo Prorsus became the Christian Bishop of Sardis.

On his deathbed, Renatus Vegetius looked around his room

at his sisters and their husbands and children, at his newly freed slaves, and at what few friends as had not preceded him in death.

About the only thing he regretted was never getting to hunt lions from a chariot in the wet marshlands of Libya.

He remembered one sunny day on a far shore half a world away, and the cry of happiness that had drifted to him out of those woods.

What was killing a few old lions compared to what he had done?

He had helped a tired old friend get home.

Vegetius was still smiling when they put the coins on his eyes.

The Boy Who
Plaited Manes
by
Nancy Springer

Here's a strange modern fairy tale, delicate and pastel-colored as a dream, but with a core of ice and iron, that suggests it's dangerous to assume that a specialist can only do that which he is best known for doing . . .

Born in Montclair, New Jersey, Nancy Springer now lives in Pennsylvania with her family. One of the most prolific fantasists of the 1980s, her adult novels include The Silver Sun, The White Hart, The Sable Moon, The Black Beast, The Golden Swan, Wings of Flame, Chains of Gold, Madbond, Mindbond, Godbond, The Hex Witch of Seldom, *and* Apocalypse. *Her novels for children and young adults, many of them about horses, include* A Horse to Love, Not on a White Horse, They're All Named Wildfire, Red Wizard, Colt, *and* The Friendship Song. *Her short fiction has been collected in* Chance: And Other Gestures of the Hand of Fate.

* * *

The boy who plaited the manes of horses arrived, fittingly enough, on the day of the Midsummer Hunt: when he was needed worst, though Wald the head groom did not yet know it. The stable seethed in a muted frenzy of work, as it had done since long before dawn, every groom and apprentice vehemently polishing. The lord's behest was that all the horses in his stable should be brushed for two hours every morning to keep the fine shine and bloom on their flanks, and this morning could be no different. Then there was also all the gear to be tended to. Though old Lord Robley of Auberon was a petty manor lord, with only some hundred of horses and less than half the number of grooms to show for a lifetime's striving, his lowly status made him all the more keen to present himself and his retinue grandly before the more powerful lords who would assemble for the Hunt. Himself and his retinue and his lovely young wife.

Therefore it was an eerie thing when the boy walked up the long stable aisle past men possessed with work, men so frantic they did not look up to glance at the stranger, up the aisle brick-paved in chevron style until he came to the stall where the lady's milk-white palfrey stood covered withers to croup with a fitted sheet tied on to keep the beast clean, and the boy swung open the heavy stall door and walked in without fear, as if he belonged there, and went up to the palfrey to plait its mane.

He was an eerie boy, so thin that he seemed deformed, and of an age difficult to guess because of his thinness. He might have been ten, or he might have been seventeen with something wrong about him that made him beardless and narrow-shouldered and thin. His eyes seemed too gathered for a ten-year-old, gray-green and calm yet feral, like woodland. His hair, dark and shaggy, seemed to bulk large above his thin, thin face.

The palfrey's hair was far better cared for than his. Its silky mane, coddled for length, hung down below its curved neck, and its tail was bundled into a wrapping, to be let down at the last moment before the lady rode, when it would trail on the ground and float like a white bridal train. The boy did not yet touch the tail, but his thin fingers flew to work on the palfrey's mane.

Wald the head groom, passing nearly at a run to see to the saddling of the lord's hotblooded hunter, stopped in his tracks and stared. And to be sure it was not that he had never seen plating before. He himself had probably braided a thousand horses' manes, and he knew what a time it took to put even a row of small looped braids along a horse's crest, and how hard it was to get them even, and how horsehair seems like a demon with a mind of its own. He frankly gawked, and other grooms stood beside him and did likewise, until more onlookers stood gathered outside the palfrey's stall than could rightly see, and those in the back demanded to know what was happening, and those in the front seemed not to hear them, but stood as if in a trance, watching the boy's thin, swift hands.

For the boy's fingers moved more quickly and deftly than
seemed human, than seemed possible, each hand by itself
combing and plaiting a long, slender braid in one smooth
movement, as if he no more than stroked the braid out of the
mane. That itself would have been wonder enough, as when a
groom is so apt that he can curry with one hand and follow after
with the brush in the other, and have a horse done in half the
time. A shining braid forming out of each hand every minute,
wonder enough—but that was the least of it. The boy inter-
wove them as he worked, so that they flowed into each other in
a network, making of the mane a delicate shawl, a veil, that
draped the palfrey's fine neck. The ends of the braids formed a
silky hem curving down to a point at the shoulder, and at the
point the boy spiraled the remaining mane into an uncanny
horsehair flower. And all the time, though it was not tied and
was by no means a cold-blooded beast, the palfrey had not
moved, standing still as a stone.

Then Wald the head groom felt fear prickling at the back of
his astonishment. The boy had carried each plait down to the
last three hairs. Yet he had fastened nothing with thread or
ribbon, but merely pressed the ends between two fingers, and
the braids stayed as he had placed them. Nor did the braids ever
seem to fall loose as he was working, or hairs fly out at random,
but all lay smooth as white silk, shimmering. The boy, or
whatever he was, stood still with his hands at his sides,
admiring his work.

Uncanny. Still, the lord and lady would be well
pleased. . . . Wald jerked himself out of amazement and
moved quickly. "Get back to your work, you fellows!" he
roared at the grooms, and then he strode into the stall.

"Who are you?" he demanded. "What do you mean coming
in here like this?" It was best, in a lord's household, never to let
anyone know you were obliged to them.

The boy looked at him silently, turning his head in the alert
yet indifferent way of a cat.

"I have asked you a question! What is your name?"

The boy did not speak, or even move his lips. Then or
thereafter, as long as he worked in that stable, he never made
any sound.

His stolid manner annoyed Wald. But though the master groom could not yet know that the boy was a mute, he saw something odd in his face. A halfwit, perhaps. He wanted to strike the boy, but even worse he wanted the praise of the lord and lady, so he turned abruptly and snatched the wrapping off the palfrey's tail, letting the cloud of white hair float down to the clean straw of the stall. "Do something with that," he snapped.

A sweet, intense glow came into the boy's eyes as he regarded his task. With his fingers he combed the hair smooth, and then he started a row of small braids above the bone.

Most of the tail he left loose and flowing, with just a cluster of braids at the top, a few of them swinging halfway to the ground. And young Lady Aelynn gasped with pleasure when she saw them, and with wonder at the mane, even though she was a lord's daughter born and not unaccustomed to finery.

It did not matter, that day, that Lord Robley's saddle had not been polished to a sufficient shine. He was well pleased with his grooms. Nor did it matter that his hawks flew poorly, his hounds were unruly and his clumsy hunter stumbled and cut its knees. Lords and ladies looked again and again at his young wife on her white palfrey, its tail trailing and shimmering like her blue silk gown, the delicate openwork of its mane as dainty as the lace kerchief tucked between her breasts or her slender gloved hand which held the caparisoned reins. Every hair of her mount was as artfully placed as her own honey-gold hair looped in gold-beaded curls atop her fair young head. Lord Robley knew himself to be the envy of everyone who saw him for the sake of his lovely wife and the showing she made on her white mount with the plaited mane.

And when the boy who plaited manes took his place among the lord's other servants in the kitchen line for the evening meal, no one gainsaid him.

Lord Robley was a hard old man, his old body hard and hale, his spirit hard. It took him less than a day to pass from being well pleased to being greedy for more: no longer was it enough that the lady's palfrey should go forth in unadorned braids. He sent a servant to Wald with silk ribbons in the Auberon colors, dark blue and crimson, and commanded that they should be plaited into the palfrey's mane and tail. This the strange boy did with ease when Wald gave him the order, and he used the ribbon ends to tie tiny bows and love knots and leave a few shimmering tendrils bobbing in the forelock. Lady Aelynn was enchanted.

Within a few days Lord Robley had sent to the stable thread of silver and of gold, strings of small pearls, tassels, pendant jewels, and fresh-cut flowers of every sort. All of these things the boy who plaited manes used with ease to dress the lady's palfrey when he was bid. Lady Aelynn went forth to the next hunt with tiny bells of silver and gold chiming at the tip of each of her mount's dainty ribbon-decked braids, and eyes turned her way wherever she rode. Nor did the boy ever seem to arrange the mane and tail and forelock twice in the same way, but whatever way he chose to plait and weave and dress it seemed the most perfect and poignant and heartachingly beautiful way a horse had ever been arrayed. Once he did the palfrey's entire mane in one great, thick braid along the crest, gathering in the hairs as he went, so that the neck seemed to arch as mightily as a destrier's, and he made the braid drip thick with flowers, roses and great lilies and spires of larkspur trailing down, so that the horse seemed to go with a mane of flowers. But another time he would leave the mane loose and floating, with just a few braids shimmering down behind the ears or in the forelock, perhaps, and this also seemed perfect and poignant and the only way a horse should be adorned.

Nor was it sufficient, any longer, that merely the lady's milk-white palfrey should go forth in braids. Lord Robley commanded that his hotblooded hunter also should have his mane done up in stubby ribboned braids and rosettes in the Auberon colors, and the horses of his retinue likewise, though with lesser rosettes. And should his wife choose to go out riding with her noble guests, all their mounts were to be prepared like hers, though in lesser degree.

All these orders Wald passed on to the boy who plaited manes, and the youngster readily did as he was bid, working sometimes from before dawn until long after dark, and never seeming to want more than what food he could eat while standing in the kitchen. He slept in the hay and straw of the loft and did not use even a horseblanket for covering until one of the grooms threw one on him. Nor did he ask for clothing, but Wald, ashamed of the boy's shabbiness, provided him with the clothing due to a servant. The master groom said nothing to him of a servant's pay. The boy seemed content without it. Probably he would have been content without the clothing as well. Though in fact it was hard to tell what he was thinking or feeling, for he never spoke and his thin face seldom moved.

No one knew his name, the boy who plaited manes. Though many of the grooms were curious and made inquiries, no one could tell who he was or where he had come from. Or even what he was, Wald thought sourly. No way to tell if the young snip was a halfwit or a bastard or what, if he would not talk. No way to tell what sort of a young warlock he might be, that the horses never moved under his hands, even the hot-blooded hunter standing like a stump for him. Scrawny brat. He could hear well enough; why would he not talk?

It did not make Wald like the strange boy, that he did at once whatever he was told and worked so hard and so silently. In particular he did not like the boy for doing the work for which Wald reaped the lord's praise; Wald disliked anyone to whom he was obliged. Nor did he like the way the boy had arrived, as if blown in on a gust of wind, and so thin that it nearly seemed possible. Nor did he like the thought that any day the boy might leave in like wise. And even disliking that thought, Wald could not bring himself to give the boy the few coppers a week which were his due, for he disliked the boy more. Wald believed there was something wrongheaded, nearly evil, about the boy. His face seemed wrong, so very thin, with the set mouth and the eyes both wild and quiet, burning like a steady candle flame.

Summer turned into autumn, and many gusts of wind blew, but the boy who plaited manes seemed content to stay, and if he knew of Wald's dislike he did not show it. In fact he showed nothing. He braided the palfrey's mane with autumn starflowers and smiled ever so slightly as he worked. Autumn turned to the first dripping and dismal, chill days of winter. The boy used bunches of bright feathers instead of flowers when he dressed the palfrey's mane, and he did not ask for a winter jerkin, so

Wald did not give him any. It was seldom enough, anyway, that the horses were used for pleasure at this season. The thin boy could spend his days huddled under a horseblanket in the loft.

Hard winter came, and the smallpox season.

Lady Aelynn was bored in the wintertime, even more so than during the rest of the year. At least in the fine weather there were walks outside, there were riding and hunting and people to impress. It would not be reasonable for a lord's wife, nobly born (though a younger child, and female), to wish for more than that. Lady Aelynn knew full well that her brief days of friendships and courtships were over. She had wed tolerably well, and Lord Robley counted her among his possessions, a beautiful thing to be prized like his gold and his best horses. He was a manor lord, and she was his belonging, his lady, and not for others to touch even with their regard. She was entirely his. So there were walks for her in walled gardens, and pleasure riding and hunting by her lord's side, and people to impress.

But in the wintertime there were not even walks. There was nothing for the Lady Aelynn to do but tend to her needlework and her own beauty, endlessly concerned with her clothes, her hair, her skin, even though she was so young, no more than seventeen—for she knew in her heart that it was for her beauty that Lord Robley smiled on her, and for no other reason. And though she did not think of it, she knew that her life lay in his grasping hands.

Therefore she was ardently uneasy, and distressed only for herself, when the woman who arranged her hair each morning was laid abed with smallpox. Though as befits a lady of rank, Aelynn hid her dismay in vexation. And it did not take her long to discover that none of her other tiring-women could serve her nearly as well.

"Mother of God!" she raged, surveying her hair in the mirror for perhaps the tenth time. "The groom who plaits the horses' manes in the stable could do better!" Then the truth of her own words struck her, and desperation made her willing to be daring. She smiled. "Bring him hither!"

Her women stammered and curtseyed and fled to consult among themselves and exclaim with the help in the kitchen. After some few minutes of this, a bold kitchen maid was dispatched to the stable and returned with a shivering waif: the boy who plaited manes.

It was not to be considered that such a beggar should go in to the lady. Her tiring-women squeaked in horror and made him bathe first, in a washbasin before the kitchen hearth, for there was a strong smell of horse and stable about him. They ordered him to scrub his own hair with strong soap and scent himself with lavender, and while some of them giggled and fled, others giggled and stayed, to pour water for him and see that he made a proper job of his ablutions. All that was demanded of him the boy who plaited manes did without any change in his thin face, any movement of his closed mouth, any flash of his feral eyes. At last they brought him clean clothing, jerkin and woolen hose only a little too large, and pulled the things as straight as they could on him, and took him to the tower where the lady waited.

He did not bow to the Lady Aelynn or look into her eyes for his instructions, but his still mouth softened a little and his glance, calm and alert, like that of a woodland thing, darted to her hair. And at once, as if he could scarcely wait, he took his place behind her and lifted her tresses in his hands. Such a soft, fine, honey-colored mane of hair as he had never seen, and combs of gold and ivory lying at hand on a rosewood table, and ribbons of silk and gold, everything he could have wanted, his for the sake of his skill.

He started at the forehead, and the lady sat as if in a trance beneath the deft touch of his hands.

Gentle, he was so gentle, she had never felt such a soft and gentle touch from any man, least of all from her lord. When Lord Robley wanted to use one of his possessions he seized it. But this boy touched her as gently as a woman, no, a mother, for no tiring-woman or maid had ever gentled her so. . . . Yet unmistakably his was the touch of a man, though she could scarcely have told how she knew. Part of it was power, she could feel the gentle power in his touch, she could feel— uncanny, altogether eerie and uncanny, what she was feeling. It was as if his quick fingers called to her hair in soft command and her hair obeyed just for the sake of the one quick touch, all the while longing to embrace. . . . She stayed breathlessly still for him, like the horses.

He plaited her hair in braids thin as bluebell stems, only a wisp of hairs to each braid, one after another with both his deft hands as if each was as easy as a caress, making them stay with merely a touch of two fingers at the end, until all her hair lay in a silky cascade of them, catching the light and glimmering and swaying like a rich drapery when he made her move her head. Some of them he gathered and looped and tied up with the ribbons which matched her dress, blue edged with gold. But most of them he left hanging to her bare back and shoulders. He surveyed his work with just a whisper of a smile when he was done, then turned and left without waiting for the lady's nod, and she sat as if under a spell and watched his thin back as he walked away. Then she tossed her head at his lack of deference. But the swinging of her hair pleased her.

She had him back to dress her hair the next day, and the next, and many days thereafter. And so that they would not have to be always bathing him, her tiring-women found him a room within the manor-house doors, and a pallet and clean blankets, and a change of clothing, plain coarse clothing, such as servants wore. They trimmed the heavy hair that shadowed his eyes, also, but he looked no less the oddling with his thin, thin face and his calm, burning glance and his mouth that seemed scarcely ever to move. He did as he was bid, whether by Wald or the lady or some kitchen maid, and every day he plaited Lady Aelynn's hair differently. One day he shaped it all into a bright crown of braids atop her head. On other days he would plait it close to her head so that the tendrils caressed her neck, or in a haughty crest studded with jewels, or in a single soft feathered braid at one side. He always left her tower chamber at once, never looking at the lady to see if he had pleased her, as if he knew that she would always be pleased.

Always, she was.

Things happened. The tiring-woman who had taken small-pox died of it, and Lady Aelynn did not care, not for the sake of her cherished hair and most certainly not for the sake of the woman herself. Lord Robley went away on a journey to discipline a debtor vassal, and Lady Aelynn did not care except to be glad, for there was a sure sense growing in her of what she would do.

When even her very tresses were enthralled by the touch of this oddling boy, longing to embrace him, could she be otherwise?

When next he had plaited her mane of honey-colored hair and turned to leave her without a glance, she caught him by one thin arm. His eyes met hers with a steady, gathered look. She stood—she was taller than he, and larger, though she was as slender as any maiden. It did not matter. She took him by one thin hand and led him to her bed, and there he did as he was bid.

Nor did he disappoint her. His touch—she had never been touched so softly, so gently, so deftly, with such power. Nor was he lacking in manhood, for all that he was as thin and hairless as a boy. And his lips, after all, knew how to move, and his tongue. But it was the touch of his thin hands that she hungered for, the gentle, tender, potent touch that thrilled her almost as if—she were loved. . . .

He smiled at her afterward, slightly, softly, a whisper of a smile in the muted half-light of her curtained bed, and his lips moved.

"You are swine," he said, "all of you nobles."

And he got up, put on his plain, coarse clothing and left her without a backward glance.

It terrified Lady Aelynn, that he was not truly a mute. Terrified her even more than what he had said, though she burned with mortified wrath whenever she thought of the latter. He, of all people, a mute, to speak such words to her and leave her helpless to avenge herself. . . . Perhaps for that reason he would not betray her. She had thought it would be safe to take a mute as her lover. . . . Perhaps he would not betray her.

In fact, it was not he who betrayed her to her lord, but Wald.

Her tiring-women suspected, perhaps because she had sent them on such a long errand. She had not thought they would suspect, for who would think that such a wisp of a beardless boy could be a bedfellow? But perhaps they also had seen the wild glow deep in his gray-green eyes. They whispered among themselves and with the kitchen maids, and the bold kitchen maid giggled with the grooms, and Wald heard.

Even though the boy who plaited manes did all the work, Wald considered the constant plaiting and adorning of manes and tails a great bother. The whole fussy business offended him, he had decided, and he had long since forgotten the few words of praise it had garnered from the lord at first. Moreover, he disliked the boy so vehemently that he was not thinking clearly. It seemed to him that he could be rid of the boy and the wretched onus of braids and rosettes all in one stroke. The day the lord returned from his journey, Wald hurried to him, begged private audience, bowed low and made his humble report.

Lord Robley heard him in icy silence, for he knew pettiness when he saw it; it had served him often in the past, and he would punish it if it misled him. He summoned his wife to question her. But the Lady Aelynn's hair hung lank, and her guilt and shame could be seen plainly in her face from the moment she came before him.

Lord Robley's roar could be heard even to the stables.

He strode over to her where she lay crumpled and weeping on his chamber floor, lifted her head by its honey-gold hair and slashed her across the face with his sword. Then he left her screaming and stinging her wound with fresh tears, and he strode to the stable with his bloody sword still drawn, Wald fleeing before him all the way; when the lord burst in all the grooms were scattering but one. The boy Wald had accused stood plaiting the white palfrey's mane.

Lord Robley hacked the palfrey's head from its braid-bedecked neck with his sword, and the boy who plaited manes stood by with something smoldering deep in his unblinking gray-green eyes, stood calmly waiting. If he had screamed and turned to flee, Lord Robley would with great satisfaction have given him a coward's death from the back. But it unnerved the lord that the boy awaited his pleasure with such mute—what? Defiance? There was no servant's bow in this one, no falling to the soiled straw, no groveling. If he had groveled he could have been kicked, stabbed, killed out of hand. . . . But this silent, watchful waiting, like the alertness of a wild thing—on the hunt or being hunted? It gave Lord Robley pause, like the pause of the wolf before the standing stag or the pause of the huntsman before the thicketed boar. He held the boy at the point of his sword—

though no such holding was necessary, for the prisoner had not
moved even to tremble—and roared for his men-at-arms to come
take the boy to the dungeon.

There the nameless stranger stayed without water or food,
and aside from starving him Lord Robley could not decide
what to do with him.

At first the boy who plaited manes paced in his prison
restlessly—he had that freedom, for he was so thin and small
that the shackles were too large to hold him. Later he lay in a
scant bed of short straw and stared narrow-eyed at the
darkness. And yet later, seeing the thin cascades of moonlight
flow down through the high, iron-barred window and puddle in
moonglades on the stone floor, he got up and began to plait the
moonbeams.

They were far finer than any horsehair, moonbeams, finer
even than the lady's honey-colored locks, and his eyes grew
wide with wonder and pleasure as he felt them. He made them
into braids as fine as silk threads, flowing together into a
lacework as close as woven cloth, and when he had reached as
high as he could, plaiting, he stroked as if combing a long mane
with his fingers and pulled more moonlight down out of the
sky—for this stuff was not like any other stuff he had ever
worked with, it slipped and slid worse than any hair, there
seemed to be no beginning or end to it except the barriers that
men put in its way. He stood plaiting the fine, thin plaits until
he had raised a shimmering heap on the floor, and then he
stepped back and allowed the moon to move on. His handiwork
he laid carefully aside in a corner.

The boy who plaited moonbeams did not sleep, but sat
waiting for the dawn, his eyes glowing greenly in the darkened
cell. He saw the sky lighten beyond the high window and
waited stolidly, as the wolf waits for the gathering of the pack,
as a wildcat waits for the game to pass along the trail below the
rock where it lies. Not until the day had neared its mid did the
sun's rays, thrust through the narrow spaces between the high
bars, wheel their shafts down to where he could reach them.
Then he got up and began to plait the sunlight.

Guards were about, or more alert, in the daytime, and they
gathered at the heavy door of his prison, peering in between the

iron bars of its small window, gawking and quarreling with each other for turns. They watched his unwavering eyes, saw the slight smile come on his face as he worked, though his thin hands glowed red as if seen through fire. They saw the shining mound he raised on the floor, and whispered among themselves and did not know what to do, for none of them dared to touch it or him. One of them requested a captain to come look. And the captain summoned the steward, and the steward went to report to the lord. And from outside, cries began to sound that the sun was standing still.

After the boy had finished, he stood back and let the sun move on, then tended to his handiwork, then sat resting on his filthy straw. Within minutes the dungeon door burst open and Lord Robley himself strode in.

Lord Robley had grown weary of mutilating his wife, and he had not yet decided what to do with his other prisoner. Annoyed by the reports from the prison, he expected that an idea would come to him when he saw the boy. He entered with drawn sword. But all thoughts of the thin young body before him were sent whirling away from his mind by what he saw laid out on the stone floor at his feet.

A mantle, a kingly cloak—but no king had ever owned such a cloak. All shining, the outside of it silver and the inside gold—but no, to call it silver and gold was to insult it. More like water and fire, flow and flame, shimmering as if it moved, as if it were alive, and yet it had been made by hands, he could see the workmanship, so fine that every thread was worth a gasp of pleasure, the outside of it somehow braided and plaited to the lining, and all around the edge a fringe of threads like bright fur so fine that it wavered in the air like flame. Lord Robley had no thought but to settle the fiery gleaming thing on his shoulders, to wear that glory and be finer than any king. He seized it and flung it on—

And screamed as he had not yet made his wife scream, with the shriek of mortal agony. His whole hard body glowed as if in a furnace. His face contorted, and he fell dead.

The boy who plaited sunbeams got up in a quiet, alert way and walked forward, as noiseless on his feet as a lynx. He reached down and took the cloak off the body of the lord, twirled it and placed it on his own shoulders, and it did not harm him. But in that cloak he seemed insubstantial, like something moving in moonlight and shadow, something nameless roaming in the night. He walked out of the open dungeon door, between the guards clustered there, past the lord's retinue and the steward, and they all shrank back from him, flattened themselves against the stone walls of the corridor so as not to come near him. No one dared take hold of him or try to stop him. He walked out through the courtyard, past the stable, and out the manor gates with the settled air of one whose business is done. The men-at-arms gathered atop the wall and watched him go.

Wald the master groom lived to old age sweating every night with terror, and died of a weakened heart in the midst of a nightmare. Nothing else but his own fear harmed him. The boy who plaited—mane of sun, mane of moon—was never seen again in that place, except that children sometimes told the tale of having glimpsed him in the wild heart of a storm, plaiting the long lashes of wind and rain.

Horse Camp

by
Ursula K. Le Guin

Ursula K. Le Guin is probably one of the best known and most universally respected SF writers in the world today. Her famous novel The Left Hand of Darkness *may have been the most influential SF novel of its decade, and shows every sign of becoming one of the enduring classics of the genre; it won both the Hugo and Nebula awards, as did Le Guin's monumental novel* The Dispossessed *a few years later. She has also won three other Hugo Awards and a Nebula Award for her short fiction, and the National Book Award for Children's Literature for her novel* The Farthest Shore, *part of her acclaimed Earthsea trilogy. Her other novels include* Planet of Exile, The Lathe of Heaven, City of Illusions, Rocannon's World, The Beginning Place, A Wizard of Earthsea, The Tombs of Atuan, *and the controversial multimedia novel* Always Coming Home. *She has had four collections:* The Wind's Twelve Quarters, Orsinian Tales, The Compass Rose, *and most recently,* Buffalo Gals and Other Animal Presences. *Her most recent novel is* Tehanu, *a continuation of her* Earthsea *series.*

In the bittersweet and evocative story that follows, she gives us a look at a familiar childhood experience, one common to millions of children, from a startlingly new perspective . . .

*   *   *

All the other seniors were over at the street side of the parking lot, but Sal stayed with Norah while they waited for the bus drivers. "Maybe you'll be in the creek cabin," Sal said, quiet and serious. "I had it second year. It's the best one. Number Five."

"How do they, when do you, like find out, what cabin?"

"They better remember we're in the same cabin," Ev said, sounding shrill. Norah did not look at her. She and Ev had planned for months and known for weeks that they were to be cabin-mates, but what good was that if they never found their

189

cabin, and also Sal was not looking at Ev, only at Norah. Sal
was cool, a tower of ivory. "They show you around, as soon as
you get there," she said, her quiet voice speaking directly to
Norah's lastnight dream of never finding the room where she
had to take a test she was late for and looking among endless
thatched barracks in a forest of thin black trees growing very
close together like hair under a hand-lens. Norah had told no
one the dream and now remembered and forgot it. "Then you
have dinner, and First Campfire," Sal said. "Kimmy's going to
be a counselor again. She's really neat. Listen, you tell old
Meredy . . ."

Norah drew breath. In all the histories of Horse Camp which
she had asked for and heard over and over for three years—the
thunderstorm story, the horsethief story, the wonderful Stevens
Mountain stories—in all of them Meredy the handler had been,
Meredy said, Meredy did, Meredy knew.

"Tell him I said hi," Sal said, with a shadowy smile, looking
across the parking lot at the far, insubstantial towers of
downtown. Behind them the doors of the Junior Girls bus
gasped open. One after another the engines of the four buses
roared and spewed. Across the asphalt in the hot morning light
small figures were lining up and climbing into the Junior Boys
bus. High, rough, faint voices bawled. "OK, hey, have fun," Sal
said. She hugged Norah and then, keeping a hand on her arm,
looked down at her intently for a moment from the tower of
ivory. She turned away. Norah watched her walk lightfoot and
buxom across the black gap to the others of her kind who
enclosed her, greeting her, "Sal! Hey, Sal!"

Ev was twitching and nickering, "Come on, Nor, come on,
we'll have to sit way at the back, come on!" Side by side they
pressed into the line below the gaping doorway of the bus.

In Number Five cabin four iron cots, thin-mattressed, grey-
blanketed, stood strewn with bottles of insect repellent and
stying mousse, T-shirts lettered UCSD and I ♥ Teddy Bears, a
flashlight, an apple, a comb with hair caught in it, a paperback
book open face down: *The Black Colt of Pirate Island*. Over
the shingle roof huge second-growth redwoods cast deep
shade, and a few feet below the porch the creek ran out into

sunlight over brown stones streaming bright green weed. Behind the cabin Jim Meredith the horse-handler, a short man of fifty who had ridden as a jockey in his teens, walked along the well-beaten path, quick and a bit bowlegged. Meredith's lips were pressed firmly together. His eyes, narrow and darting, glanced from cabin to cabin, from side to side. Far through the trees high voices cried.

The Counselors know what is to be known. Red Ginger, blonde Kimmy, and beautiful black Sue: they know the vices of Pal, and how to keep Trigger from putting her head down and drinking for ten minutes from every creek. They strike the great shoulders smartly, "Aw, get over, you big lunk!" They know how to swim underwater, how to sing in harmony, how to get seconds, and when a shoe is loose. They know where they are. They know where the rest of Horse Camp is. "Home Creek runs into Little River here," Kimmy says, drawing lines in the soft dust with a redwood twig that breaks. "Senior Girls here, Senior Boys across there, Junior Birdmen about here."—"Who needs 'em?" says Sue, yawning. "Come on, who's going to help me walk the mares?"

They were all around the campfire on Quartz Meadow after the long first day of the First Overnight. The counselors were still singing, but very soft, so soft you almost couldn't hear them, lying in the sleeping bag listening to One Spot stamp and Trigger snort and the shifting at the pickets, standing in the fine, cool alpine grass listening to the soft voices and the sleepers shifting and later one coyote down the mountain singing all alone.

"Nothing wrong with you. Get up!" said Meredy, and slapped her hip. Turning her long, delicate head to him with a deprecating gaze, Philly got to her feet. She stood a moment, shuddering the reddish silk of her flank as if to dislodge flies, tested her left foreleg with caution, and then walked on, step by step. Step by step, watching, Norah went with her. Inside her body there was still a deep trembling. As she passed him, the handler just nodded. "You're all right," he meant. She was all right.

Freedom, the freedom to run, freedom is to run. Freedom is galloping. What else can it be? Only other ways to run, imitations of galloping across great highlands with the wind. Oh Philly sweet Philly my love! If Ev and Trigger couldn't keep up she'd slow down and come round in a while, after a while, over there, across the long, long field of grass, once she had learned this by heart and knew it forever, the purity, the pure joy.

"Right leg, Nor," said Meredy. And passed on to Cass and Tammy.

You have to start with the right fore. Everything else is all right. Freedom depends on this, that you start with the right fore, that long leg well balanced on its elegant pastern, that you set down that tiptoe middle-fingernail so hard and round, and spurn the dirt. Highstepping, trot past old Meredy, who always hides his smile.

Shoulder to shoulder, she and Ev, in the long heat of afternoon, in a trance of light, across the home creek in the dry wild oats and cow parsley of the Long Pasture. "I was afraid before I came here," thinks Norah, incredulous, remembering childhood. She leans her head against Ev's firm and silken side. The sting of small flies awakens, the swish of long tails sends to sleep. Down by the creek in a patch of coarse grass Philly grazes and dozes. Sue comes striding by, winks wordless, beautiful as a burning coal, lazy and purposeful, bound for the shade of the willows. Is it worth getting up to go down to get your feet in the cool water? Next year Sal will be too old for a camper, but can come back as a counselor, come back here. Norah will come back a second-year camper, Sal a counselor. They will be here. This is what freedom is, what goes on, the sun in summer, the wild grass, coming back each year.

Coming back from the Long Pack Trip to Stevens Mountain weary and dirty, thirsty and in bliss, coming down from the high places, in line, Sue jogging just in front of her and Ev half asleep behind her, some sound or motion caught and turned Norah's head to look across the alpine field. On the far side under dark firs a line of horses, mounted and with packs—"Look!"

Ev snorted, Sue flicked her ears and stopped. Norah halted in line behind her, stretching her neck to see. She saw her sister going first in the distant line, the small head proudly borne. She was walking lightfoot and easy, fresh, just starting up to the high passes of the mountain. On her back a young man sat erect, his fine, fair head turned a little aside, to the forest. One hand was on his thigh, the other on the reins, guiding her. Norah called out and then broke from the line, going to Sal, calling out to her. "No, no, no, no!" she called. Behind her Ev and then Sue called to her. "Nor! Nor!"

Sal did not hear or heed. Going straight ahead, the color of ivory, distant in the clear, dry light, she stepped into the shadow of the trees. The others and their riders followed, jogging one after the other till the last was gone.

Norah had stopped in the middle of the meadow, and stood in grass in sunlight. Flies hummed.

She tossed her head, turned, and trotted back to the line. She went along it from one to the next, teasing, chivying, Kimmy yelling at her to get back in line, till Sue broke out of line to chase her and she ran, and then Ev began to run, whinnying shrill, and then Cass, and Philly, and all the rest, the whole bunch, cantering first and then running flat out, running wild, racing, heading for Horse Camp and the Long Pasture, for Meredy and the long evening standing in the fenced field, in the sweet dry grass, in the fetlock-shallow water of the home creek.

His Coat So Gay
by
Sterling E. Lanier

Although he has published novels—most notably the well-received Hiero's Journey, *its sequel,* The Unforsaken Hiero, *and, most recently,* Menace Under Marswood—*Sterling E. Lanier is probably best known in the fantasy and science fiction fields for his long sequence of stories describing the odd adventures of Brigadier Donald Ffellowes, which have been collected in* The Peculiar Exploits of Brigadier Ffellowes *and* The Curious Quests of Brigadier Ffellowes.

Unusually well crafted examples of that curious sub-genre known as the "club story" or "bar story"—whose antecedents in the fantasy field go back at least as far as Lord Dunsany's stories of the clubman Jorkens, and include subsequent work by Arthur C. Clarke, L. Sprague De Camp and Fletcher Pratt—Lanier's Ffellowes stories are erudite, intelligent, witty, fast-paced—and often just plain scary.

In "His Coat So Gay," one of the most suspenseful and chilling of all the Brigadier Ffellowes stories, Ffellowes is invited to a remote valley for a week of hunting, but instead finds himself the prey of the monstrous, relentless, clip-clopping black shape of the Dead Horse . . .

* * *

There had been a big spread in the newspapers about a British duke going through bankruptcy proceedings and his third divorce simultaneously. The divorce was contested, the evidence was sordid and those giving it equally so. The nobleman in question came out of the whole thing very badly, it being proved, among other things, that he had run up huge debts to tradesmen, knowing damn well when he did it that he couldn't hope to pay them. There was lots more, though, including secret "orgies," which seem to have been dirty parties of the sort to have passed quite unnoticed in Los Angeles.

One of the members tapped his newspaper. A few of us were

sitting upstairs in the library after dinner. It was a hot night in New York, but the club was air-conditioned and very pleasant.

"Good thing," said the man with the paper, "that Mason Williams isn't here to shout about this. He'd love to give General Ffellowes a hard time. Can't you hear him? 'Rotten bunch of degenerates! Lousy overbearing crooks and cadgers! Long line of aristocratic bums and swindlers!' It would be the best opportunity he's had in years for trying to annoy the brigadier."

"I notice you were smart enough to say 'trying'!" said someone else. "He's never managed to annoy Ffellowes yet. I doubt if this would do it either."

"Who wants to annoy me, eh?" came the easy, clipped tones of our favorite English member. He had come up the narrow back stairs at the other end of the room and was now standing behind my own back. He always moved silently, not I feel certain out of a desire to be stealthy, but from a lifetime's training. Ffellowes' years in (apparently) every secret as well as public branch of Her Majesty's service had given him the ability to walk like a cat, and a quiet one at that.

I jumped and so did a couple of others, and then there was a moment of embarrassed silence.

Ffellowes is very quick. He saw the newspaper headline in my neighbor's lap and began to chuckle.

"Good heavens, is that supposed to offend me? What a hope! I suppose someone thought our friend Williams might make use of it to savage the British Lion, eh?" He moved from behind my chair and dropped into a vacant seat, his eyes twinkling.

"Item," he said, "the man in question's a Scot, not English. Most important distinction. A lesser and unstable breed." This was said with such dead-pan emphasis that we all started to laugh at once. Ffellowes' smooth, ruddy face remained immobile, but his blue eyes danced.

"If you won't be serious," he said, when the laughter died away, "I shall have to explain why Chattan's little peccadilloes are unlikely to move me to wrath. Or anyone else with any real knowledge, for that matter.

"You know, Richard the Lion Heart was a bad debtor on a

scale that makes anyone modern look silly. All the Plantagenets were, for that matter. Richard seems to have been a quite unabashed queer as well, of course, and likewise William the Second, called Rufus. When, at any rate, one asked those lads for monies due, one had better have had a fast horse and a waiting ship. They canceled debts rather abruptly. There are thousands more examples, but I mention the kings as quite a fairish sample. Now Chattan's an ass and his sexual troubles are purely squalid, fit only for headlines in a cheap paper. But there are other cases no paper ever got to print. Not so long ago, one of your splashier magazines ran a purely fictional piece about an aged nobleman, Scots again, who was sentenced never to leave his family castle, as a result of an atrocious crime, not *quite* provable. The story happens to be quite true and the verdict was approved by the Lords in a closed session. The last pope but two had a South Italian cardinal locked up in his own palace for the remainder of his life on various charges not susceptible of public utterance. The old man only died ten years ago. So it goes, and there are dozens more cases of a similar nature.

"The fact is, persons in positions of power often abuse that power in the oddest and most unpleasant ways. The extent of caprice in the human mind is infinite. Whenever public gaze, so to speak, is withdrawn, oddities occur, and far worse than illicit sex is involved in these pockets of infection. Once off the highways of humanity, if you care for analogies, one finds the oddest byways. All that's needed is isolation, that and power, economic or physical." He seemed to brood for a moment.

Outside the windows, the haze and smog kept even the blaze of Manhattan at night dim and sultry looking. The garish electricity of New York took on something of the appearance of patches of torch and fire light in the heat and murk.

"Haven't you left out one qualification, sir?" said a younger member. "What about time? Surely, to get these Dracula-castle effects and so on, you have to have centuries to play with a complaisant bunch of peasants, hereditary aristocrats, the whole bit. In other words, a really *old* country, right?"

Ffellowes stared at the opposite wall for a bit before

answering. Finally he seemed to shrug, as if he had come to a decision.

"Gilles de Rais," he said, "is perhaps the best example known of your Dracula syndrome, so I admit I must agree with you. In general, however, only in general. The worst case of this sort of thing which ever came to my personal knowledge, and very personal it was, took place in the early 1930's in one of your larger Eastern states. So that while time is certainly needed, as indeed for the formation of any disease, the so-called modern age is not so much of a protection as one might think. And yet there was great age, too."

He raised his hand and the hum of startled comment which had begun to rise died at once.

"I'll tell you the story. But I'll tell it my way. No questions of any sort whatsoever. There are still people alive who could be injured. I shall cheerfully disguise and alter any detail I can which might lead to identification of the family or place concerned. Beyond that, you will simply have to accept my word. If you're interested on that basis . . . ?"

The circle of faces, mine included, was so eager that his iron countenance damned near cracked into a grin, but he held it back and began.

"In the early days of your, and indeed everyone's, Great Depression, I was the most junior military attache of our Washington embassy. It was an agreeable part of my duties to mix socially as much as I could with Americans of my own age. One way of doing this was hunting, fox hunting to be more explicit. I used to go out with the Middleburg Hunt, and while enjoying the exercise, I made a number of friends as well.

"One of them was a man whom I shall call Canler Waldron. That's not even an anagram, but sounds vaguely like his real name. He was supposed to be putting in time as junior member of your State Department, my own age and very good company.

"It was immediately obvious that he was extremely well off. Most people, of course, had been at least affected a trifle by the Crash, if not a whole lot, but it was plain that whatever Can's financial basis was, it had hardly been shaken. Small comments were revealing, especially his puzzlement when, as often happened, others pleaded lack of funds to explain some inability to take a trip or to purchase something. He was, I may add, the most generous of men financially, and without being what you'd call a 'sucker,' he was very easy to leave with the check, so much so one had to guard against it.

"He was pleasant looking, black haired, narrow faced, dark brown eyes, a generalized North European type, and, as I said, about my own age, barely twenty-one. And what a magnificent rider! I'm not bad, or wasn't then, but I've never seen anyone to match Canler Waldron. No fence ever bothered him and he always led the field, riding so easily that he hardly appeared to be conscious of what he was doing. It got so that he became embarrassed by the attention and used to pull his horse in order to stay back and not be first at every death. Of course he was magnificently mounted; he had a whole string of big black hunters, his own private breed he said. But there were others out who had fine 'cattle' too; no, he was simply a superb rider.

"We were chatting one Fall morning after a very dull run, and I asked him why he always wore the black hunting coat of a non-hunt member. I knew he belonged to some hunt or other and didn't understand why he never used their colors.

" 'Highly embarrassing to explain to you, Donald, of all people,' he said, but he was smiling. 'My family were Irish and very patriotic during our Revolution. No pink coats ('pink' being the term for hunting red) for us. Too close to the hated redcoat army in looks, see? So we wear light green, and I frankly get damned tired of being asked what it is. That's all.'

"I was amused for several reasons. 'Of course I understand. Some of our own hunts wear other colors, you know. But I thought green coats were for foot hounds, beagles, bassetts and such?'

" 'Ours is much lighter, like grass, with buff lapels,' he said. He seemed a little ill at ease for some reason, as our horses shifted and stamped under the hot Virginia sun. 'It's a family hunt, you see. No non-Waldron can wear the coat. This sounds pretty snobby, so again, I avoid questions by not wearing it except at home. Betty feels the same way and she hates black. Here she comes now. What did you think of the ride, Sis?'

" 'Not very exciting,' she said quietly, looking around so that

she should not be convicted of rudeness to our hosts. I haven't
mentioned Betty Waldron, have I? Even after all these years,
it's still painful.

"She was nineteen years old, very pale, and no sun ever
raised so much as a freckle. Her eyes were almost black, her
hair midnight, and her voice very gentle and sad. She was
quiet, seldom smiled, and when she did my heart turned over.
Usually, her thoughts were miles away and she seemed to walk
in a dream. She also rode superbly, almost absentmindedly, to
look at her."

Ffellowes sighed and arched his hands together in his lap, his
gaze fixed on the rug before him.

"I was a poor devil of an artillery subaltern, few prospects
save for my pay, but I could dream, as long as I kept my mouth
shut. She seemed to like me as much, or even more than the
gaudy lads who were always flocking about, and I felt I had a
tiny, the smallest grain of hope. I'd never said a thing. I knew
already the family must be staggeringly rich and I had my
pride. But also, as I say, my dreams.

"'Let's ask Donald home and give him some real sport,' I
suddenly heard Can say to her.

"'When?' she asked sharply, looking hard at him.

"'How about the end of the cubbing season? Last week in
October. Get the best of both sports, adult and young. Hounds
will be in good condition, and it's our best time of year.' He
smiled at me and patted his horse. 'What say, limey? Like some
real hunting, eight hours sometimes?'

"I was delighted and surprised, because I'd heard several
people fishing rather obviously for invitations to the Waldron
place at one time or another and all being politely choked off.
I had made up my mind never to place myself where such a
rebuff could strike me. There was a goodish number of
fortune-hunting Europeans about just then, some of them
English, and they made me a trifle ill. But I was surprised and
hurt, too, by Betty's reaction.

"'Not this Fall, Can,' she said, her face even whiter than
usual. 'Not—this—Fall!' The words were stressed separately
and came out with an intensity I can't convey.

"'As the head of the family, I'm afraid what I say goes,' said

Canler in a voice I'd certainly never heard him use before. It was heavy and dominating, even domineering. As I watched, quite baffled, she choked back a sob and urged her horse away from us. In a moment her slender black back and shining topper were lost in the milling sea of the main body of the hunt. I was really hurt badly.

" 'Now look here, old boy,' I said. 'I don't know what's going on, but I can't possibly accept your invitation under these circumstances. Betty obviously loathes the idea, and I wouldn't dream of coming against her slightest wish.'

"He urged his horse over until we were only a yard apart. 'You must, Donald. You don't understand. I don't like letting out family secrets, but I'm going to have to in this case. Betty was very roughly treated by a man last year in the Fall. A guy who seemed to like her and then just walked out, without a word, and disappeared. I know you'll never speak of this to her, and she'd rather die than say anything to you. But I haven't been able to get her interested in things ever since. You're the first man she's liked from that time to this, and you've got to help me pull her out of this depression. Surely you've noticed how vague and dreamy she is? She's living in a world of unreality, trying to shut out unhappiness. I can't get her to see a doctor, and even if I could, it probably wouldn't do any good. What she needs is one decent man being kind to her in the same surroundings as she was made unhappy in. Can you see why I need you as a friend so badly?' He was damned earnest and it was impossible not to be touched.

" 'Well, that's all very well,' I mumbled, 'but she's still dead set against my coming, you know. I simply can't come in the face of such opposition. You mentioned yourself as head of the family. Do I take it that your parents are dead? Because if so, then Betty is my hostess. It won't do, damn it all.'

" 'Now, look,' he said, 'don't turn me down. By tomorrow morning she'll ask you herself, I swear. I promise that if she doesn't, the whole thing's off. Will you come if she asks you and give me a hand at cheering her up? And we are orphans, by the way, just us two.'

"Of course I agreed. I was wild to come. To get leave would be easy. There was nothing much but routine at the embassy anyway, and mixing with people like the Waldrons was as much a part of my duties as going to any Fort Leavenworth maneuvers.

"And sure enough, Betty rang me up at my Washington flat the next morning and apologized for her behavior the previous day. She sounded very dim and tired but perfectly all right. I asked her twice if she was sure she wanted my company, and she repeated that she did, still apologizing for the day before. She said she had felt feverish and didn't know why she'd spoken as she had. This was good enough for me, and so it was settled.

"Thus in the last week in October, I found myself hunting the coverts of—well, call it the valley of Waldrondale. What a glorious, mad time it was! The late Indian summer lingered, and each cold night gave way to a lovely misty dawn. The main Waldron lands lay in the hollow of a spur of the Appalachian range. Apparently some early Waldron, an emigrant from Ireland during the '16, I gathered, had gone straight west into Indian territory and somehow laid claim to a perfectly immense tract of country. What is really odd is that the red men seemed to feel it was all fine, that he should do so.

"'We always got along with our Indians,' Canler told me once. 'Look around the valley at the faces, my own included. There's some Indian blood in all of us. A branch of the lost Erie nation, before the Iroquois destroyed them, according to the family records.'

"It was quite true that when one looked, the whole valley indeed appeared to have a family resemblance. The women were very pale, and both sexes were black haired and dark eyed, with lean, aquiline features. Many of them, apparently local farmers, rode with the hunt and fine riders they were, too, well mounted and fully familiar with field etiquette.

"Waldrondale was a great, heart-shaped valley, of perhaps eight thousand acres. The Waldrons leased some of it to cousins and farmed some themselves. They owned still more land outside the actual valley, but that was all leased. It was easy to see that in Waldrondale itself they were actually rulers. Although both Betty and Can were called by their first names, every one of the valley dwellers was ready and willing to drop whatever he or she was doing at a moment's notice to oblige either of them in the smallest way. It was not subservience exactly, but instead almost an eagerness of the sort a monarch might have got in the days when kings were also sacred beings. Canler shrugged when I mentioned how the matter struck me.

"'We've just been here a long time, that's all. They've simply got used to us telling them what to do. When the first Waldron came over from Galway, a lot of retainers seem to have come with him. So it's not really a strictly normal American situation.' He looked lazily at me. 'Hope you don't think we're too effete and baronial here, now that England's becoming so democratized?'

"'Not at all,' I said quickly and the subject was changed. There had been an unpleasant undertone in his speech, almost jeering, and for some reason he seemed rather irritated.

"What wonderful hunting we had! The actual members of the hunt, those who wore the light green jackets, were only a dozen or so, mostly close relatives of Canler's and Betty's. When we had started the first morning at dawn, I'd surprised them all for I was then a full member of the Duke of Beaufort's pack, and as a joke more than anything else, I had brought the blue and yellow-lapelled hunting coat along. The joke was that I had been planning to show them, the Waldrons, one of our own variant colors all along, ever since I had heard about theirs. They were all amazed at seeing me not only *not* in black, but in 'non-red,' so to speak. The little withered huntsman, a local farmer, named McColl, was absolutely taken aback and for some reason seemed frightened. He made a curious remark, of which I caught only two words, 'Sam Haines,' and then made a sign which I had no trouble at all interpreting. Two fingers at either end of a fist have always been an attempt to ward off the evil eye, or some other malign spiritual influence. I said nothing at the time, but during dinner I asked Betty who 'Sam Haines' was and what had made old McColl so nervous about my blue coat. Betty's reaction was even more peculiar. She muttered something about a local holiday and also that my coat was the 'wrong color for an Englishman,' and then abruptly changed the subject. Puzzled, I looked up, to notice that all conversation seemed to have died at the rest of the big table. There were perhaps twenty guests, all the regular hunt members and some more besides from the outlying parts of the valley. I was struck by the intensity of the very similar faces, male and female, all staring at us, lean, pale and dark eyed, all with that coarse raven hair. For a moment I had a most peculiar feeling that I had blundered into a den of some dangerous creature or other, some pack animal perhaps, like a wolf. Then Canler laughed from the head of the table and conversation started again. The illusion was broken, as a thrown pebble shatters a mirrored pool of water, and I promptly forgot it.

"The golden, wonderful days passed as October drew to a close. We were always up before dawn and hunted the great vale of Waldrondale sometimes until noon. Large patches of dense wood had been left deliberately uncleared here and there and made superb coverts. I never had such a good going, not even in Leicestershire at its best. And I was with Betty, who seemed happy, too. But although we drew almost the entire valley at one time or another, there was one exception, and it puzzled me to the point of asking Can about it one morning.

"Directly behind the Big House (it had no other name) the ground rose very sharply in the direction of the high blue hills beyond. But a giant hedge, all tangled and overgrown, barred access to whatever lay up the slope. The higher hills angled down, as it were, as if to enclose the house and grounds, two arms of high, rocky ground almost reaching the level of the house on either side. Yet it was evident that an area of some considerable extent, a smallish plateau in fact, lay directly behind the house, between it and the sheer slopes of the mountain, itself some jagged outlier of the great Appalachian chain. And the huge hedge could only have existed for the purpose of barring access to this particular piece of land.

"'It's a sanctuary,' Canler said when I asked him. 'The family has a burial plot there, and we always go there on—on certain days. It's been there since we settled the area, has some first growth timber among other things, and we like to keep it as it is. But I'll show it to you before you leave if you're really interested.' His voice was incurious and flat, but again I had the feeling, almost a sixth sense, if you like, that I had somehow managed to both annoy and, odder, amuse him. I changed the subject and we spoke of the coming day's sport.

"One more peculiar thing occurred on that day in the late afternoon. Betty and I had got a bit separated from the rest of the hunt, a thing I didn't mind one bit, and we also were some distance out from the narrow mouth of the valley proper, for the fox had run very far indeed. As we rode toward home under the warm sun, I noticed that we were passing a small, white, country church, wooden, you know, and rather shabby. As I looked, the minister, parson, or what have you, appeared on the porch, and seeing us, stood still, staring. We were not more than thirty feet apart for the dusty path, hardly a road at all, ran right next to the church. The minister was a tired-looking soul of about fifty, dressed in an ordinary suit but with a Roman collar, just like the C. of E. curate at home.

"But the man's expression! He never looked at me, but he stared at Betty, never moving or speaking, and the venom in his eyes was unmistakable. Hatred and contempt mingled with loathing.

"Our horses had stopped and in the silence they fidgeted and stamped. I looked at Betty and saw a look of pain on her face, but she never spoke or moved either. I decided to break the silence myself.

"'Good day, padre,' I said breezily. 'Nice little church you have here. A jolly spot, lovely trees and all.' I expect I sounded half-witted.

"He turned his gaze on me and it changed utterly. The hatred vanished and instead I saw the face of a decent, kindly man, yes, and a deeply troubled one. He raised one hand and I thought for a startled moment he actually was going to bless me, don't you know, but he evidently thought better of it. Instead, he spoke, plainly addressing me alone.

"'For the next forty-eight hours this church will remain open. And I will be here.'

"With that, he turned on his heel and re-entered the church, shutting the door firmly behind him.

"'Peculiar chap, that,' I said to Betty. 'Seems to have a bit of a down on you, too, if his nasty look was any indication. Is he out of his head, or what? Perhaps I ought to speak to Can, eh?'

" 'No,' she said quickly, putting her hand on my arm. 'You mustn't; promise me you won't say anything to him about this, not a word!'

" 'Of course I won't, Betty, but what on earth is wrong with the man? All that mumbo jumbo about his confounded church being open?'

" 'He—well, he doesn't like any of our family, Donald. Perhaps he has reason. Lots of people outside the valley aren't too fond of the Waldrons. And the Depression hasn't helped matters. Can won't cut down on high living and of course hungry people who see us are furious. Don't let's talk any more about it. Mr. Andrews is a very decent man and I don't want Canler to hear about this. He might be angry and do something unpleasant. No more talk now. Come on, the horses are rested, I'll race you to the main road.'

"The horses were *not* rested and we both knew it, but I could never refuse her anything. By the time we rejoined the main body of the hunt, the poor beasts were blown, and we suffered a lot of chaff, mostly directed at me, for not treating our mounts decently.

"The next day was the thirty-first of October. My stay had only two more days to run and I could hardly bear to think of leaving. But I felt glorious too. The previous night, as I had thrown the bedclothes back, preparatory to climbing in, a small packet had been revealed. Opening it, I had found a worn, tiny cross on a chain, both silver and obviously very old. I recognized the cross as being of the ancient Irish or Gaelic design, rounded and with a circle in the center where the arms joined. There was a note in a delicate hand that I knew well, since I'd saved every scrap of paper I'd ever received from her.

"Wear this for me always and say nothing to anyone.

"Can you imagine how marvelous life seemed? The next hunt morning was so fine it could hardly have been exceeded. But even if it had been terrible and I'd broken a leg, I don't think I'd have noticed. I was wearing Betty's family token, sent to *me*, secretly under my shirt, and I came very close to singing aloud. She said nothing to me, save for polite banalities, and she looked tired, as if she'd not slept too well.

"As we rode past a lovely field of gathered shocks of maize, your 'corn,' you know, I noticed all the jolly pumpkins still left lying about in the fields and asked my nearest neighbor, one of the younger cousins, if the local kids didn't use them for Hallowe'en as I'd been told in the papers.

" 'Today?' he said, and then gobbled the same words used by the old huntsman, 'Sam Haines,' or perhaps 'Hayne.'

" 'We don't call it that,' he added stiffly and before I could ask why or anything else, spurred his horse and rode ahead. I was beginning to wonder, in a vague sort of way, if all this isolation really could be good for people. Canler and Betty seemed increasingly moody and indeed the whole crowd appeared subject to odd moods.

"Perhaps a bit inbred, I thought. *I must try and get Betty out of here.* Now apparently I'd offended someone by mentioning Hallowe'en, which, it occurred to me in passing, was that very evening. 'Sam Haines' indeed!

"Well, I promptly forgot all that when we found, located a fox, you know, and the chase started. It was a splendid one and long, and we had a very late lunch. I got a good afternoon rest, since Canler had told me we were having a banquet that evening. 'A farewell party for you, Donald,' he said, 'and a special one. We don't dress up much, but tonight we'll have a sort of hunt ball, eh?'

"I'd seen no preparations for music, but the Big House was so really big that the London Symphony could have been hidden somewhere about.

"I heard the dinner gong as I finished dressing, and when I came down to the main living room, all were assembled, the full hunt, with all the men in their soft-emerald green dress coats, to which my blue made a mild contrast. To my surprise, a number of children, although not small ones, were there also, all in party dress, eyes gleaming with excitement. Betty looked lovely in an emerald evening dress, but also very wrought up, and her eyes did not meet mine. Once again, a tremendous desire to protect her and get her out of this interesting but rather curious clan came over me.

"But Can was pushing his way through the throng and he took me by the elbow. 'Come and be toasted, Donald, as the only outsider,' he said, smiling. 'Here's the family punch and the family punch bowl too, something few others have ever seen.'

"At a long table in a side alcove, stood an extraordinary bowl, a huge stone thing, with things like runes scratched around the rim. Behind it, in his 'greens,' but bareheaded, stood the little withered huntsman, McColl. It was he who filled a squat goblet, but as he did so and handed it to me, his eyes narrowed, and he hissed something inaudible over the noise behind me. It looked like 'watch!' I was alerted, and when he handed me the curious stone cup, I knew why. There was a folded slip of paper under the cup's base, which I took as I accepted the cup itself. Can, who stood just behind me, could have seen nothing.

"I'm rather good at conjuring tricks, and it was only a moment before I was able to pass my hand over my forehead and read the note at the same instant. The message was simple, the reverse of Alice's on the bottle.

" 'Drink nothing.' That was all, but it was enough to send a thrill through my veins. I was sure of two things. McColl had never acted this way on his own hook. Betty, to whom the man was obviously devoted, was behind this. And something else too.

"I was in danger. I knew it. All the vague uneasiness I had suppressed during my stay, the peculiar stares, the cryptic remarks, the attitude of the local minister we had seen, all coalesced into something ominous, inchoate but menacing. These cold, good-looking people were not my friends, if indeed they were anyone's. I looked casually about while pretending to sip from my cup. Between me and each of the three exits, a group of men were standing, chatting and laughing, accepting drinks from trays passed by servants, but *never moving*. As my brain began to race overtime, I actually forgot my warning and sipped from my drink. It was like nothing I have had before or since, being pungent, sweet and at the same time almost perfumed, but not in an unpleasant way. I managed to avoid swallowing all but a tiny bit, but even that was wildly exhilarating, making my face flush and the blood roar through my veins. It must have showed, I expect, for I saw my host half smile and others too, as they raised their cups to me. The sudden wave of anger I felt did not show, but now I really commenced to think.

"I turned and presented my almost full goblet to McColl again as if asking for more. Without batting an eye, he *emptied* it behind the cover of the great bowl, as if cleaning out some dregs, and refilled it. The little chap had brains. As again I raised the cup to my lips, I saw the smile appear on Can's face once more. My back was to McColl, blocking him off from the rest of the room, and this time his rasping, penetrating whisper was easy to hear.

"'After dinner, be paralyzed, stiff, frozen in your seat. You can't move, understand?'

"I made a circle with my fingers behind my back to show I understood, and then walked out into the room to meet Canler who was coming toward me.

"'Don't stand at the punch all evening, Donald,' he said, laughing. 'You have a long night ahead, you know.' But now his laughter was mocking, and his lean, handsome face was suddenly a mask of cruelty and malign purpose. As we moved about together, the faces and manners of the others, both men and women, even the children and servants, were the same, and I wondered that I had ever thought of any of them as friendly. Under their laughter and banter, I felt contempt, yes, and hatred and triumph too, mixed with a streak of pure nastiness. I was the stalled ox, flattered, fattened and fed, and the butchers were amused. They knew my fate, but I would not know until the door of the abattoir closed behind me. But the ox was not quite helpless yet, nor was the door quite slammed shut. I noticed Betty had gone, and when I made some comment or other, Can laughed and told me she was checking dinner preparations, as indeed any hostess might. I played my part as well as I could, and apparently well enough. McColl gave me bogus refills when we were alone, and I tried to seem excited, full of *joie de vivre*, you know. Whatever other effect was expected was seemingly reserved for after dinner.

"Eventually, about nine I should think, we went in to dinner, myself carefully shepherded between several male cousins. These folk were not leaving much to chance, whatever their purpose.

"The great dining room was a blaze of candles and gleaming silver and crystal. I was seated next to Betty at one end of the long table, and Canler took the other. Servants began to pour wine and the dinner commenced. At first, the conversation and laughter were, to outward appearances, quite normal. The shrill laughter of the young rose above the deeper tones of their elders. Indeed the sly, feral glances of the children as they watched me surreptitiously were not the least of my unpleasant impressions. Once again and far more strongly, the feeling of being in a den of some savage and predatory brutes returned to me, nor, this time, did it leave.

"At my side, Betty was the exception. Her face never looked lovelier, ivory white in the candle glow, and calm, as if whatever had troubled her earlier had gone. She did not speak much, but her eyes met mine frankly, and I felt stronger, knowing that in the woman I loved, whatever came, I had at least one ally.

"I have said that as the meal progressed, so too did the quiet. I had eaten a fairish amount, but barely tasted any of the wines from the battery of glasses at my place. As dessert was cleared off, amid almost total silence, I became aware that I had better start playing my other role, for every eye was now trained at my end of the table.

"Turning to the girl, an unmarried cousin, on my other side, my right, I spoke slowly and carefully, as one intoxicated.

"'My goodness, that punch must have been strong! I can scarcely move my hand, d'you know. Good thing we don't have to ride tonight, eh?'

"Whatever possessed me to say *that,* I can't think, but my partner stared at me and then broke into a peal of cold laughter. As she did so, choking with her own amusement, the man on her far side, who had heard me also, repeated it to his neighbors. In an instant the whole table was a-ripple with sinister delight, and I could see Can at the far end, his white teeth gleaming as he caught the joke. I revolved my head slowly and solemnly in apparent puzzlement, and the laughter grew. I could see two of the waiters laughing in a far corner. And then it ceased.

"A great bell or chime tolled somewhere, not too far off, and there was complete silence as if by magic. Suddenly I was aware of Canler, who had risen at his place and had raised his hands, as if in an invocation.

" 'The hour returns,' he cried. 'The Blessed Feast is upon us, the Feast of Sam'hain. My people, hence to your duties, to your robes, to the sacred park of the *Sheade!* Go, for the hour comes and passes!'

"It was an effort to sit still while this rigmarole went on, but I remembered the earlier warnings and froze in my seat, blinking stupidly. It was as well, for four of the men servants, all large, now stood behind and beside my chair. In an instant the room was empty, save for these four, myself and my host, who now strode the length of the table to stare down at me, his eyes filled with anger and contempt. Before I could even move, he had struck me over the face with his open hand.

" 'You, you English boor, would raise your eyes to the last princess of the Firbolgs, whose stock used yours as the meat and beasts of burden they are before Rome was even a village! Last year we had another one like you, and his polo-playing friends at Hicksville are still wondering where he went!' He laughed savagely and struck me again. I can tell you chaps, I learned real self-control in that moment! I never moved, but gazed up at him, my eyes blank, registering vacuous idiocy.

" 'The mead of the *Dagda* keeps its power,' he said. 'Bring him along, you four, the Great Hour passes!'

"Keeping limp, I allowed myself to be lifted and carried from the room. Through the great dark house, following that false friend, its master, we went, until at last we climbed a broad stairway and emerged under the frosty October stars. Before us lay the towering, overgrown hedge, and now I learnt the secret of it. A great gate, overgrown with vines so as to be invisible when shut, had been opened, and before me lay the hidden place of the House of Waldron. This is what I saw:

"An avenue of giant oaks marched a quarter mile to a circular space where towered black tumuli of stone rose against the night sky. As I was borne toward these monoliths, the light of great fires was kindled on either side as I passed, and from them came an acrid, evil reek which caught at the throat. Around and over them leapt my fellow dinner guests and the servants, wearing scanty, green tunics, young and old together, their voices rising in a wild screaming chant, unintelligible, but regular and rhythmic. Canler had vanished momentarily, but now I heard his voice ahead of us. He must have been gone longer than I thought, for when those carrying me reached the circle of standing stones, he was standing outlined against the largest fire of all, which blazed, newly kindled, behind him. I saw the cause of the horrid stench, for instead of logs, there were burning white, dry bones, a great mountain of them. Next to him stood Betty and both of them had their arms raised and were singing the same wild chant as the crowd.

"I was slammed to the ground by my guards but held erect and immovable so that I had a good chance to examine the two heirs of the finest families in the modern United States.

"Both were barefoot and wore thigh-length green tunics, his apparently wool, but hers silk or something like it, with her ivory body gleaming through it almost as if she were nude. Upon her breasts and belly were marks of gold, like some strange, uncouth writing, clearly visible through the gauzy fabric. Her black hair was unbound and poured in waves over her shoulders. Canler wore upon his neck a massive circular torque, also of gold, and on his head a coronal wreath, apparently of autumn leaves. In Betty's right hand was held a golden sceptre, looking like a crude attempt to form a giant stalk of wheat. She waved this in rhythm as they sang.

"Behind me the harsh chorus rose in volume, and I knew the rest of the pack, for that's how I thought of them, were closing in. The noise rose to a crescendo, then ceased. Only the crackling of the great, reeking fire before me broke the night's silence. Then Canler raised his hands again in invocation and began a solitary chant in the strange harsh tongue they had used before. It was brief, and when it came to an end, he spoke again, but in English this time.

"I call to Sam'hain, Lord of the Dead. I, Tuathal, the Seventieth and One Hundred, of the line of Miled, of the race of Goedel Glas, last true *Ardr'i* of ancient Erin, Supreme Vate of the *Corcu Firbolgi*. Oh, Lord from Beyond, who has preserved my ancient people and nourished them in plenty, the bonefires greet the night, your sacrifice awaits you!" He fell silent and Betty stepped forward. In her left hand she now held a small golden sickle, and very gently she pricked my forehead three times, in three places. Then she stepped back and called out in her clear voice.

"I, Morrigu, Priestess and Bride of the Dead, have prepared the sacrifice. Let the Horses of the Night attend!"

"D'you know, all I could think of was some homework I'd done on your American Constitution, in which Washington advocated separation of church and state? The human mind is a wonderful thing! Quite apart from the reek of the burning bones, though, I knew a stench of a spiritual sort. I was seeing something old here, old beyond knowledge, old and evil. I felt that somehow not only my body was in danger.

"Now I heard the stamp of hooves. From one side, snorting and rearing, a great black horse was led into the firelight by a half-naked boy, who had trouble with the beast, but still held him. The horse was saddled and bridled, and I knew him at once. It was Bran, the hunter I'd been lent all week. Behind him, I could hear other horses moving.

"'Mount him,' shouted Canler, or Tuathal, as he now called himself. With that, I was lifted into the saddle, where I swayed, looking as doped and helpless as I could. Before I could move, my hands were caught and lashed together at the wrists with leather cords, then in turn tied loosely to the headstall, giving them a play of some inches but no more. The reins were looped up and knotted. Then my host stepped up to my knee and glared up at me.

"The Wild Hunt rides, Slave and Outlander! You are the quarry, and two choices lie before you, both being death. For if we find you, death by these,' and he waved a curious spear, short and broad in the blade.

"But *others* hunt on this night, and maybe when Those Who Hunt Without Riders come upon your track, you will wish for these points instead. Save for children's toys, the outside world has long forgotten their Christian Feast of All Hallows. How long then have they forgotten that which inspired it, ten thousand and more years before the Nazarene was slain? Now—ride and show good sport to the Wild Hunt!"

"With that someone gave Bran a frightful cut over the croup, and he bounded off into the dark, almost unseating me in the process. I had no idea where we were going, except that it was not back down the avenue of trees and the blazing fires. But I soon saw that at least two riders were herding me away at an angle down the hill, cutting at Bran's flanks with whips when he veered from the course they had set. Twice the whips caught my legs, but the boots saved me from the worst of it.

"Eventually, we burst out into a glade near the southern spur of the mountain, and I saw that another, smaller gate had been opened in the great hedge. Through this my poor brute was flogged, but once through it, I was alone. The Big House was invisible around a curve of the hill, and no lights marked its presence.

"'Ride hard, Englishman,' called one of my herdsmen. 'Two deaths follow on your track.' With that, they turned back and I heard the gate slam. At the same time, I heard something else. Far off in the night I heard the shrill whinnying of a horse. Mingled with it and nearer was the sound of a horn, golden and clear. The horse cry was like that of no horse I have ever heard, a savage screaming noise which cut into my ear drums and raised the hackles even further on my neck. At the same time I made a new discovery.

"Some sharp thing had been poking into my left thigh ever since I was placed on the horse. Even in the starlight I now could see the reason. The haft of a heavy knife projected under my leg, apparently taped to the saddle! By stretching and bending my body, I could just free it, and once free, I cut the lead which tethered my wrists to the headstall. As I did so, I urged Bran with my knees downhill and to the right, keeping close to the trees which grew unclipt at the base of the mountain spur. I knew there was little time to waste, for the sound of galloping horses was coming through the night, far off, but drawing nearer by the instant! It might be the Twentieth Century outside the valley, but I knew it would be the last of me if that pack of green-clad maniacs ever caught up with me. The Wild Hunt was not a joke at this point!

"As I saw it, I had three secret assets. One, the knife, a sturdy piece of work with an eight-inch blade, which I now held in my teeth and tried to use to saw my wrists free. The other was the fact that I have a good eye for ground and I had ridden the length and breadth of the valley for a week. While not as familiar with the area as those who now hunted me over it like a rabbit, I was, nevertheless, not a stranger and I fancied I could find my way even at night. My third ace was Betty. What she could do, I had no idea, but I felt sure she would do something.

"The damned leather cords simply could not be cut while Bran moved, even at a walk, and I simply was forced to stop. It only took a second's sawing, for the knife was sharp, and I was free. I was in deep shadows, and I listened intently, while I unknotted the reins.

"The sound of many horses galloping was still audible through the quiet night, but it was no nearer, indeed the reverse. It now came from off to my left and somewhat lower down the valley. I was baffled by this, but only for a moment. Canler and his jolly group wanted a good hunt. Drugged as I was supposed to be, it would never do to follow directly on my track. Instead, they were heading to cut me off from the mouth of the valley, after which they could return at leisure and hunt me down. All of this and much more passed through my mind in seconds, you know.

"My next thought was the hills. In most places the encircling wall of mountain was far too steep for a horse. But I could leave Bran behind, and most of the ground ought to be possible for an active chap on foot. By dawn I could be well out of reach of this murderous gang. As the thought crossed my mind, I urged Bran toward the nearest wall of rock. We crossed a little glade and approached the black mass of the slope, shrouded in more trees at the base, and I kept my eye peeled for trouble. But it was my mount who found it.

"He suddenly snorted and checked, stamping his feet, refusing to go a foot forward. I drew the knife from my belt, also alerted, and by a sudden awakening of a sense far older than anything merely physical. Ahead of us lay a menace of a different sort than the hunters of Waldrondale. I remembered my quondam host, threatening me that something else was hunting that night, and also the men who had driven me through the hedge called after me that *two* deaths were on my track.

"Before me, as I sat, frozen in the saddle, something moved in the shadows. It was large, but its exact shape was not easy to make out. I was conscious of a sudden feeling of intense cold, something I've experienced once or twice. I now know this to mean that one of what I'll call an Enemy from Outside, a foe of the spirit, is about. On my breast there was a feeling of heat, as if I'd been burnt by a match. It was where I wore Betty's gift. The cross, too, was warning me. Then, two dim spots of yellow phosphorescence glowed at a height even with mine. A hard sound like a hoof striking a stone echoed once.

"That was enough for Bran! With a squeal of fright which sounded more like a hare than a blood horse, he turned and bolted. If I had not freed my hands, I would have been thrown off in an instant, and as it was I had the very devil of a time staying on. He was not merely galloping, but bounding, gathering his quarters under him with each stride as if to take a jump. Only sheer terror can make a trained horse so forget himself.

"I did my best to guide him, for through the night I heard the golden questing note of a horn. The Wild Hunt was drawing the coverts. They seemed to be quite far down the valley, and fortunately Bran was running away across its upper part, in the same direction as the Big House.

"I caught a glimpse of its high, lightless gables, black against the stars as we raced over some open ground a quarter mile below it, then we were in the trees again, and I finally began to master the horse, at length bringing him to a halt. Once again, as he stood, sweating and shivering, I used my ears. At first there was nothing, then, well down the vale to my right front came the sound of the questing horn. I was still undiscovered.

"You may wonder, as I did at first, why I had heard no hounds. Surely it would have been easy for this crew to keep some bloodhounds, or perhaps to smear my clothes or horse with anise and use their own thoroughbred foxhounds. I can only say I don't know. At a guess, and mind you, it's only a guess, there were other powers or elements loose that night which might have come into conflict with a normal hunting pack. But that's only a guess. Still, there were none, and though I was not yet sure of it, I was fairly certain, for even the

clumsiest hound should have been in full cry on my track by
now. The Wild Hunt then, seemed to hunt at sight. Again the
clear horn sounded. They were working up the slope in my
direction.

"As quietly as possible, I urged Bran, who now seemed less
nervous, along the edge of the little wood we were in and down
the slope. We had galloped from the hill spur on the right, as
one faced away from the house, perhaps two thirds of the way
across the valley, which at this point was some two miles wide.
Having tried one slope and met—well, whatever I *had* met, I
would now try the other.

"My first check came at a wooden fence. I didn't dare jump
such a thing at night, as much for the noise as for the danger of
landing badly. But I knew there were gates. I dismounted and
led Bran along until I found one, and then shut it carefully
behind me. I had not heard the mellow horn note for some time
and the click of the gate latch sounded loud in the frosty night.
Through the large field beyond I rode at a walk. There was
another gate at the far side, and beyond that another dark clump
of wood. It was on the edge of this that I suddenly drew rein.

"Ahead of me, something was moving down in the wood. I
heard some bulky creature shoulder into a tree trunk and the
sound of heavy steps. It might have been another horse from
the sound. But at the same moment, up the slope behind me,
not too far away came the thud of hooves on the ground, many
hooves. The horn note blew, not more than two fields away, by
the sound. I had no choice and urged Bran forward into the
trees. He did not seem too nervous, and went willingly enough.
The sound ahead of me ceased, and then, as I came to a tiny
glade in the heart of the little wood, a dim shape moved ahead
of me. I checked my horse and watched, knife ready.

"'Donald?'" came a soft voice. Into the little clearing rode
Betty, mounted on a horse as dark as mine, her great black
mare. I urged Bran forward to meet her.

"'I've been looking for you for over an hour,' she whispered,
her breath warm on my cheek. I was holding her as tightly as
I could, our mounts standing side by side, amiably sniffing one
another. 'Let me go, Donald, or we'll both be dead. There's a
chance, a thin one if we go the way I've thought out.' She freed

herself and sat looking gravely at me. My night vision was
good and I could see she had changed into a simple tunic of
what looked like doeskin and soft, supple, knee boots. Sock-
eted in a sling was one of the short, heavy spears, and I reached
over and took it. The very heft of it made me feel better. The
glimmering blade seemed red even in the dim tree light, and I
suddenly realized the point was bronze. These extraordinary
people went in for authenticity in their madness.

"'Come on, quickly,' she said and wheeled her horse back
the way she had come. I followed obediently and we soon came
to the edge of the forest. Before us lay another gentle slope, but
immediately beneath us was a sunken dirt road, which mean-
dered away to the left and downhill, between high banks, their
tops planted with hedge. We slid down a sandy slope, and our
horses began to walk along the road, raising hardly any dust.
Betty rode a little ahead, her white face visible as she turned to
look back at intervals. Far away a cock crowed, but I looked at
my watch and it was no more than 3 AM. I could hear nothing
uphill and the horn was silent. We rode through a little brook,
only inches deep. Then, as we had just passed out of hearing of
the gurgle of the stream, a new sound broke the quiet night.

"It was somewhere between a whinny and a screech, and I
remembered the noise I had heard as the two riders had driven
me through the hedge. If one could imagine some unthinkable
horse creature screaming at the scent of blood, eagerly,
hungrily seeking its prey, well, that's the best I can do to
describe it.

"'Come on, we have to ride for our lives!' Betty hissed.
'They have let the Dead Horse loose. No one can stand against
that.'

"With that, she urged her mount into a gallop and I followed
suit. We tore along the narrow track between the banks, taking
each twist at a dead run, always angling somehow downhill and
toward the valley mouth.

"Then, the road suddenly went up and I could see both ahead
and back. Betty reined up and we surveyed our position. At the
same time the horn blew again, but short, sharp notes this time,

and a wild screaming broke out. Three fields back up the long gentle slope, the Wild Hunt had seen our black outlines on the little swell where we paused. I could see what looked like a dozen horsemen coming full tilt and the faint glitter of the spears. But Betty was looking back down along our recent track.

"From out of the dark hollows came a vast grunting noise, like that of a colossal pig sighting the swill pail. It was very close.

"Betty struck her horse over the withers and we started to gallop again in real earnest. Bran was tired, but he went on nobly, and her big mare simply flew. The Hunt was silent now, but I knew they were still coming. And I knew too, that something else was coming. Almost, I felt a cold breath on my back, and I held the spear tightly against Bran's neck.

"Suddenly, Betty checked, so sharply that her horse reared, and I saw why as I drew abreast. We had come very close to the mouth of the valley and a line of fires lay before us, not three hundred yards away on the open flat. Around them moved many figures, and even at this distance I could see that a cordon was established, yet from the hats and glint of weapons, I knew they were not the Waldrons or their retainers. Apparently the outside world was coming to Waldrondale, at least this far. We had a fighting chance.

"Between us and the nearest fire, a black horseman rode at us, and he was only a hundred feet off. The raised spear and the bare head told me that at least one of the valley maniacs had been posted to intercept me, in the unlikely event of my getting clear of the rest.

"I spurred the tired hunter forward and gripped the short spear near its butt end, as one might a club. The move was quite instinctive. I knew nothing of spears but I was out to kill and I was a six-goal polo player. The chap ahead, some Waldron cousin, I expect, needed practice which he never got. He tried to stab at me, overhand, but before our horses could touch, I had swerved and lashed out as I would on a long drive at the ball. The heavy bronze edge took him between the eyes and, really, that was that. His horse went off to one side alone.

"Wheeling Bran, I started to call to Betty to come on, and as

I did, I saw that which she had so feared had tracked us down.

"I am still not entirely certain of what I saw, for I have the feeling that part of it was seen with what Asiatics refer to as the Third Eye, the inner 'eye' of the soul.

"The girl sat, a dozen yards from me, facing something which was advancing slowly upon us. They had called it the Dead Horse, and its shifting outlines indeed at moments seemed to resemble a monstrous horse, yet at others, some enormous and distorted pig. The click of what seemed hooves was clear in the night. It had an unclean color, an oily shifting, dappling of grey and black. Its pupilless eyes, which glowed with a cold, yellow light, were fixed upon Betty, who waited as if turned to stone. Whatever it was, it had no place in the normal scheme of things. A terrible cold again came upon me and time seemed frozen. I could neither move nor speak, and Bran trembled, unmoving between my legs.

"My love broke the spell. Or it broke her. God knows what it must have cost her to defy such a thing, with the breeding she had, and the training. At any rate, she did so. She shouted something I couldn't catch, apparently in that pre-Gaelic gibberish they used and flung out her arm as if striking at the monster. At the same instant it sprang, straight at her. There was a confused sound or sounds, a sort of *spinning*, as if an incredible top were whirling in my ear, and at the same instant my vision blurred.

"When I recovered myself, I was leaning over Bran's neck, clutching him to stay on, and Betty lay silent in the pale dust of the road. A yard away lay her horse, also unmoving. And there was nothing else.

"As I dismounted and picked her up, I knew she was dead, and that the mare had died in the same instant. She had held the thing from Outside away, kept it off me, but it had claimed a price. The high priestess of the cult had committed treason and sacrilege, and her life was the price. Her face was smiling and peaceful, the ivory skin unblemished, as if she were asleep.

"I looked up at the sound of more galloping hoofbeats. The Wild Hunt, all utterly silent, were rounding a bend below me and not more than a hundred yards away. I lifted Betty easily, for she was very light, and mounted. Bran still had a little go

left, and we headed for the fires, passing the dead man lying
sprawled in his kilt or whatever on the road. I was not really
afraid any longer, and as I drew up at the fire where a dozen
gun barrels pointed at me, it all felt unreal. I looked back and
there was an empty hill, a barren road. The riders of Waldrondale had vanished, having turned back apparently at the sight of
the fires and the armed men.

"'He's not one! Look at the gal! That crowd must have been
hunting *him*. Call the parson over or Father Skelton, one of
you. Keep a sharp lookout, now!'

"It was a babble of voices and like a dream. I sat staring
stupidly down and holding Betty against my heart until I
realized a man was pulling at my knees and talking insistently.
I began to wake up then, and looking down, recognized the
minister I had seen when Betty and I had ridden past a day
earlier. I could not remember his name, but I handed Betty
down to him when he asked for her, as obediently as a child.

"'She saved me, you know,' I said brightly. 'She left them
and saved me. But the Dead Horse got her. That was too much,
you see. She was only a girl, couldn't fight *that*. You do see,
don't you?' This is what I am told I said at any rate, by Mr.
Andrews, the Episcopal minister of the little Church of the
Redeemer. But that was later. I remember none of it.

"When I woke, in the spare bed of the rectory the next day,
I found Andrews sitting silently by my bed. He was looking at
my bare breast on which lay the little Celtic cross. He was fully
dressed, tired and unshaven, and he reeked of smoke, like a
dead fireplace, still full of coals and wood ash.

"Before I could speak, he asked me a question. 'Did she, the
young lady, I mean, give you that?'

"'Yes,' I said. 'It may have saved me. Where is she?'

"'Downstairs, in my late wife's room. I intend to give her a
Christian burial, which I never would have dreamt possible.
But she has been saved to us.'

"'What about the rest of that crowd?' I said. 'Can nothing be
done?'

"He looked calmly at me. 'They are all dead. We have been
planning this for three years. That Hell spawn have ruled this
part of the country since the Revolution. Governors, senators,

generals, all Waldrons, and everyone else afraid to say a word.'
He paused. 'Even the young children were not saved. Old and
young are in that place behind the house. We took nothing from
the house but your clothes. The hill folk, who live to the West,
came down on them just before dawn, as we came up. Now
there is a great burning, the house, the groves, everything. The
State Police are coming, but several bridges are out for some
reason, and they will be quite a time.' He fell silent, but his eyes
gleamed. The prophets of Israel were not all dead.

"Well, I said a last good-bye to Betty and went back to
Washington. The police never knew I was there at all, and I was
apparently as shocked as anyone to hear that a large gang of
bootleggers and Chicago gangsters had wiped out one of
America's first families and got away clean without being
captured. It was a six day sensation and then everyone forgot it.
I still have the little cross, you know, and that's all."

We sat silent, all brooding over this extraordinary tale. Like
all of the brigadier's tales, it seemed too fantastic for human
credibility, and yet—and *yet!*

The younger member who had spoken earlier could not resist
one question, despite Ffellowes' prestory ban on such things.

"Well, sir," he now said. "Why, this means that one of the
oldest royal families in the world, far more ancient than King
Arthur's, say, is only recently extinct. That's absolutely amaz-
ing!"

Ffellowes looked up from his concentration on the rug and
seemed to fix his gaze on the young man. To my amazement he
did not become irritated. In fact, he was quite calm and
controlled.

"Possibly, possibly," he said, "but of course they all appear
to have been Irish or at least Celts of some sort or other. I have
always considered their reliability open to considerable doubt."

Further Reading

Novels
(There must be hundreds of novels about horses that have some trace of fantasy or a fantastic element to them, many of them children's and young adult novels—far too many to attempt any sort of comprehensive listing here. So we will limit ourselves to saying that among those fantasy novels that deal with horses or horselike creatures, some of the more central are:)
The Last Unicorn, Peter S. Beagle
Unicorn Mountain, Michael Bishop
Winds of Fate, Mercedes Lackey
Black Unicorn, Tanith Lee
A Swiftly Tilting Planet, Madeline L'Engle
Stalking the Unicorn, Mike Resnick
The Heavenly Horse from the Outermost West, Mary Stanton
A Wind in Cairo, Judith Tarr
Brothers of the Wind, Jane Yolen
(And we can't end this listing without mentioning what may well be the only two *science fiction* horse novels ever written:)
The Island Stallion Races, Walter Farley
Overlay, Barry N. Malzberg

Anthologies
Horse Fantastic, edited by Martin H. Greenberg and Rosalind M. Greenberg
Herds of Thunder, Manes of Gold, edited by Bruce Coville
Unicorns!, edited by Jack Dann and Gardner Dozois
Unicorns II, edited by Jack Dann and Gardner Dozois
The Unicorn Treasury, edited by Bruce Coville
Bestiary!, edited by Jack Dann and Gardner Dozois

Other Short Fiction

"The Rocking Horse," Cezarija Abartis, *Twilight Zone Magazine*, Sept./Oct. 1984

"Snow Horse," Joan Aiken, *A Whisper in the Night*

"Rocinante," Steven R. Boyett, *Elsewhere III*

"Bellerophon," Kevin Christensen, *Destines*, Spring 1980

"The Horse with One Leg," George Alec Effinger, *Idle Pleasures*

"Driving the Chevy Biscayne to Oblivion," Kandis Elliot, *Asimov's Science Fiction*, March 1993

"The Wild One," Max Evans, *The New Frontier*

"Spud and Cochise," Oliver La Farge, *A Decade of F&SF*

"Royal Licorice," R.A. Lafferty, *Orbit 14*

"The Magic White Horse with His Heart in His Mouth," Phyllis MacLennan, *Best from F&SF 21*

"Kehailan," Judith Tarr, *Arabesques*

"Al-Ghazalah," Judith Tarr, *Arabesques 2*

"Redwall is both a credible and
ingratiating place, one to which readers
will doubtless cheerfully return."
—New York Times Book Review

BRIAN JACQUES

SALAMANDASTRON
—————— A Novel of Redwall ——————

*"The Assassin waved his claws in the air. In a trice
the rocks were bristling with armed vermin behind him.
They flooded onto the sands of the shore and stood like
a pestilence of evil weeds sprung there by magic: line
upon line of ferrets, stoats, weasels, rats and foxes.
Banners of blood red and standards decorated their
skins, hanks of beast hair and skulls swayed in the light
breeze.*

The battle for Salamandastron was under way...."
—excerpted from <u>Salamandastron</u>

__ 0-441-00031-2/$4.99